THE WANDERERS

KATE ORMAND

Sky Pony Press
New York

For my parents, with love
and for Andy, always

———————

Sky Pony Press books may be purchased in bulk at special discounts for sales promotion, corporate gifts, fund-raising, or educational purposes. Special editions can also be created to specifications. For details, contact the Special Sales Department, Sky Pony Press, 307 West 36th Street, 11th Floor, New York, NY 10018 or info@skyhorsepublishing.com.

Sky Pony® is a registered trademark of Skyhorse Publishing, Inc.®, a Delaware corporation.

Visit our website at www.skyponypress.com.

10 9 8 7 6 5 4 3 2 1

Library of Congress Cataloging-in-Publication Data is available on file.

Cover design by Georgia Morrissey
Cover photo credit: ArcAngel Images

ISBN: 978-1-63450-201-6
Ebook ISBN: 978-1-63450-914-5

Printed in the United States of America

CONTENTS

CONTENTS

CONTENTS

DUSTY CURTAINS

"Flo, you're up next."

I start when I hear my name called, even though I've been expecting it. That doesn't mean I'm ready, though.

"Flo?" the person shouts again. I recognize the voice as Ava's now. It's softer than Nora's. "Are you back here?"

I keep quiet and hope she'll go away and let me think. "Twenty minutes," Ava adds. I hear soft footfalls as she walks away.

She didn't see me, and I didn't see her, but I'm sure she knew I was hiding between the red and green striped curtains. I part them now and watch the lions in the ring beyond. Ava better hurry if she's going to get out there in time.

A net drops down around the ring for this act. Real lions would get through it in a heartbeat if they chose to, but the audience is in no danger here, not with us.

The music plays loud and grand—the steady beat of drums and the flare of trumpets. The sound of the portable stereo crackles a bit if you listen close enough. It's hidden behind the curtains directly across the ring from me. The underage circus members take turns controlling the volume and stopping and starting the tracks.

As the notes dramatically climb, the powerful frame of a lion is silhouetted between parted curtains. That's Hari. He stalks into the ring, taking center stage.

The lights are working tonight, so they fade in slowly until spotlights rest on Ava and Nora—the two lionesses sitting on podiums on either side of the ring—and one on Hari. The sparkly blue bows around their necks catch the light, dazzling. Well, they're supposed to dazzle. And maybe they would if everything wasn't so cheap.

The audience claps when they see the animals. The lions bring in the most cheers every night. Owen stands patiently beside the central lion, letting the audience's applause die down before beginning the act. The smile on his face is genuine—he loves performing. At fifteen, he doesn't have an act of his own yet, but he worked hard to get a spot as a lion tamer, and he does a good job.

Owen takes the lion over to a thin beam, while the two lionesses circle the ring. Hari's black claws scratch the worn wood of the beam as he walks along it. Owen keeps in step beside the lion, clapping his hands in the air. He tries to match his claps to the rhythm of the music, but he doesn't quite manage. Nothing's ever quite perfect with us.

Once the lion reaches the other side of the beam, Owen turns to face the audience, removes his tamer's black and silver top hat, and bows low. A thundering round of applause follows.

The other two lions come forward, approaching the beam, ready for their next trick. The lights dim again to a soft red hue. Low music plays while they get into position, somber and moody. It was my job, sometimes, to fade the music in and out. I'd just watch through the curtain like I'm doing now and turn the dial on cue. I'd rather be doing that than performing.

The sound of cellos pours softly from the speakers, so low that I can hear the rustling of popcorn bags and hot dog wrappers coming from the audience. The lights are angled toward the ring so the crowd is only very dimly lit, but I can see them shuffling and fussing, trying to get comfortable on the hard wooden seats.

The lions are nearing the end of their act now, which means I've got about ten minutes left until I go out there. And even though I know I should get ready, I don't seem to be able to make myself move and do it. I want to stay where I am. Right here, out of sight.

I run shaking fingers over the curtain that hides me, releasing dust into the air. I cough and flap my hand in front of my face. The circus isn't the most glamorous place, though I imagine it could be. I've seen a movie about a circus on Hari's portable DVD player. It was a magnificent place—confetti and fireworks, gymnasts in glittering costumes, and a tent five times the size of this one.

Here, the surrounding curtains, the same design that stretches around the outside of the ring, are striped dark green and maroon. Inside, it's a suede kind of material that gathers and traps dust. Outside, it's more plastic and crinkles when I touch it. It's noisy when it rains.

Mismatched curtains section off separate areas and give us privacy backstage. The sectioned-off areas are mostly changing rooms. Not that many shifters are all that concerned about others seeing them naked—something I have never been comfortable with.

Some of the curtains back here that make up these areas are created from old materials—worn, holey blankets we can't use anymore, the waterproof fabric from umbrellas left behind at the end of the night. Some have holes in them, some are frayed along the edges, some smell damp and moldy, causing a lingering musky scent in the tent. No, *this* circus is definitely not glamorous.

It's a wonder that anyone actually comes to watch us. Though I suppose they don't know how bad it smells until they get here, by which time they've already paid. The elders are strict on keeping the audience area looking nice, so at least they don't see what we see.

Out there, four rows of wooden benches in a semi-circle face the ring. The first row is ground level, then they go up, up, up. The last two rows are perfect for crawling underneath and taking people's belongings on a slow night—a cell phone, a fancy pair of leather gloves, a wallet from a coat pocket—not that I have any part in that kind of thing. We don't steal *every* night, but if money's tight and the circus isn't making much (which it doesn't), and we're running low on food (which we are), what else are we to do? We have to survive somehow and our options are limited.

I move from foot to foot. The lions are almost done now, so I sink back into the shadows a little more. From my place behind the curtain, I have a perfect view of the ring, but nobody can see me. I am invisible, or at least that's how it seems. I can hear everything, see everything, *feel* everything.

The rest of the circus members don't really come here, near the audience. They all hang out outside at the back of the tent, in the changing areas, or by the stage entrance. We have a cast of nineteen members, with another twelve not yet old enough to perform. That number changes all the time with newcomers, the ones that grow up, form their own packs, and move on, and the odd few stupid enough to run away. Oh, sure, I've thought about it myself. In fact, I've thought about it almost every day for the past few weeks, with my first performance creeping up on me. But I'm not dumb enough to actually risk it.

Now that I've turned sixteen, I'm required to take part in the performances. And as the newest performer, my act is the finale. I have to suffer through the entire thing before it's my turn to go up. I can't think of anything worse for my nerves.

They'll introduce me to the crowd and I'll take my place in the ring. Not as a girl, though. My limbs tingle in antici-pation, but my mind shuts down the thought. I've been practicing for this moment for so long, but I'm still not ready, and I feel like I never will be. My tongue feels as dry as sandpaper, my throat as scratchy. *It shouldn't be this hard.*

Everyone keeps telling me the nerves will get better, fade with the more performances I do, the more experience I get. But that doesn't help me now, not tonight. Not at this moment, when I'm seconds away from my first appearance.

"And now," I hear from the other side of the curtain. My stomach drops. That was both the longest and the fastest ten minutes of my life. It's actually time to go out there. My knuckles are white, squeezing the material, and my palms sweat onto the fabric. "The moment you have all been waiting for—I am proud to introduce the newest addition to the show!"

Me.

The crowd explodes with applause. They whistle and cheer in their excitement, captivated by the experience of the circus. I'd probably be doing the same if I were one of them, seeing it for the first time, unaware of the secrets hidden behind the dusty curtains. I really should move, start to make my way up, but my feet are glued to the ground, sinking into the mud—mud I hope will swallow me whole.

The sound of clapping starts to fade, then dies down completely.

I'm introduced again, but I still don't move an inch. I'm safe, standing here in my robe. It's familiar. Not like out there, not in front of all those people. I can imagine Nora's face right now—she'll be embarrassed, angry, standing there with her arms up in the air, frozen in a moment of uncertainty. She's the strictest of the elders, always quickest to lose her temper. The general unofficial rule is to avoid her altogether.

Move, I think. *Get out there. Get it out of the way. Everyone else did it.*

My breathing racks my entire body. My legs are numb and unresponsive to my mind's commands to move, go, walk, *anything.* Someone will come and get me any second, surely.

I've forgotten everything, though. I can't remember my act—the sequence, the cues. Blank. I can't even remember how to shift, though I've been doing it most of my life. I don't think I'd even be able to handle fading the music in and out the way I'm feeling right now.

The darkness back here becomes suffocating, closing in around me. The dusty air fills my throat and tickles my nose. The tent smells of hot dogs and buttery popcorn, making my stomach turn over. It's a cold night, but the air in the tent is thick and humid. I feel like everything is in super-focus, every sense overwhelmed. I need to get out of here.

My mind is made—I'm leaving the tent—but before I can even turn around, someone's hand touches my arm.

No.

The touch is gentle, though, nonthreatening. Still, all I can think is, *Someone's found me. I missed my chance.*

I hold my breath and wait for what comes next. Will they talk me into performing or simply drag me out there? Whoever it is, soft touch or not, no one will let me get away with leaving this tent. It's like I'm the only one here who's pretending.

"Flo, are you okay?" says the person behind me. I can breathe again. Jett.

Momentarily relaxed by his presence, I take a peek back through the curtains at the fidgeting audience and an angry-looking ringmaster. Nora's seething, I can tell by the way her lips are pursed, her eyebrows pulled together. Her gaze searches the darkness, looking closely at the curtains. I step back and let go before she sees me.

"No," I say, shaking my head. "No, I'm not okay. I can't do this. I can't go out there."

"Sure you can," Jett says. "You've been practicing for months just for this one show. You know what you're doing. And you can't really keep them waiting any longer."

"*Why?* Why do I have to do it?" I argue.

"We all do. You know that. We all have to support each other." He rubs his hand over his mouth. "Flo, we can't pick and choose who performs and who doesn't. Do you think I like going out there? Having everyone laugh at me riding that tiny bicycle around in circles? It's humiliating. But I do it. Because if I didn't, I wouldn't deserve to stay here, and where else could I go?"

I frown.

"Come on, Flo. "

"I can't," I growl, annoyed by him. He's always been my best friend, and now I think we're something more, so he really should know what to say to me by now, how to comfort me. He should know not to coax me out of hiding and into doing something I desperately don't want to do. I know it's the pressure of the circus, the stress of show night—we all feel it—but that's no excuse. This is the first time I'll be in my horse form in front of strangers. That's not something you just *do*.

If I want to go, I should already be gone. So I turn and run away from him without warning. I don't *care* about how we look. I don't *care* if we lose money. I burst through the curtains and head for the woods, and I don't look back.

2

LYDIA THE WOLF

I pass the bearded lady as I make my way around the circus tent.

She spots me straight away. "Hey, Flo!" she calls as I approach her stand. I don't plan on stopping, though.

No one's sure what Ruby's shape actually is. She's old enough to perform now, but she's the only one of us who can't fully transform into an animal. When she shifts, she grows hair on her face and her hands and feet, but she doesn't change shape. I often wonder what it must feel like for her, stuck in that in-between stage, working the door while the rest of us perform in the ring. She sits alone out here throughout the entire show. Her job is to greet customers, taking their tickets or their money at the start of the night, then see them out again at the end. They love her. They crowd her, taking photographs and looking closely to see if the hair is fake.

"How'd it go?" she asks, sitting beside a sign that swings on rusty bars and reads: COME ONE! COME ALL! TO THE ANIMAL CIRCUS! Except some of the painted letters have peeled over time, making it difficult to read. I ignore bearded Ruby and keep moving toward the woods.

I hurry into the bushes that surround our camp, pushing through the foliage hard and carelessly. Branches snag my robe and cut my skin, like hands with sharp fingers, claws even, trying to drag me back to the tent. But I hardly feel any of it, and I don't stop running.

Somewhere out here is a lake, quiet and private. In recent weeks (and, really, any time we stop at this location), I've spent some time sitting by the lake when I want to get away from the camp for a while. I have a me-place at all the circus locations. Only Jett ever knows where I am when I disappear from camp for a while. Only Jett would notice.

We'll be moving on from here tomorrow. Tonight was our last show in the area. And I ruined it.

I make it to the lake and drop to my knees on a carpet of crusty leaves, even though it's fall and it's freezing. Gulping air into my lungs, I try to steady my heartbeat. Watching the lake helps, but it's dark now and the inky black water is still. I like it more in the daytime, when the sun catches the surface.

In the quiet, I calm down. My pulse slows after the rush from the tent, but speeds back up when I think of the mess I left behind. What will happen when they find me? Will they punish me? How? I don't know what the punishment is for what I did. I've never known anyone who refused to perform before, never known anyone who hasn't taken part once they became old enough. Even some of the underage shifters are desperate to turn sixteen and officially join the circus, but I've never seen the appeal. I don't want to perform—it scares me.

I often think of the world beyond this, as terrifying as it is. I look at the audience each night and wonder where they live, where they work, what their houses are like. I have no one outside of this bubble, though. And hardly anyone inside it. No family, nowhere to go. The circus is all I have, and I might have just jeopardized my future here. But is it a future I even want?

I don't know the answer to that.

I've never fully felt like I belong here; perhaps that's why I long for an alternative. We can actually leave when we're older. When we reach twenty-one, the elders offer a choice. Few take it. Some stay a few years until their group is old enough before leaving together to form a new pack. I've never properly considered that decision, being so far from the choosing age, but I doubt Jett and I would leave. It's safest for us here, as much as I'd like a fresh start.

The circus shifters tend to stick with their own species group. When I joined, there were no other horses, and there still aren't. Jett's the only bear, so I've always figured he must have felt bad for me in the beginning, knowing how it is to be the only one. He befriended me when we were old enough to grasp the way things worked, and we've remained close since. You stick with your group. It's just the way it is.

Jett steps into the clearing now, and my eyes find him immediately. "Hi," he says.

"Hi," I reply.

"Ruby said she saw you run off into the woods. I figured you'd be here." He lowers himself down next to me.

"Does anyone else know?" I ask.

Jett shakes his head. "Only Ruby, but she won't say anything. You owe her an apology, by the way."

I look at the ground, ashamed. "I know. She'll get it." I crush some dried leaves between my fingers. "Do you know what they're going to do to me?"

"No," he says. "I left just as they closed the show. They're furious, though. That much I do know. Maybe you shouldn't go back tonight. You could stay out here and give the elders some distance to cool off."

I look around, horrified at the thought of staying in the dark woods all night by myself. I'll miss a hot supper and the comfort of my small tent, exchanging it for sitting out here on damp soil in nothing but a robe. The trees suddenly look a lot more menacing—the shadows between them, and the sounds of animals scratching and rustling in the branches. The woods transform into a sinister rather than welcoming place when I'm faced with a night alone here.

I shake my head no. "I don't want to stay here alone," I say. I don't mean to sound like I'm suggesting Jett stay with me, but I don't protest when he tells me he will.

What if the camp packs up and leaves before we make it back in the morning? This is the last night, after all. They'll already be preparing to move on.

He edges closer and puts his arm around me. I hadn't realized how much I was shivering, and not just from the chill in the air. I rest my head against his chest and breathe in his scent. He smells clammy and musky, like the circus, not like Jett—like lemon and fresh mint. I suppose I must smell the same.

He trails his fingertips across my collarbone and up my neck. I close my eyes and whisper, "What am I going to do?"

Jett sighs heavily. "I suppose you go and apologize to the elders and do things right tomorrow."

I nod. I have a lot of people to apologize to in the morning.

"Like it or not, Flo, you'll be in the next show, you'll be the finale, and you'll have to do it right. I'm sorry. . . . I know that isn't what you want to hear."

I squeeze my eyes shut. "Do you think they'll give me more time?"

"Afraid not, little pony. This is our life."

That's what I thought.

I lean back against him and sink my head into his chest, staring at the crispy leaves surrounding my mud-caked feet. "Tell me a story," I say.

"It'll only give you nightmares," he says. And he's right. The stories of shifters have always given me bad dreams. They rarely have good endings. But tonight I can't settle and I don't want to fall asleep wondering what'll happen when I return to camp or thinking of the show tomorrow night. Those things make for worse nightmares. I need a distraction.

The elders tell us stories of shifters who ran away from the circus, captured or killed by hunters, rejected and slaughtered by other packs. It's dangerous outside our own circle, and the elders make sure we know it.

"It doesn't matter," I say. "Just tell me one. Any one."

"All right," Jett says, then falls silent, thinking. "How about 'Lydia the Wolf'?"

The story of Lydia and the hunters is one of the most frightening, set hundreds of years in the past when humans first discovered our kind and the hunters formed. It's the first story we learn, and the one the elders most often remind us of during evenings around the campfire. I'm certain they believe it'll make any lingering doubts about the way we live our lives fizzle away into the flames. But I don't hear it the way they intend it to be heard. They say Lydia was a fool and should never have done what she did. They say she doomed us all, but I kind of see myself in Lydia—she was pressured by her pack, like I am by the circus, but she was courageous and tried to break free, and I love that about her. Even if it did go horribly wrong, at least she followed her heart.

"Lydia the Wolf was wise and brave, as a shifter should be," Jett begins. He idly moves his fingers up and down my spine and I have trouble listening to the story at all. "She didn't want to live apart from humans. Though she loved her pack, she was not willing to miss out on so much, on the life she wanted, just to protect her identity. She was selfish. Convinced she had a hold on herself, she ventured into a small town one evening and into the town's tavern."

I close my eyes and imagine the village as I have done a thousand times before. It's all so familiar to me now. My mind fills with the scene of the story—the day has turned to night and the sky outside is black. Inside, the tavern is dimly lit with the buttery yellow glow of lanterns and candles. Lydia makes her way through the crowd.

"She was beautiful," Jett continues. "And she attracted plenty of attention. The new girl—mysterious, attractive, exciting." He kisses my neck after each word and my stomach somersaults three times over. "There was but one man. One who did not push his way through the others in an attempt to grab Lydia's interest. And by doing just that, he gained it. He was kind, handsome, caring, and, as she got to know him, she fell for him and his charms, his manner, his affection.

"The other shifters saw what she had, and they moved into the village, too. They were a youthful group and immediately raised suspicion. They were assumed witches. And as she was associated with them, Lydia was labeled a witch, too.

"When Lydia trusted the man she cared for fully, she told him what she *really* was. She begged him to leave with her, for it was becoming unsafe. She wished to start a new life. But he despised her for revealing her true self, for what she was. He said she was a demon, cursed. He confided in his three closest friends, all affection for Lydia lost in that one sentence she uttered. Together, the man and his friends vowed to destroy the cursed ones. And the lives of shifters have been endangered since."

He stops, his fingers still tracing lazy circles on my back. "That's not the end," I say.

"I know," he whispers. "I thought you were getting tired."

"I am," I say with a smile. "But I can keep awake until the end of the story. Go on."

Jett takes a deep breath and picks up where he left off. "Lydia received a message that the man wanted to meet her. She agreed, hoping he'd changed his mind about her, but when she arrived, he was not there. She waited and waited, thinking they were leaving together that evening, until someone finally came. But it was not him. It was another member of her pack, then another, and another. Their clothes were stained with blood, their mouths dripping and their hair matted with it. 'What have you done?' she asked. One man stepped forward and took her hands. She was shaking. 'What have you done?!' This time she screamed the words.

"'What was necessary,' the man replied. 'Come, Lydia. He would've hurt you. And then us. Come with your own. It is not safe for us here.' The pack took her deep into the forest, encouraged her to find her old ways and not to long for life as a human, for humans cannot be trusted."

Jett takes my hand in his, lacing his fingers through mine. "The three surviving men found the body of their friend, torn to pieces, shredded by animals, and they swore to catch the beasts that did it. The three of them rallied together and labeled themselves hunters. They recruited a fourth hunter—the eldest son of their murdered friend. They taught their own sons, and their sons taught their sons, and so on. This line of hunters has existed ever since."

I blink a few times, my eyes heavy. "Lydia had terrible friends," I comment.

"Lydia had smart friends," Jett counters.

"They ripped up a human, stole her back, and took off into the woods, leaving the whole mess behind. If they'd just been more careful . . ."

Jett sits up straighter, his posture now stiff. "Don't be foolish, Flo. We can't trust humans."

I sit up, too. "I know that. But that doesn't excuse Lydia's friends killing—"

"A hunter," Jett interrupts. "They killed a hunter."

"A human," I argue.

"No," he says, and holds his palms flat out in front of him. "Here are your humans. Then rats, cockroaches," he lowers his hand each time, then plummets it to the ground. "There are your hunters."

"All right," I say, trying not to roll my eyes. "I get it. I just sometimes want to believe there's more than this."

Jett rises to his feet. "There's not."

"Stop!" I demand. "You always do this. You always change the subject or abandon it altogether when we talk about hunters. This is important to me, Jett."

He stops. Takes a breath. Shaking his head, he says, "You don't understand. You haven't been around humans the same way I have. You haven't seen . . ."

"Haven't seen what?" I ask. "Jett, if I don't understand, then help me, because all I see is—"

"I just wish you'd stop filling your head with all these impossible hopes. It hurts me to see you thinking this way when I know it'll only lead to disappointment. The road is our home."

"How can I just switch off like that? What aren't you telling me?" I stand, too. "I know you, Jett. I know when you're hiding something. I thought we had no secrets."

Jett draws a deep breath, lifts up his shirt at the side, and turns his body toward me. In the dying light, I move around him to get a better look. There's a long scar—a pattern of links, like a chain. It's thin, pale, hard to make out, but there. "What is this?" I say, running my finger over it. He flinches, but doesn't move away.

"A hunter did it to me," he whispers.

I pull my hand back quickly, as if it could burn me. "When?"

"My family was attacked by them." He pauses. "They wrapped my parents in chains, my mother screamed as the silver burned and sank into her skin."

"You told me you never knew your family. You told me Hari found you abandoned and you grew up here."

Jett shakes his head.

I want to reach out to him but I can't move.

He keeps talking.

"My father tried to comfort her, even though he was burning, too. I was separated from them. I struggled. I fought. I tried to get to them. So the hunters wrapped me in chains, too. The rest is a blur. I was so young I don't remember much else."

"Why did you keep this from me?"

"I didn't want to tell you about it! I didn't want to tell anyone. But I think it's important now. . . . With the way you're thinking." He sighs, runs a hand through his hair. "I've never told any of the others, only the elders know. Hari did find me. Abandoned. The hunters left me behind after they did whatever they did to my parents. The metallic stench of blood and burned skin is something I'll never forget. Hari told me he was like me, and about the circus.

He told me he'd protect me. So I went with him. I didn't have a lot of choice. I didn't really understand what was going on."

I run my hands lightly over his arm. He moves away. "Let's not, okay?"

"What?" I ask, confused.

"Just . . . don't do that. Don't feel sorry for me. I don't want that. Everyone here has been through something similar, whether they remember it or not."

"But, Jett—"

"Flo, please."

I stare at him for a long moment, at the distance he put between us just now. I battle with myself over what to say next. I know what it feels like to touch silver. The elders introduced me to it once I was old enough to understand. They told me that shifters can't touch it. They told me it's our greatest weakness. They told me it can stop us shifting, pull us from our shapes. Then they made me touch it.

It singed the ends of my fingertips, melted the skin clean off. I've never felt such intense pain. Even though shifters heal fast, the soreness lasted for days. The silver left its mark, a reminder of what it can do. Not that I could ever forget.

Squeezing my eyes shut, I will the image of burning flesh out of my head. Everything around me is still, silent.

3

INTO THE LIONS' DEN

Pink and purple light shines faintly through the treetops.

Leaves are stuck to my cheek and tangled in my hair. My bare legs are pink from the cold. Jett's sitting upright, leaning against a tree trunk. "Morning," he says. My eyes flick to his chest, the image of his burned flesh flashing through my mind. I push it back. He's right—we've all been through something similar. I just didn't know Jett remembered so much of his life before he was brought here.

I look around the clearing for the source of the sound that woke me. Splashing and laughing comes from the lake, too far out for me to see who it is. The sun breaks through the clouds and makes the water sparkle. I catch sight of a seal, which I think is Star, drifting lazily on the surface. I smile a little as I watch her, then worry that she'll be disappointed in me. Star loves my act—she begs the elders to let her watch when I practice—and I know I must have let her down.

Around Star, there are three other shifters in their human forms. They chase each other, ducking under the water to avoid being splashed, somersaulting and giggling.

I used to play out here like this with Jett and the triplets. Until one of the brothers ducked me under and I swallowed so much lake water, I puked.

I hear heavy footsteps crunching on the leaves before someone else bursts into the clearing. Pru, one of the tiger girls, stands there with her hands on her hips, staring straight ahead with a scowl on her face. She hasn't noticed me yet, still on the ground. I back up quietly so the trees shield me from her view.

"What the hell are you doing?" Pru yells across the water. "Nora said take a bath, not play moronic games. Come on! You've been here ages."

Star shifts back and swims to shore. The others reluctantly follow. Pru continues to yell across the water. "You're going to hold us all up, you know? There's loads left to do before we leave."

Behind the tree, I stand gingerly and brush the dirt and leaves from my robe. Jett pulls himself to his feet and does the same. Then I hear Star ask Pru about me. "Has anyone found Flo yet?"

"Who cares?" Pru responds. "Let's go."

I shake my head and make my way back through the trees to camp before the others see me, gesturing for Jett to follow. The last thing I need is Pru's attention.

Dew-covered leaves stick to the soles of my feet, slimy and slippery. I don't make any effort to hurry; even though I'm afraid of them leaving without us, I'm equally afraid of the elders being there, waiting for me to get back.

"Are you okay?" Jett asks.

"I think so," I say.

I tug my robe together against my body and walk out into camp before I change my mind and bolt again.

On our return, the camp is being cleared and packed away. The huge tent we hold the circus inside—a maze of curtains and props—is no longer standing. The air is thick with smoke from the extinguished campfire.

The old muddy cars we use, scratched, rusty, and dirty, are lined up on the side of the road, doors open, piled high with our belongings. It's a sight I see all too often. But that's my life, packing up and moving on, never staying in the same place for too long, nothing but a tent and a backpack of clothes to my name. I get so sick of running sometimes.

The elders have two trailers between them—Hari in one, and Ava and Nora share the other—and the rest of us sleep in small tents. It often works out two to a tent, but I somehow wound up with one of my own, which is one of the only ones still standing now.

In the center of the camp is the fire pit, where we gather on logs or chairs (if you're lucky enough to get one). I can't remember a night before last that I didn't sit around the fire with the rest of the circus after the show. I don't usually wander off at nighttime.

Almost everything is packed away now, though the evidence of our stay remains—patches of flattened grass, scorched earth, a circle of logs around a pile of blackened wood.

The three elders stand in a row, looking into the forest, undoubtedly waiting for me to emerge. When they see me, they turn their backs to me and walk away, clearly expecting me to follow. Here I go, into the lions' den (literally).

Jett puts his hand on the small of my back. He kisses the side of my head. "It'll be all right."

I nod and follow the elders. They lead me down a thin path. The rough, uneven ground is lined with prickly bushes and overgrown weeds. They scratch my bare legs as I walk by them. Once the four of us are out of earshot and sight of the others, the elders turn to face me and I almost crash into them.

The elders are in their forties and fifties, so they aren't actually *old*. Ava and Nora both have short pale-blond, almost white, hair. Hari's is a much darker blond and streaked with gray. When they shift into their lion shapes, Hari's mane is tawny-brown, and Ava and Nora's pelts are as light as sand.

Nora glares at me. I remember the look on her face last night and try not to tremble under her gaze. Ava stands beside her with her arms folded across her chest. Hari steps forward and regards me silently. I swallow, desperate to take a step back, but I don't move.

"What happened last night?" Hari asks, surprisingly calm. I expected someone to shout at me.

"I panicked. I'm sorry," I answer pathetically.

"You were ready, Flo," Ava says. "You've been practicing for a long time now, longer than anyone else practiced before their first show."

What's that supposed to mean? I wonder. Am I not as good as everyone else? Don't I learn as quickly, perform as well? My head swims with a thousand questions, but do the answers really matter?

"I know," I say, instead of voicing my questions. "I'm sorry. I was nervous."

"We all get nervous," Ava continues. "Every one of us has been through this, or has it to come. We perform because we have to. This is how our group works—you know that. We have to stick together, we have to keep moving. We support each other here, Flo. This is how it is for our kind. This is how it is for *us*. This is how we get by."

Her speech sounds rehearsed, like she's said it many times. I nod at the three of them and apologize again. Owen comes running down the path before I can say anything else. He skids to a stop when he sees us and catches his breath. "There . . . you are."

I wonder which of us he's talking to. "What is it?" Nora snaps.

"Jonah's here," Owen wheezes out. "I've looked . . . everywhere . . . for you. He's waiting."

"Right," Nora says. "Off you go. Tell him we're coming." Owen takes off in the opposite direction. Seeming satisfied with my apology, Nora adds, "Flo, go back to camp and practice for tonight until we leave. Which will be soon."

I turn and head back. I will be in tonight's show at the next location, then, and I won't get away with letting them down a second time.

4
DANGEROUS

Jett's waiting for me when I get back to camp.

He holds open his arms and I walk straight into them. "What did they say?"

I wrap my arms around him, remembering the scars on his side as my hands pass over them. "As expected," I say. "I'm performing tonight—no excuses."

Jett steps back and meets my eyes. "Come on. I'll help you get ready to go." He picks a leaf out of my hair and crumples it up in his hand. The ripped pieces are carried to the ground by the wind, scattered and broken.

"I can't," I say. "I have to practice for tonight until it's time to leave."

"Then I'll help you do that," he says simply. "We've got about half an hour."

"Aren't you supposed to be helping them pack up?" I ask, nodding my head toward the disassembled circus tent. "I'm not actually sure I'm allowed any help."

"Did they say you weren't?"

"Well, not exactly—"

"Then I'm helping you," he says with a grin.

I tug on his arm. "Fine. Come on."

The elders walk by us but don't look my way. Jonah stands on the edge of camp next to his flashy car. He's our agent for this area—he sets up the performances around here for anywhere between two weeks and two months and takes a cut of anything we make. He must have plenty of other clients to afford a car like that. There's no way he's getting a decent enough wage out of us. We're usually quite popular around here, though, so he must be doing something right. Hari hands him the books, and Nora gives him an envelope of money.

Jett and I leave the camp. We squeeze through a hedge and come out the other side in a large clearing. "Okay. Shift," he says when we stop.

I blush. "Turn around first," I say, fiddling with the tie on my robe.

He holds his hands over his eyes and turns so his back is to me. I slip out of the robe and let it fall to the ground. It's ruined anyway. The cold air bites my bare skin. I close my eyes and will my shape to come.

The world blurs around me, eventually surrounding me in darkness, nothingness, which is why I close my eyes. When I was younger, and just beginning to learn how to take my shape, I'd fall over all the time from the dizzying sensation that comes with what we call the Blackout. It's as if the shape takes you, picks you off the planet, and sends you somewhere else. I've seen others shift, their bodies blurring out of focus so they're nothing more than lines and smudges of color.

Wherever we're taken during the transformation is cold. Goosebumps flare up on my bare flesh, pins and needles prickle beneath my skin, and I feel like I've been dropped into a dimension of black ice.

Then I start to take shape, to leave my human skin behind, and I'm on fire. My insides are electric, sparking and sizzling. My long chestnut-brown hair grows and travels along my body, coating every part of my skin, wrapping me in its warmth. My heart feels like it's expanding in reaction to the change. It beats differently, at a quicker rate, pumping more forcefully.

When I open my eyes, the world looks different. I can see and hear so clearly; everything is suddenly sharp and intensified. My senses are overloaded. Sound crashes into my ears, making them twitch. Jett's foot against the hard mud, the rustle of his jacket as his arm moves, the noise of him breathing through his nose, the sound of his heart beating—I can hear it all, and all too well.

I can see for hundreds of yards to each side, but Jett's standing right in front of me and almost completely out of sight. I turn my head so I can see him properly. Having eyes on the side of my head is usually the most difficult thing to get used to when I shift—the way the world looks so different when I open them again, throwing me off balance. Walking on four legs takes some getting used to as well.

Sunbeams break through the clouds like spotlights. I know my coat will be shimmering and glossy in this early morning light. I shake my head, fanning out my dark-brown mane, and swish my tail.

"Are you ready?" Jett turns around slowly. He looks at me and smiles. I smile back, I think, by curling back my upper lip. Warm breath surrounds my face in a thin cloud, visible in the crisp air for a second before disappearing altogether.

Jett takes a step toward me and carefully reaches out to me. He runs his hand down my long nose and I tilt my head to let him, nuzzling his side. He laughs. "You're so beautiful," he says. The girl in me loves to hear him say that.

I stamp my hind leg and move away from him, trotting off into the opening to warm up and get used to my form. Tonight, this is the skin I will wear.

While I warm up, Jett sets up a hurdle—the one they will light on fire tonight. It's easy to jump when it's unlit. There's no danger other than tripping over it. But if I trip once it's on fire, I could burn myself or knock it over and set the tent ablaze.

To say that I'm afraid of this trick is an understatement. It took me a long time to overcome the fear enough to face it. When I first began my training, I'd run up to the flames but come to a screeching halt just before the jump. They had me clear the unlit hurdle endlessly before I finally managed to do it lit, and even then we didn't stop. I can't count how many times I have done this now. The elders were right: I have had more training on my act than is usual. No one else seemed to give them this much of a problem. This is big, though. Dangerous. And it's a risk on a new act. Any number of things could go wrong, and each runs through my head right before I jump.

I wonder if the elders are pushing me too far—too much too soon. But I've convinced myself they know what they're doing. They have their reasons, and they know what's best for us. If they say I can do it, then I must.

I jump and clear the hurdle over and over and over. It's too easy. I know I can do it here and now, but what about when it's on fire and I'm not just jumping in front of Jett, but in front of a whole audience of strangers?

Hari shows up in the clearing just as I jump and clear the hurdle again. He claps his hands together as he approaches me. I can't tell if he means it, or if he's mocking me in some way. Hari's the nicest of the elders, though. I'd only *really* expect that kind of thing from Nora. So I decide he's pleased with me.

"Very good, Flo," Hari says. "Very good, indeed. You're certainly ready, my dear, though I knew that already." He continues walking until he's only inches from me. He stops and strokes along my side. "It's only you who has to believe that now."

He turns and shouts over to Jett. "Pack up the hurdle and bring the equipment back." Then he faces me again. "You can shift back when you're ready and rejoin us in camp. We're almost all set to leave for the next location. Violet Bay—you like it there, don't you, Flo?"

I nod. I do. We've visited before when we've performed in that area. I always want to go back there. It's close to a beach, and sometimes we're allowed to go sit on the sand if it's quiet and there aren't many humans around. I like all the locations in that area, but Violet Bay is the only site that backs onto the beach.

As Hari leaves, I trot back over to Jett. My robe is beside him in a heap on the floor. I nudge Jett with my nose, turning his back to me. "That tickles!" he says, laughing. I nudge him a little more for good measure; I like hearing him laugh.

Once his back is to me, I close my eyes and shift back. The
Blackout returns, everything's in reverse. The heat first, then
the cold as my coat is shed. There's a shrinking sensation that
doesn't last long, and isn't uncomfortable, but I am aware of
it. Some shifters say they can't feel that, but I can. It's only
there a moment, then it's gone and I'm human again.

When I open my eyes, I grab my robe immediately off
the ground and cover myself up. The rush makes me dizzy,
but the moment quickly passes.

"You can turn around now," I say to Jett, finding my
voice again.

He does, then clears the distance between us and wraps
his arms around me, packing my stomach chock-full of
manic butterflies same as every other time he touches me.
I swallow and lean into him. "That was amazing, Flo. You
cleared the jump every time."

It's not the jump that rattles me, though; it's the flames.
"Do you think it needs to be on fire?" I ask.

"I guess," Jett says with a shrug. "It's not much of a
show if it's not, I suppose. You know, it has to be 'shock-
ing' and 'something the audience will remember,'" he says,
quoting the elders and making his voice higher.

I laugh. "That's a pretty good impression. Which one
were you impersonating?"

"Nora, of course," Jett says with a smirk. He strokes my
arm, catching his hand in one of the rips on the sleeve of
my robe. His fingers brush along my bare skin. "Seriously,
Flo, you'll be fine. You cleared it by a mile; those flames
aren't getting near you. Is that what you're worried about?"

I nod.

"Don't," he says, as if it's *that* simple. Like my fear could so easily disappear, just like that. "You'll clear them, I know you will."

He wraps an arm around my shoulder, the other around the hurdle, and we start walking back toward camp. "After you've changed, will you come ride in the car with me and the guys?"

I whine, "I hate those guys!"

Jett laughs. "They know you do. If you weren't so obvious about it, they'd probably leave you alone."

I frown. That's what he always says. Still, it's hard not to react. "Why don't you stick up for me?" I ask.

"I do!" Jett says. "I always say something to them when they get going. You four have been giving me a headache since we were five years old, seriously."

I can't help but laugh and let it go. "Fine. I'll meet you by the car. I'm guessing they'll have a lot to say after last night, though."

"I'll speak to them while you're getting ready," Jett says. "Leave them to me." He kisses me on the cheek and we go separate ways—Jett to the car, me to my tent.

5

THE FLAMING HORSE INN

I wash up as best as I can with a cloth and soap before the buckets are packed away.

When I'm done, I go back to my tent and look through some freshly washed clothes someone's laid out for me. It must have been Ava or Nora, which means one of them rummaged through my backpack while I was out practicing. I don't exactly have much that's my own, so I don't like the idea of someone else looking through it.

I guess they were only trying to help—or hurry me along. I slip into a pair of black jeans and boots, an oversize checkered shirt that used to be Jett's, and a brown coat with a fake fur hood. It feels nice to be wrapped up warm after wearing just a thin robe since last night.

I zip up my backpack and toss it out of the tent, then roll up my sleeping bag and do the same with that. Jett comes to help take the tent down and carries some of my things over to the car for me. I pull my hair into a band and follow him.

"Hey, Flo," says Lucas. I roll my eyes and brace myself for what's coming.

Jett whispers something to him, but I don't catch it. Then I hear him say, "Be nice," under his breath.

I sigh and say, "Hey," back.

"I didn't realize you were a disappearing act," Lucas says, grinning.

"What did I just say?" Jett hisses. Lucas ignores him. I narrow my eyes and open my mouth to snap back, but Jett claps his hands together and says, "Okay. Let's get going."

Lucas laughs and climbs into the back with Lance and Logan—triplets, elephants. The three of them are total morons. I raise my eyebrows at Jett, then go around the car to the front passenger seat.

Inside, Jett taps my knee. "You okay?" he mouths. I shrug and put my seat belt on. The other cars, which had been waiting for us, start moving off more or less as soon as we get into our seats. Jett starts the car, puts it into gear, and follows the rest of the circus along the winding roads and on to the next site.

Jett turns the music on, which I'm grateful for—it keeps the triplets from talking about last night. I have enough to worry about without their teasing the whole way to Violet Bay.

I keep thinking about those flames on the hurdle, stretching up and licking the space above. Of the heat grazing my stomach as I leap over them. In the tent, I won't get as much space to run before the jump. Why has no one else thought of that? I'm more convinced than ever that the elders are wrong on this. But I know they won't listen to me. They'll think I'm making excuses to get out of the show.

Sweat trickles down my spine and I open the window a crack, feeling nauseated. Jett glances at me. I can tell he knows something's wrong. He always knows. But he doesn't ask while the brothers are in the back, in case they overhear. I don't want them, of all people, knowing how much this is affecting me. So Jett and I turn our attention to the road before us, keeping our eyes trained ahead and our thoughts to ourselves.

The triplets and I have never really gotten along. We just didn't click as children. The brothers liked playing pranks, which I thought were mean and often ended up sabotaging to protect someone else's feelings. They started calling me "spoil sport" after a while and turned their attention to me. I was never "in" on pranks anymore, so I couldn't stop them, and a lot of them were played on me instead. Like the time they moved my tent, put costume makeup on me while I slept, filled my shoes with sand—stupid things that *no one* finds funny.

Jett's stuck in the middle and always has been. He keeps the peace and sorts out the arguments. We don't actually argue all that often now we've grown up. But the three still pick on me whenever they find something worth picking on. Seems I did a lot more of the "growing up" than they did.

After a while, we pass through a sleepy village, going slowly over a cobblestone road. There's an old English inn with wooden tables and benches outside littered with pint glasses and beer bottles, empty except for froth at the bottom. Beer mats are ripped into tiny pieces and blowing around in the wind. Snack wrappers, stuck in the gaps of the wooden planks on the table, attract birds for the crumbs. The sign above the door creaks in the breeze, displaying a worn painting of a horse surrounded by fire.

I do a double take, certain I've imagined it. The scratchy letters below read: THE FLAMING HORSE INN. I shudder and turn my attention to the rest of the village, trying to forget the foreboding image on the old sign.

The road is narrow, and a group of people have to step to the side, pressing their backs up against the stone walls of the stores and houses to let us pass. They're dressed in coats and hats and scarves, walking boots on their feet and large backpacks strapped to their backs. I wonder what it'd be like to be one of those people, wrapped up and out for a walk in the mountains, then maybe stopping off for a drink and lunch at the warm inn. Maybe not the inn we just passed, though. No one should go there.

The cars in front turn off the road and pull onto a dirt parking lot. We bump across and park, too. The other shifters climb from their vehicles and stretch. The elders walk by the front of the car. Hari bangs his hand on the bonnet twice and Nora looks in and grins at me.

"Why are we stopping?" I say to Jett.

"For lunch," Lance answers.

"Oh, have you changed your name to Jett?" I say, turning in my seat. The other two brothers laugh, their blond hair falling over their faces. Seventeen and still huddled together laughing and picking on girls. I roll my eyes. "Grow up, guys. Seriously."

The brothers get out of the car and slam their doors, harder than necessary. I unclip my seat belt and pull the door handle. Jett puts his hand on mine. "Wait," he says. "I can tell something's up with you. What is it? The show?"

"No. It's nothing," I say, but I know that won't wash with him.

He tilts his head. "Flo, it's me. You can tell me."

I sigh and shuffle around in my seat to face him. "I'm still worried about the fire. I haven't practiced enough with the hurdle lit. I'll have to jump higher to clear the flames. I don't know if I'll get enough height. And I'll have less distance to run into the jump. I'm freaking out, Jett."

"That's okay," he soothes. "It's natural to be nervous. Do you want to speak to the elders? I'll come with you. I'll even do the speaking if you want."

"No," I say quickly. I appreciate him sticking up for me, but sometimes he looks after me too much. Even if I did want to talk to the elders, I don't need someone to speak *for* me. "If I wanted to talk to them, don't you think I'd have done it myself already? I am capable, you know."

"I didn't mean it like that. You're just not yourself lately, and I'm trying to look out for you. I'll do whatever you need me to do."

I close my eyes and sigh. "Just be there with me. I have to do it, and I guess it'll be over by this time tomorrow." I shake my head, banishing thoughts of the show. "Let's just go for lunch. I'm starving."

Jett opens his door, letting a gust of chilly air into the car. I follow suit and he holds out his hand. I take it and he squeezes it in his, then we walk together in the direction the others went in. "Where did they go?" I ask.

Jett points ahead with his free hand, directly at The Flaming Horse. "To that old inn over there."

36

6

BEAR ATTACK

"Spooky," Jett says under his breath as we pass through the doorway of the inn.

He looks up at the sign swinging in the wind. I keep my head down as we enter the old building. I don't want to look at it again. Spooky doesn't even cover it. No doubt it was Nora's idea to stop here for lunch. I remember the way she smirked as she walked past the car.

It's warm and cozy inside the inn. I almost forget my unease, but the sign creaks again as the door swings shut and a chill runs through me. The big room with its stone walls is lit with a yellow-orange glow from the various mismatched table lamps and candles. Two fireplaces are lit, both with comfy armchairs and a coffee table positioned in front of them. The triplets have claimed one of those spots for themselves. The smell of hot pastry and the tang of ale fills the air, adding to the comfort. Jett and I join the triplets on the squishy chairs beside one of the crackling log fires. "What did they say we could have?" I ask.

"One drink, one meal from this side of the menu," Lucas says, pointing at the SANDWICHES AND LIGHT BITES section. Jett and I both order a soft drink and a sandwich for lunch.

The elders sit in the corner away from the rest of us. The pack is then split up into smaller groups throughout the room—the tigers with the tigers, the seals with the seals, the baboons with the baboons (making too much noise, as usual). Those too young to perform, or the only one of their species in the circus, tend to stick together, too.

I envy the younger ones right now. I want to be at that table with them, knowing that I only have to watch the show tonight, not be in it. Funny thing is, I'll bet any one of them would trade places with me in a second. Maybe that'd change when the time came to perform, though. I was never all that nervous about it until it crept up on me, and suddenly I was to go out into the ring with the fire and the cheers and the dozens of eyes watching . . . watching.

Our order arrives and I eat quickly, staring into the fire in front of me and not really tasting anything that goes into my mouth. *Chew, chew, chew, swallow.*

I can hear the elephant triplets bickering among themselves, involving Jett here and there. They mention my name once or twice, probably followed by something insulting, but I'm not paying enough attention for what they're saying to register. Their voices sound distant and muffled, like an invisible barrier stands between them and me. I suppose it does. Their words pass over me, and I only catch some of them: *fire, jump, run away, scared.*

Jett touches my leg. I jump, blink. The triplets snigger, but I only look at Jett. My eyes are dry, and I blink some more to work the moisture back. "Are you all right in here, Flo?" Jett asks quietly then shoots an irritated look at the triplets.

"Yes," I say. But my expression must say otherwise because Jett doesn't seem convinced.

"We can wait back at the car if you want to," he says. "Everyone's almost done anyway."

I stand up and put my plate on the coffee table. The fire glows off its white surface, flickering and hot. I look away and head for the door.

"I'll just let the elders know," Jett says.

I wait for him outside. The creaky sign above my head groans in the wind and I will him to hurry. Wrapping my arms around myself to keep warm, I lean back against the wall.

Before long, Jett steps out into the cold. "Okay, let's go," he says. My teeth chatter and I move closer to Jett.

"How long will they be?" I ask.

"Not long, but we can enjoy some quiet before we set off again. Sometimes it's hard to get away from all the noise."

I smile. "Thank you." I'm concerned that peace and quiet will give me more time with my thoughts than is welcome, but the chatter and bustle of the circus can be deafening at times. Especially when we're all packed into one room like the inn.

"Don't mention it," Jett says as he unlocks the car. He opens the passenger door for me before running around to the driver's side and jumping in, closing the door quickly to cut off the flow of cold air blowing in. He puts the keys in the ignition and turns the heat on. I clasp my hands together, but Jett takes them from me and holds them in his own, rubbing them to warm them up. "That better?" he asks.

I nod. "Yeah. Thanks."

He moves closer to me. "You're welcome. Here," he says, pulling off his scarf and draping it around my neck. He leans over while he pulls it around me, so close that I can feel the warmth of his breath on my cheek. I close my eyes. "There," he says, moving back. My hair is stuck under the scarf and he leans over again to fix it, letting it fall over my shoulders.

This time, when he starts to move back onto his seat, I stop him. I cup my hand around his elbow, keeping him close to me, our faces inches apart. Being this near to him still makes my heart hammer in my chest, makes my stomach flutter, and I'm overwhelmed with a mixture of nerves and excitement. I lose myself in his dark eyes, run a shaky hand through his dark hair. He takes a deep breath and puts his hand on my thigh. His eyes close, breaking the connection. I swallow and move back. Only slightly, but he notices.

"Sorry," I say quickly. I ball my hands together on my lap and turn my body to face forward rather than toward him. "I'm just worried about tonight. It's like a huge weight on me and I can't . . ."

"Flo, you don't need to be sorry. I—"

Fists knock against the car window, stopping Jett from finishing his sentence. He sighs and turns to unlock the doors and let the triplets inside. "Brr!" Lance says—at least I think it is Lance—as he rubs his hands together and holds them out to the heater. "You shouldn't keep us waiting out there."

"I didn't keep you waiting," Jett says flatly. "I opened the door as soon as you knocked."

"Jeez, lighten up. We didn't interrupt something, did we?" Lucas says with a smirk. Neither Jett nor I answer. "Anyway, no more breaks now. So if either of you need anything, now's your chance."

Jett looks at me and I shake my head. "I'll just be a minute," he says, opening the car door and dashing out. He crosses the road to the village, heading for a little store on the corner. We can get a tiny allowance—the smallest cut imaginable from the circus's takings—and that's only if we do something that really earns it. I have nothing. I've never bought myself anything. I have the clothes I was given by the elders, the essentials that they provide, but I have nothing of my own. It takes a lot of saving up to be able to afford anything.

I watch Jett enter the store with the dark blue sign. The gold lettering reads: THE HORSE ON THE MOUNTAIN. What is it with this village and horses? I glance up at the mountaintop.

"So, Flo," one of the triplets says. They all sound the same, so if I'm not looking at them, I'm never sure who's speaking. The three of them lean forward, resting their arms on the front two seats. "What's the deal with running away last night? Everyone wants to know."

"The elders haven't said a thing," another says.

"Did you get in trouble?"

"No," I say, sighing heavily. "I'm not talking about it."

"Why?"

"What was the problem?"

"I've seen your act. I was looking forward to it."

I turn to face them. "Oh, what? In case I tripped, is that it?"

Lucas smirks. "Something like that."

"You know, you guys are so—"

The car door opens and Jett slides into his seat hurriedly. "Guys, look at this." He unfolds two of the free local newspapers and throws one into the back for the triplets, spreading the other across our laps. The front-page headline reads: MAN SURVIVES VICIOUS BEAR ATTACK.

"Jett, what is this?" I ask, wondering what a bear attack has to do with us. We only just got here.

"Read here," Jett says, pointing to a paragraph on the page.

A twenty-four-year-old man is recovering in the hospital after being mauled by two bears outside his home. The bears charged at him as he was putting out the garbage for pick-up. If it wasn't for the courage of three passersby, the victim may not have been so fortunate. The three men who arrived on the scene are yet to be identified, but are urged to come forward. Police and officials are still hunting the bears. People in the area are advised to be extra vigilant at this time.

I frown, trying to make sense of it.

42

"Doesn't it seem odd to you? It says here that the closest zoo is over twenty miles away from the place where it happened, and none of their animals were reported missing," Jett says, pointing his finger to a different part of the article.

"What about the mountains?"

Jett shakes his head. "The guy's house isn't anywhere near the mountains. The bears would surely have been spotted between here and there."

"Are you thinking shifters did this?" Lucas asks.

"I don't know," Jett replies. "I'm going to speak to the elders before we set off."

"It does seem likely, though," I say. "Doesn't it? And the three passersby that showed up on time and disappeared right after. Hunters?"

Jett scratches his forehead. "Maybe. I'll be right back." He hops out of the car again, taking the newspaper with him.

This time the triplets are quiet when Jett leaves. They're still reading the newspaper article spread across their laps. I stare ahead and watch Jett approach Hari's trailer and knock at the door on the side.

I've heard of shifters like this before, if that's who it was. There are rogue packs of shifters who enjoy letting their animal sides take over. They lose themselves and often end up hurting people. These shifters are the easiest for the hunters to track down. They're messy. They leave trails. It's these kinds of shifters who put the rest of us in danger. And this time, their trail ends in the same area we're staying in for two months.

I look back at the article the triplets are holding and imagine the scene. The attack, the human victim, the hunters. Fighting is engraved into our animal natures. Some shifters get a rush from letting their instincts take over. They don't know how to control it.

Growing up in the circus, our behavior as animals was the hardest thing to overcome during our training with the elders. Sometimes, because I didn't know what I was doing, it took me a long time to return to human. When I took my shape, I was barely aware of my human self, but I learned to control my actions and to find myself, which is something these shifters must never have accomplished. This skill is necessary as a performer. Shifters can't lose their heads in the ring, get lost in their shapes, be actual animals inside a tent full of humans. Now, as a horse, I am more myself than ever. I even find it difficult to give in to my animal instincts after training so hard to suppress them.

Ava and Nora have joined Jett and Hari outside Hari's trailer now. They're holding the newspaper open between the three of them while Jett makes his way back to the car. He climbs in and sighs. "Ready to go?" he says.

"What did they say?" I ask.

"Not a lot. They think the bears were shifters, too."

"And? What are they going to do about it?"

"Nothing. They said that the hunters will find the bears before the police do, if they haven't already." He clicks his seat belt on and adjusts the rearview mirror, wiping it with his sleeve.

"And then what?" I ask.

"The hunters will kill the shifters and all will be forgotten."

"Except it won't," I mutter.

"Flo, this happens all the time. Not all shifters are decent. They brought this on themselves."

"But they're bears!" I say. "And it happened close to our next location. Doesn't that worry you?"

Jett nods once, his mouth a thin line. "Yes, it does. Hopefully they've caught them and moved on. There's not a lot we can do." The first cars start to drive away, joining the cobblestone road in a single line of traffic. Jett looks at the triplets in the rearview mirror. "Buckle up."

We set off again, along the rickety roads of the small village for a short while, then on to straight, flat roads through the city and toward the coast. Violet Bay, with salty air and the wind from the sea, is by far my favorite of our locations. I wish the shifter attack hadn't spoiled our return.

Jett doesn't say another word about the article, and I don't bring it up again either. It doesn't stop me thinking about it though. Shifters like the bears that attacked that man usually come from packs that live wild. They still travel, like we do, but they're less civilized. They hide away in secluded areas and they have little regard for human life. Humans have so much while we have so little even though we are stronger than they are. Why are they the dominant species? Why do *they* control *us*? Why do I both so desperately want to be one and fear them at the same time?

Humans would see us as a threat, and it's true that some of us are. We could never reveal our existence to all of them. The hunters, a secret government-funded organization, know about us, about what we are and what we can do. Some are even descendants from a long line of hunters brought into this life and trained from an early age, like the ones in the story "Lydia the Wolf." They know secrets of this world that many wouldn't be able to handle.

It's hard to imagine what'd happen if our existence became public knowledge. It'd tip the balance of the human world. They wouldn't know what to believe anymore. Myths and legends and fairy tales and nightmares would all be up in the air. It'd raise so many questions: *What else exists? What's real and what isn't?* They wouldn't understand. So we're kept secret and kept in check by the ones who do understand.

I think about this for most of the journey. It really worries me that the bears attacked a human so close to where our next camp is, drawing hunters to the area. *But hunters are everywhere,* I remind myself. That's why we keep moving.

7

BOYCOTT THE CIRCUS

There are protestors outside the entrance to our camp in Violet Bay.

We drive past slowly as they wave signs over their heads. The posters read: CRUELTY UNDER THE BIG TOP. BOYCOTT THE CIRCUS! CRUELTY IS NOT ENTERTAINMENT. I have to look away.

I keep my eyes cast down, listening to the shouting outside. We've dealt with protests before and it's never easy. There's no telling how long they'll stay out here for, or how often they'll come back. "See what they're like," Nora tells us every time we encounter protestors. "The humans. Hostile and intimidating, the whole lot of them."

I have to agree, but I can sympathize on some level with their efforts. We're not an animal circus, though. Not *really*. If we could just go out there and tell them we're here willingly, not kept in cages and used for entertainment. But we can't—this is just another situation where there's nothing we can do but let it ride out its course.

The cages and trucks follow us into the site. The bars are covered, seeing as they don't contain any real animals— we use them for storage instead, and to sit or sleep inside when the weather's really bad. The protestors steer clear of them, respectful of the animals they think are inside.

I flinch at the sound of a palm smacking against the window right by my head. They don't steer clear of us.

A girl catches my eye. She holds my gaze, a white sign up above her head, which reads: ANIMAL CIRCUS = ANIMAL ABUSE in red paint. There's a fierce look in her eyes, an unquestionable belief in what she stands for. I can see the use of animals for entertainment upsets her, and I know I can't take away her sadness and worry without revealing what we are, and that's out of the question. I wonder if she, if all of them, knew about us—about how the hunters track us down, treat us worse than animals—would they campaign to stop that, too?

I turn away from the girl as Jett parks. I don't want to get out of the car, but no one else is letting the protest stop them. Violet Bay looks like most of the other places we stop at—fairly secluded, but not hard to find or too out of the way. There's a large, clear space surrounded by bushes and trees. Enough land to put the tent up, set up camp around the back, and allow customers to park in front.

"Flo, you're with me this afternoon," Nora says as I get out of the car. It's hard to hear her over the shouts from the crowd at the entrance. "Just ignore them," she snaps. "Come on."

Jett and the triplets have to go help set up camp and the circus tent while Nora takes me over to a field and sets up the hurdle for me to practice. Once we pass through a thick row of bushes, we're out of sight from the protestors. I can hear the waves crashing nearby and I close my eyes, breathing in the salt air and longing to go down to the beach. Nora snaps her fingers. "Concentrate. There will be plenty of time to spend on the beach while we're here."

I open my eyes. "How did you know that's what I was thinking?"

She tilts her head. "We've been here seven times. You behave the same way every time we arrive. But today isn't like all those other times, today is the day of your first performance. That's what you need to concentrate on. The beach can wait."

I take off my boots and socks. The ground is sludge beneath my bare feet, the mud cold and gooey. "Ugh."

"Come on, Flo. Hurry. I've got a lot of other things to do, you know."

I stop undressing. "Then I'll practice on my own."

She shakes her head. "No. I'm watching you do it now so there are no excuses for running away again later. You better not, Flo."

"I won't!" I look over at the hurdle. "What about the fire?" I ask.

"What about it?" Nora replies, crossing her arms.

"Aren't you going to set the hurdle on fire?"

"That's for the show."

"But I want to practice *before* the show." My voice sounds whiny and I instantly regret speaking to her in that tone. Nora's face turns sour (well, more sour than usual) and she narrows her eyes at me.

"It's a waste," she snaps. "You've done it with the fire plenty times. I will not set the hurdle alight now, not with the protestors at the entrance. You've had enough time to practice with the flames; just practice clearing it so you're ready for the show."

She says *ready for the show* with emphasis, which makes me feel embarrassed.

"Okay," I say resentfully. I bite my tongue against saying anything else about the fire. What's the point in practicing this way? I've done this a thousand times. I could clear the hurdle with my eyes closed.

I undress completely. Nora watches me the whole time, and I'm not brave enough to ask her to turn around.

When we begin, I focus my practice on running at the hurdle from a lesser distance, as the space will be restricted inside the tent. Cleared, cleared, cleared.

I keep going until Nora waves her hands when time's up. I shift back to my human form and get dressed quickly. "Good. No excuses tonight, then. Go set up your tent now and get yourself sorted."

I do as she says.

Back in camp, the protests continue. Jett runs over when he sees me. "Flo! How did it go?" he asks.

"Fine. I suppose," I answer. After looking forward to coming to Violet Bay, it hasn't exactly started out as I hoped, what with the bear attacks and the protestors and training with Nora.

Jett tilts his head. "Supper is almost ready. Sit with me?"

"Okay." My feet follow him, but my mind is elsewhere.

We collect our bowls of soup and plates of warm buttered bread and take our places around the campfire. The cars and the tents that are standing provide some privacy between us and the humans gathered on the edge of the site. I wonder when they'll leave. Maybe they'll stay for the show, hassle customers as they come to watch. It's not like that kind of thing hasn't happened before. The elders must be fuming.

The steam from the soup drifts up around my face. I lift the spoon to my lips and swallow the hot liquid. There's a strong peppery taste, which means Ava cooked tonight rather than Hari.

"Just an hour until the public arrive," Jett says, then seems to think better of it and adds, "Sorry. Not what you want to hear."

I shake my head. "It's fine." It's something I have to face up to; it won't just go away if no one mentions it. Jett's cheeks flush, or it could just be the glow from the campfire. I rest my head on his shoulder. "Really. It's okay."

"I can do your dishes. You know, if you need some time," he offers.

I sit up and finish my meal, then hand Jett the soup-smeared bowl and crumb-covered plate. "Thank you," I say. No one needs to offer twice to do my dishes for me. I hate washing them, and we all have to do our own. I hand them over gladly.

"Okay, then," Jett says, stacking the dishes up in his hands. "Anything else?" I shake my head. "Well, I'll see you in a little while, then." He kisses my cheek. "Everything will be fine."

I wish he knew that for sure.

8

THE BEAR CLAW AND THE HORSESHOE

An hour later, I walk barefoot to the big tent.

Wrapped in my robe, I stand in my usual spot where no one can see me, watching the stage, watching the crowd. But soon they will see me, all of them.

I draw a deep breath. The elders are probably looking for me, wanting to keep me close and in sight so I don't take off again. But I don't plan to. This will never go away; I just have to face it.

I feel the same way I did last night—sweaty, nervous, nauseous. With added pressure. This time I'm going out there, no excuses, no way out.

As I peer through the gap, watching the elephant triplets balancing on podiums, two shadows appear on either side of me. I jump and whip around. It's Nora and Ava. Here, no doubt, to make sure I'm ready.

"Flo, how are you feeling?" Ava asks with unexpected sympathy. But I know better—they are here to check up on me; they don't feel sorry for me.

"I think I'm okay," I tell them.

Nora frowns. "Well, which is it? Are you okay or aren't you?"

"Yes, I'm fine," I say quickly.

"And you know when you're to go on. Someone will come get you and escort you to the stage entrance," Ava says.

I scowl. "I know when I'm to go on. After you two and Hari."

"Correct," Nora says. "Don't try anything, I've got people keeping an eye on you tonight."

I look around, squinting into the shadows. "Where?"

Nora tuts. "Just don't screw up," she says, then the two of them stalk off like . . . well, like lions. They speak to other acts as they pass by them, then they're out of sight again. But now I have this weird feeling—is someone watching me right now? "Hello?" I say. "Who's there?"

When I receive no answer, I stick my head back through the curtain. Jett is performing now, riding a small bicycle around in circles. He's wearing a red waistcoat and a cone-shaped hat. There's a yellow star printed on the back of the waistcoat and another on the front of the hat. Each star has a glitter outline, which catches the light and sparkles. *Everything's got to have sparkle:* stars on the hats and jackets, glitter, fairy lights, and confetti. We have to collect as much of the confetti back up as we can at the end of the night to use again. Nothing goes to waste.

Jett squeezes a horn attached to the handlebars of the bike, and I look at the audience. They're smiling and laughing. Adults lean down to their children and point at Jett. One man sits with his daughters—one on his knee and the other on the bench beside him. The one on his lap has her face painted like a bear and she is watching Jett with a huge smile on her face. I guess some people in town aren't afraid of bears right now. The other has tiger face paint. She's laughing and scooping popcorn into her mouth. She's so absorbed by the performance that most of the popcorn pieces miss her mouth and drop to the floor. I wonder who's on cleaning duty tonight.

A while later, the monkeys burst into the ring with juggling balls and hula-hoops. Someone taps my shoulder. I let go of the curtain and step back, knocking into Jett. "Hey," he says, steadying me. "All okay?"

"I suppose."

"I know you're nervous, but this is a good night. It's a good audience out there." He unfolds two chairs and places them beside each other. We sit down and I lean my head on his shoulder.

We stay like that for a while. I have my eyes closed, concentrating on breathing and clearing my mind. The moment feels too short, though, as excited cheers from the crowd attract my attention.

I sit upright. A growl rips through the tent.

Lions.

I get up, but I don't look, can't look, because it means I'm on next. I put my hand on the folding chair beside me, and my other on my chest. It feels tight and I can't catch my breath. Jett stands, too, and places his hand on my back. "Flo? Are you going to faint?" he asks, concern lacing his words.

"No," I breathe. "No. It's fine."

He starts to rub my back. It's meant to feel soothing, but nothing could calm me now. "Flo?" he says, shaking me gently. "Flo, can you hear me?"

"What? Did you say something?"

A worried look passes over his face. "Yes. I said you better get 'round there and get ready to go on. They're setting up for you; you need to shift."

I whimper. Over his shoulder I can see Pru and her friends making their way over. Pru stops and raises an eyebrow when she sees me. They must be here to "escort" me to the stage. Nora couldn't have picked a worse person for the job.

"Let's go, let's go," Pru says, clapping her hands together.

Jett turns to look at her. "We're coming. Give us some room."

Pru rolls her eyes and leaves us to it. She doesn't go far, though, keeping me in her sight.

"I'll be with you, Flo," Jett whispers. "I'll stay with you the whole time."

"Will you come out there with me?" I ask hopelessly.

"I can't do that," he says sadly. "You know I can't. One of the elders will be walking you out." I already know that, though. I just wish it were him. "I'll be with you until you go out there, and I'll be waiting for you right by the curtain when you get back." He takes my head in each of his hands squashing my hair against my cheeks. Kissing my forehead, he reaches for my hand, then leads me to the stage entrance, passing Pru and the others on the way there.

"Okay, Flo," Jett says when we stop by the ring with just one more curtain to go through before I'm out there for everyone to see. "Shift."

"Turn away first," I say. He smiles and spins around. I untie the rope that holds my robe together and place the robe on a hook. Then I close my eyes and shift. The cool ice prickling across my skin offers momentary relief, then slaps me awake. Then the heat comes, like a warm blanket with the promise of safety.

"Let's go, Flo," Nora says, smacking my side.

Jett turns around at the sound of her voice. "You can do it," he whispers.

Nora wears a bright topcoat and tails—red with gold trim, black pants, and a gold glittery top hat with a thick black feather on the side. She attaches a blue-and-white feather headpiece around my nose and ears and makes sure it's straight. Then she leads me through the curtain into the ring to face the crowd.

The spotlight finds me and I can't see ahead. I realize I've stopped breathing and let out a long puff of air, my lips fluttering. The smell of grease and salt and so many bodies packed into the tent is overwhelming. I can almost taste it on my tongue.

I'm paraded around in front of the audience. The sound of my own heartbeat fills my ears. Nora invites some of the children from the first row to stand and stroke me. Six small hands pat at my nose and my sides. I see the girl with the tiger face paint. Her bag of popcorn spills on the floor in her hurry to come closer. She's smiling, though, and strokes me gently and confidently.

Nora leads me away now. There is a gap at the side of the tent, a curtain pulled back. It leads outside. I'm to go through it and wait for my cue to start running back into the tent and jump the flaming hurdle. So my concerns about the running distance were unnecessary. I should have just asked.

It's too warm in the tent with so many people crammed inside, shoulder to shoulder, knee to knee. And that heat is intensified once the hurdle is lit. A chorus of cheers responds to the fire. I stare at it, transfixed. Nora tugs at my reins and takes me to Ava. Ava leads me to my starting point.

Outside, I can breathe again, but the relief of fresh, cool air doesn't last for long. Ava turns me around and points at the circus tent. "You know what to do," she says, then slaps my side. "Go!"

I hesitate for a moment, just for a moment, then start to run. Faster, faster, I pick up speed. This is it. Once I make this jump, I'll become a true member of the circus. The headpiece feels heavy. One of the feathers flutters down and startles me. I falter for a second then pick up my pace again. I can't let anything go wrong this time. I have to do this.

I see the fire in front of me the moment I burst back into the tent. With only a half-second until I jump, I panic again. I can feel the heat as I get closer to the hurdle. I want to turn around and run back outside and away from all of this. But I remember my training, and I know I can do it. I have to believe that I can.

Jump.

The world pauses while I'm in the air. All four hooves leave the ground. I'm high enough, I know I am. I pass over the fire; the flames don't get near me. Then I land heavily on the other side and slow my pace. The crowd explodes with applause.

I did it! I jumped. I cleared the hurdle. I cleared the flames.

Nora brings me to the front of the ring again and bows. Then the show is over.

My first show, over.

I really did it. I look out at the audience as they cheer for me. After seeing them applaud so many acts, it's strange to be the one they're celebrating. It's exhilarating and surreal and frightening all rolled into one. The audience merges into a mass of noise and color. I scan the front row and find the little girl with the face paint. She's standing on her dad's knee, clapping her hands and waving to me.

I trot behind the curtain and shift back to human form, yanking my robe from the hook and quickly covering my body with it. Jett is the first person I see. He ducks under a curtain and comes sprinting toward me. He swoops me into his arms, lifting me off the ground and spinning me around. I squeal as he whirls us around and around. "Amazing, amazing, amazing," he says with each twirl, spinning until I feel dizzy. I lose my balance when he sets me down. He laughs and steadies me. "I'm so proud of you, Flo!"

My face hurts from smiling.

"Come on, it's time to celebrate! Your dress is through here." He holds the curtain aside. He looks gorgeous in a gray suit and open-collar white shirt, with his dark hair brushed back away from his face. "You look good," I say with a smile.

He grins back and takes my hand. "This way."

I go with him through the gap into a small space sectioned off for me to get ready for my party. All shifters get a party after their first show. Mine should have been last night, but instead I spent it in the woods by the lake after running away. It all seems so long ago. And it all seems so stupid now, the fuss I made over performing. The show went really well, and now I can celebrate and stop worrying.

I gasp when I see the dress. It's scorching-red with full-length bell-sleeves. Jett smiles and teases it carefully from its hanger. He holds it against me. "Perfect," he whispers.

"When did they get this?" I ask, running my hand down the soft material.

He rubs the back of his neck. "Um. It's one of Nora's. She has a chest of clothing stored away in her trailer. She got this out of her collection for you."

My face falls. They usually buy shifters their own outfits that we can keep and treasure as our own in memory of our first show. "So I have to give it back tomorrow?"

"Well, yeah. I'm sorry, Flo."

"What happened to keeping one, like everyone else?"

Jett looks at the ground, worrying his lips with his teeth. "They did buy you something, but they took it away to save for the next shifter because of what you did last night."

I swallow the lump in my throat. "This is my punishment then."

"I'm so sorry. It's yours tonight, at least."

"You don't need to be sorry," I say. "I just thought I'd finally have something of my own, with good memories attached to it." I try to smile, but I feel sad that I'm the only shifter who hasn't been given their own outfit to wear and keep. The only shifter who hasn't deserved to be treated, spoiled, on just this one night.

"When would you wear it, anyway?" Jett says in an attempt to make me feel better. "To breakfast around the campfire?"

I stifle a small laugh. "I know, I know. It's just a nice thing to have."

"Well, I picked something up for you this afternoon. So it looks like you will have something of your own with good memories attached to it. Turn around."

I grin at him. "You really got me something?"

"Yes. Turn around!" Jett insists.

I do as he says. He gathers up my hair, draping it over one shoulder. His warm fingertips graze my skin and he attaches a clasp at the back of my neck. "A necklace?" I say, wrapping my fist around it and heading over to the mirror.

The mirror is scratched and old with no frame. It distorts my reflection unless I stand in just the right place. Around my neck is a gold chain with two pendants hanging from it. One is a horseshoe, the other a claw. In the mirror's reflection, I see Jett approach me from behind. "It's meant to be a bear claw," he says. "And the horseshoe, you know. You."

I smile. "I love it. Where did you get this? You must have spent everything you had."

He kisses my neck, his lips brushing over the thin chain. "It's worth it." He rests his chin on my shoulder. "I found it in the gift store this afternoon. I just wanted to get you something for tonight and there it was! I bought the chain and chose the two pendants from a selection in the store."

"It's perfect," I say. "It couldn't be more perfect."

Jett straightens up. "I'm glad you like it," he says softly. "And that's something you can keep. It'll always remind you of your first show, your own party—"

"And of you," I finish, turning around to face him. I push up onto my tiptoes.

"I'm not going anywhere," he says against my lips.

Pru bursts into the space. I start and jump away from Jett like we were doing something wrong, which makes me feel stupid. *Why does she keep showing up everywhere? I think angrily.*

"I was sent to see if you were ready," she says coldly. "Everyone's waiting for you out there."

"Almost," I say. "I won't be long." Pru looks from me to Jett then turns and hurries back through the curtain.

Jett turns around without prompting while I take my robe off. I unzip the dress and slip it over my head. It fits well enough. The hem brushes softly against my calves, a slight frill showing at the bottom. The neckline is perfect for my new necklace.

"You can turn around now," I say. He does, slowly. I watch his gaze drift over me, taking in the dress. He doesn't speak right away. My heart beats at least three times its normal rate. When the intimacy of his stare becomes too much, I turn my back to him and pull the material together. "Will you zip the back? I can't reach."

I look over my shoulder. Jett shakes his head like he's trying to clear it. "Yes. Of course." He holds the zip in one hand while the other grazes my back, warm and gentle. He pulls the zip up slowly and fastens the clasp then reaches around for the lace tie, knotting it into a bow at the back. The dress hugs my waist. "There," Jett breathes, taking a step back.

I turn to face him. We look at each other for a long moment. Jett clears his throat. "The color suits you," he says. "Brings out your . . . eyes."

I can't help but laugh. "My eyes are green!"

"Yes. They are. And green and red are contrasting colors, so put together each appears more vivid."

"Oh, I see," I say, still grinning. "Anything else?"

"Yes. Your hair kind of matches the dress color, too."

"My hair 'kind of matches the dress color.' Thank you! I am blown away by your compliments," I tease.

Jett pulls me to him. "You know I think you're beautiful." He kisses me once. His lips linger on mine.

When he steps back, he holds out his hand. I discreetly wipe my palm on the side of the dress before taking it. Then we make our way to my party.

9

STRANGERS AND FRIENDS

The party is held inside the circus tent.

The shifters are gathered and waiting in the ring. When I step out from behind the curtain with Jett, Ava and Nora approach. "We're so proud of you," Ava says.

"Yes," Nora adds. "Well done, Flo."

I smile and thank them, then the speakers crackle to life and the music starts up. Jett and I go to the buffet table to get a drink.

The multicolored stage lights are still on, the audience area a dark mass of black wood. Shifters are scattered on the benches in small groups, talking and drinking from red plastic cups. The music plays loudly, and the buffet table holds an assortment of food and drink—chips, dips, soda, and even pizza—which is a welcome change from hot soup or stew and bread around the campfire.

"Hey, Jett." I turn around at the same time Jett does. The triplets are holding plastic cups of the fizzy red punch from the bowl on the table. Logan is tossing pieces of popcorn into the air and catching them in his mouth. Most miss and fall on the floor around his feet. He doesn't bother picking them up. I wonder who'll have to tidy up the mess *he's* making. "Want to come see Ruby shift?" Lucas asks.

The bearded lady never shifts in front of anyone. "Why is she shifting?" I ask.

Lucas shrugs. "She's weird."

I glare at him. "Don't say that about her!" Sometimes the triplets go too far. "How would you like it if all you did was grow a trunk on your face and big ears on the side of your head when you shifted?"

"Jeez, Flo. I wasn't being serious."

"Just don't call her, or anyone else here, *weird*. If she's weird, you are too."

"How'd you work that out?" he asks.

I roll my eyes.

"Whatever," he says. "Anyway, I'm not making her shift. She always does this at parties."

I fold my arms across my chest. Jett puts his hand on my shoulder. "Well, I've never seen her do it," I say.

"You've never been invited to watch." Lucas turns to Jett. "So are you coming?"

"No," Jett says shortly.

"Suit yourself." The triplets walk together to the benches and disappear beneath them. I cluck my tongue and turn away. Idiots.

I take a sip of the sweet red punch. Jett's face glows blue under one of the show lights. "Shall we dance?" he asks, placing his cup down on the side.

I hesitate and take another drink from mine. I'm not much of a dancer, but the song is fast and, looking around, everyone seems to be throwing their hands in the air and swaying their hips. That can't be too hard. I set my cup down next to Jett's. "All right."

I don't want to be watched by those sitting on the sidelines, so we go into the middle of the makeshift dance floor. I join in the fist-pumping and hip-shaking. Jett laughs as I throw my hands up above my head. He copies my moves and bumps my hip with his. I laugh, too.

Before long, the song ends and a slow one begins. I don't know what to do now the fist-pumping and hip-shaking has stopped.

"Oh," I say, looking over my shoulder to where we left our drinks. I turn to leave, but Jett reaches for me and gently pulls me to him. He guides my hands up over his shoulders and places his on my waist. My cheeks feel hot. I don't want him to see me blush, so I look at the ground and copy his footwork.

Jett lifts my chin and looks at me with hooded eyes. Is he going to kiss me? Here in front of everyone? My eyes meet his and he simply smiles at me. I smile back and rest my head on his chest.

I close my eyes and think about our first kiss. It happened a few months back while we were dismantling the circus tent on a warm summer morning. I even remember exactly what I was wearing that day—my jeans with a striped vest and white sandals. Jett was shirtless, pulling pegs out of the ground. A section of the tent came down on top of us. We dropped to a crawl under the fallen curtain, laughing as we made our way out from under it. The buckle on my sandal caught on some rope. Jett untangled it, and then it just *happened*. The laughter stopped, Jett's gaze traveled to my lips. He offered me a small smile and waited for me to return it. When I did, he let go of my shoe and moved toward me, sliding his arms around my waist. My breath caught and my chest tightened when I realized what was coming. I think we both knew it would happen eventually.

I parted my lips and relaxed into the circle of his arms. I held on to him as the kiss deepened, growing more hungry, like there was so much lost time to make up for. My entire body warmed, responding to his touch. I could feel his heart beating just as fast as mine as we pressed up against each other. I lost myself entirely in the moment, and I never wanted it to end. It was just about the two of us and no one else. When his lips touched mine, the world fell away, and I wanted it to stay gone for a while. But before long, we drew back, breathless. Then we crawled out. He took my hand to help me stand and didn't let go when I found my feet.

I open my eyes and watch the other dancers. I see Nora and Ava with two of the triplets. Hari twirls Ruby under his arm beside them. Lance sits on the benches, talking to Ursula. They're all here for me. To celebrate my first show. I smile again, listening to the soft music and focusing on the feel of Jett's arms wrapped around me. Even if the dress is only on loan, I feel good in it, and it feels good to be here, wearing it, with everyone together.

The song ends too soon. Jett and I step to the side, out of the way of others who continue dancing to the next song. "Would you like another drink?" Jett asks.

"We left ours over there." I point to where we'd set them down, but they're gone. Either taken by accident or thrown away. "Oh. Then yes."

Jett makes his way to the refreshments table.

I sit on the lions' beam with my legs dangling off the edge. I kick them absently. "Hello!" I look down to see Pru looking up at me. Her greeting is uncharacteristically cheery.

Two other tiger shifters stand slightly behind her. All three are too young to perform. I know the elders are desperate to get them into the circus, counting the days until their sixteenth birthdays. They've been practicing an act in secret for the past few months; it's meant to be spectacular, but I can't comment. I haven't been invited to watch. Just like I've never been asked to see Ruby shift at past parties. The tiger girls could probably start performing now, really, but rules are rules. They can't break the age rule for one act and not for another.

"Hi, Pru."

"So, did I interrupt something between you and Jett back there?" she asks, nodding her head to the side.

"Not really," I reply. I'm not giving Pru any cause to dig for details.

"*So*, he's available, then? You two aren't a thing?" My insides feel all muddled. *Just say yes*, I tell myself. But it's none of her business!

I'm quiet for too long, prompting Pru to ask me again. "Flo?" She glances over at Jett, who is making his way back. "How hard is it?" she says impatiently. "Either you are or you aren't."

"I—"

Jett returns with a plastic cup in each of his hands. "Hey, Pru," he says, handing one of the drinks to me. She narrows her eyes when I take it, then she looks back to Jett and her face softens. "What are you two talking about?"

"Pru was—"

"Um, I was just asking Flo what her first show was like," Pru says, cutting me off. "I can't wait until it's my turn. Have you seen us practice, Jett?"

Nice lie. They roll so easily off her tongue. She's the elders' little darling—and an absolute horror to everyone else. Unless she wants something. Or *someone*.

"Not yet," Jett responds, taking a sip of his drink.

"Oh, you should!"

"All right. Thanks," Jett says passively.

Pru looks from me to him. I start to feel jealous, but Pru can do what she wants; Jett won't respond in the way she wants him to. I have nothing to worry about. I think.

"Did you see Ruby shift earlier?" Pru asks Jett. "It was so funny."

"It's not funny, Pru," I say.

"Of course it is! She doesn't mind. She does it all the time at parties."

"And would you hang out with her if she didn't?"

Pru shrugs. "Can you imagine, though! I'd probably still look good even if I couldn't shift the whole way. Cat's eyes and—"

"Claws?" I finish for her. Some of the anger from listening to the triplets earlier returns. I can't stand hearing people put each other down. The same way I could never stand back and watch the triplets prank someone. We're together forever; why make it hard to live with each other?

Jett chokes on a laugh and almost spills his drink. Pru glares at me. She's not the type of person you want to get on the wrong side of—she's very short-tempered and quick to react. "You'd look hilarious, Flo. You'd probably have these big buck teeth and—"

"Pru, stop," Jett interrupts.

"What?" she snaps. "I was only joking. And she did it to me!" She exhales sharply. "Whatever," she says, then stalks off back to the other tigers, who abandoned her in favor of the buffet table minutes earlier.

"Just ignore her," Jett says.

"Always do," I reply, still annoyed by her comments.

"Claws, though," he says. "Nice comeback."

I snort. "They're always out anyway. Jeez."

I'm still smiling when Ursula and Owen approach us. "Hey Flo," Ursula says.

"Everyone's been waiting to come and congratulate you," Owen adds. Which I translate to: "Everyone's been waiting for Pru to move away." She upsets everyone and the other shifters tend to avoid her where possible.

Ursula and Owen are siblings, zebras. Ursula was five when she arrived at the circus, and Owen three. We ask Ursula about it all the time—their life before, what happened, where they came from. But she's too hazy on details to make much sense of it all. At five, Ursula is the oldest ever recruit.

"How was it?" Ursula asks.

I hop down from the beam and put my cup down on top of it. "Scary at first, but I think I did okay."

"You did more than okay," Jett says, nudging me with his elbow.

"He's right, Flo," Owen says. "You were great! You're so lucky having your party. I can't wait until it's my turn."

"Enjoy the build-up to it," Ursula says to Owen. She shakes her head. "Always in a hurry to grow up. You really were great tonight, Flo." She reaches out to hug me. Owen does the same.

The baboons and the seals join us in a big group. They congratulate me same as Ursula and Owen. One of the seals, eight-year-old Star, wraps her arms around my waist while the others talk to me. They have to pull her off when they leave.

"See," Jett says. "Everyone's really proud of you."

"Yeah, tonight," I say shyly, unsure how long this attention will last. I have a pretty good idea, though. "Tomorrow things will just go back to normal and no one will care anymore."

Jett frowns. "I'll care."

I shift my gaze to his face and find he's watching me. I turn and my arms go around his neck, his around my waist. He grins: lopsided, adorable. I put my head against his chest, soothed by his heartbeat, by his words. *I'll care.*

I smile and cling to this moment.

10
CHALK

The party continues late into the night.

It's after midnight now. The seals were the first to leave, carrying a sleeping Star out with them. Ava and Nora went next, and others started to filter out slowly after that, making their way back to their tents and trailers to sleep. Now the only people remaining are the triplets—messing around on the circus equipment—and Jett.

Lance and Lucas are playing rock-paper-scissors. By the look on his face, Lucas is losing. On his third go, he keeps his hand in a fist—rock—then punches his brother in the stomach. Not too hard, but hard enough. Lance launches himself at Lucas and they roll around on the floor, scuffling. Logan goes over to break them up.

Jett and I sit on the dark benches. "Did you have a good night?" he asks.

"Yes," I say. And I really did.

"Good," Jett replies, reaching up to touch the necklace he gave me earlier. "What do you want to do now?"

"Sleep, mostly," I say, yawning at the thought of crawling into my sleeping bag inside my cozy little tent. I never stay late at parties. I'm usually one of the first to turn in.

Jett stands. "Let me walk you back?"

We make our way down the benches, jumping onto each one. "What about them?" I say, pointing to the triplets. All three are sitting on the floor. Lance's shirt is torn. Someone will be in trouble for that when the elders notice.

Jett laughs. "They do this at every party. They're always the last to leave. They'll be fine."

We walk to my tent in silence. My eyes are heavy and my body aches after everything it's been through—the traveling, the shifting, the practice, the performance, the dancing. It's been a long day.

"Here we are," Jett says when we reach my little yellow tent.

"Thank you," I say. "And for the necklace, too. I really do love it."

Jett slides his arms around me and I push up onto my tiptoes to kiss him. But before our lips meet, someone clears their throat.

The sound startles me in the dark and I look in the direction it came from. A flashlight turns on, pointing right at me. I shield my eyes from the glare. Then something hits me in the face, going into my mouth and down the front of the dress, tickling my skin. I shriek and stumble backward. The light goes out again, and I hear people running.

"Flo?"

I spit some of the chalky powder onto the floor. "What is this stuff?" I say, rubbing it off my chin. A door bangs open and another light fills the space around us.

"What are you two *doing?*" Nora scolds, Ava hovering behind her, holding her own small flashlight. "What do you have all over you? All over my dress!"

Ava steps in front of her sister and comes over to examine me. "What happened? Where did the powder come from?"

"Someone threw it at us," Jett says, brushing the white stuff off his shirt.

"Then what?"

"Then they ran away," I say.

Ava turns to Nora. "The protestors, do you think?"

Nora nods sharply. "Most likely. This wouldn't be the first time."

"You two go wash up," Ava says. "We'll find out what happened, and I'll get some of the older ones on guard for the night. Don't worry."

I'm not actually worried. Just angry, and surprised. "Wash that dress before you hand it back to me, Flo," Nora says as they leave.

I sigh. "I'm going to grab my robe, then go wash up before bed. Are you coming?"

"Yes," Jett says, removing his shirt.

I take a towel from my pack and change into my robe, folding Nora's dress up neatly by the door of my tent. Then I go back outside to take a shower before bed. Jett and I make our way over to the bathing area beneath the trees. I feel exposed in the dark, not knowing who's around. Jett seems to sense my hesitation. "I'll stand watch while you shower, then you do the same for me?"

"Stand and watch?" I say teasingly, in an attempt to lighten the mood.

"You know what I mean," Jett replies with a smile, turning his back while I undress. I step into one of the metal buckets. The one I chose is behind a large rock and sheltered beneath a tree, so it offers the most privacy. Still, I'm making this quick.

The metal watering can above is tied to a branch with a piece of rope, another piece tied to the spout. I pull on the spout end and the cold water rushes out, prickling my skin with each drop. I gasp.

"What is it?" Jett whisper-shouts over his shoulder.

"Cold," I hiss back. My teeth chatter.

Using a piece of lemon-scented soap, I scrub away at my body, running the suds up into my hair. I stand there until the large can is drained, then towel off. I put my robe back on before I'm fully dry and it sticks to my skin.

"Done," I say. "Your turn."

Jett and I trade places. He sets up one of the other showers while I stand in the wet grass, hugging my arms to my body to keep warm. I should replace the water I used, but I'm hoping I'll be excused given the circumstances. I stare into the darkness and will Jett to hurry so I can go back to the safety of my tent and zip myself in.

II
FOOLISH ACTIVITIES
OF MONKEYS

The zip on my tent opens a fraction the next morning.

"Flo?" Jett whispers.

"I'm awake," I say. "Just a second."

I finish getting dressed in the clothes I had on yesterday then crawl out of the tent with Nora's dress slung over my shoulder. "I thought you might have overslept. Breakfast will be ready in ten."

"I'm going to make a start on washing this dress. I'll meet you over there."

"Do you need any help?"

"It's fine," I reply. "Thanks. Do we know what happened yet?"

Jett frowns, nods. "Protestors. Like Ava said."

"What were they doing? Why were they here in the night?"

"They'd been snooping around the animal cages. One was found open."

"But there aren't any animals! What now? Did someone catch them?"

"Nora did. Ava made her let him go. He didn't say anything, but he dropped the flour he poured over us."

"Oh."

"I know. It's scary," he says.

"Yeah. It is. I wonder if they'll come back."

Jett shakes his head. "I don't know for sure. But would you come back after facing Nora?"

I grin. "No way."

"Exactly," he says, smiling back.

I step forward and kiss him lightly. "See you at breakfast."

His smile widens. "Don't be late."

Jett heads off to the campfire to wait for breakfast and get us a decent seat, and I head to the laundry area by the showers. I look up at the sky. It's an ugly color, promising rain. I try to forget about the protestors. We've had plenty of run-ins with them, but they've never staged anything like this. They're getting more daring, and the worse they get, the louder they become, and the more attention falls on us.

I pass Nora on my way. "Don't forget to fill those shower cans back up. And you left the soap on the floor. In the mud. You know the purpose of soap, right?"

I stop myself from glaring. Nora's mood is always at its worst in the morning. "I'll sort it all out."

She nods once. "Be careful with that dress. Some of the fabric is delicate. Ruby is good at laundry; maybe if you're nice to her she'll do it for you and then we'll both be sure you aren't going to return it tattered and damaged."

"I'm always nice to Ruby," I tell her, but she doesn't seem to be listening. She leaves without another word.

How am I supposed to fill the water cans, clean the soap, and wash Nora's dress in ten minutes? If you're late for breakfast, you don't get any.

I rush over to the laundry area first. Ruby is there, checking off baskets. "Are you on laundry duty today?" I ask.

"Not just me," she says coldly. I remember I haven't apologized to her yet for ignoring her the night I ran away.

"I've been meaning to come and find you, actually. To say sorry for the way I treated you the other night. I didn't mean to ignore you like I did. You were being nice, and I was freaking out. I just ran. I'm sorry."

"Apology accepted," she says, simple as that.

"Really?"

"I said so, didn't I?" she says with a smile. "So what is it you need washing?"

I hold up the red dress. "Nora's dress. I wouldn't usually ask but she said I might ruin it if I wash it myself. I think I'd be okay, I'm just not sure I want to take the chance. I can do something for you in return? Swap a chore?"

She takes the dress, running her hands over the material. "This is very delicate," she agrees, peering at it closely. "One wrong move and it's had it. Okay, I'll wash it, and I'll think on what you can do for me in return."

"Thank you, Ruby," I say. "I owe you."

"Yes. You do."

Next, I dash over to the watering cans. I wash the dirt off the soap inside one of the metal tubs, then drag the ones Jett and I used over to the bushes, emptying them out.

I peer back over at camp, checking if they've started serving breakfast yet. They haven't.

I pull the tarp off a barrel of water at the side of the shower area and refill the two used hanging cans, drenching my arms in the process. Once I'm done, I hurry back over to camp, shaking out my sleeves to let them dry off by the fire.

Owen and Ursula are on cooking duty. They scramble eggs, fry potatoes, and toast bread. As Ursula plates it up, Owen adds a thick bean sauce and hands out portions. My stomach rumbles as the smell wafts from the fire. I dig in as soon as I'm handed a plate, savoring each mouthful. The meals here are a little hit and miss, so I make sure I enjoy it when we get a good one.

Jett eats in silence beside me. We're both on cleaning duty this morning. So last night, when I was wondering who was going to be the one to pick the popcorn off the floor, the answer was *me*.

Those under sixteen have a schooling session this morning with Hari, who I haven't seen much since we arrived here. I look around for him, but he isn't nearby. I spot Nora and Ava talking to Iris—the agent for this area. The chatter around the campfire dies down as everyone tries to listen in on their conversation about the flour attack last night.

The three of them soon notice and approach us. Nora calls the group to attention, not that our attention needed calling. "Iris informs us that the protestors have moved on. So it's business as normal. Go back to your breakfast."

I catch her thanking Iris as they step away again to speak privately. Hari comes out of his trailer not long after. He speaks to Iris briefly, then makes his way over to collect the underaged for their school session. "The rest of you have chores, so clean up and get going," he says.

I offer to wash Jett's plate as payback for him taking mine last night before the show. He doesn't let me, though. The two of us head over to the washing bowl together and scrub our plates and cutlery clean, then lay them out to dry. We go straight to the circus tent afterward to start cleaning.

Itch, one of the monkey shifters, is waiting outside the tent for us. "Hey. I'm on cleaning duty with you two," he says. "Oscar is supposed to be here, too, but he hasn't finished eating yet."

Oscar is another one of the monkeys old enough to perform. When I was twelve, Oscar and I dated for a day. Jett stopped speaking to me, Oscar wouldn't stop following me around, and it ended by showtime the same night. We held hands for thirty seconds. That's the closest I ever got to a boyfriend before Jett.

"Go get him while we get started," Jett says. "Breakfast is over."

Itch takes off in search of Oscar while Jett and I go inside. It's worse than I remembered. Spilled food and drink on the floor and tables. Empty cups dotted around all over the benches and circus equipment. The mats in the ring are all rumpled up and skewed. A bag in the corner is bursting with garbage. I roll up my still-damp sleeves.

Itch and Oscar come into the tent. Itch lets out a low whistle. "This place is a mess."

Oscar folds his arms across his chest. "How did we get stuck on cleaning duty? It stinks in here."

"There are worse chores," Jett says.

"Name one," Oscar retorts.

"Cleaning the portable toilet," Itch says with a cheeky grin.

Oscar wrinkles his nose. "Ugh. Way to lower the tone, Itch."

"It was pretty low already," Itch retorts.

Oscar flicks Itch on the nose. "Ow!" he shouts, cupping his face in his hands.

"Can we get started?" I say, stopping them from fooling around any longer. We only have until lunch to get this place looking presentable again. I don't want to be in trouble with the elders for goofing around and not getting the job done. I also don't want to be in here when I have a free two hours after lunch. I want to enjoy them on the beach and not have to come back and finish up here.

Jett brings a trash bag over and holds it open for me while I throw things into it. I spot Itch throwing food into one. "Stop!" I yell. Itch freezes and the two monkeys look at me. "Don't throw the food away. We never throw food away."

"But some of it's stale," Oscar says. "It's been sitting out all night."

"So? You two should know this—keep it separate and give it to the elders when we've finished. They'll decide what to save and what to discard. Honestly, Itch."

"Don't look at me like that! I've never been on cleaning duty after a party before. I didn't know." He fishes out the food he threw in the garbage bag and lays it on a tray. "Better?"

I raise my eyebrows. It doesn't look the slightest bit appetizing. "Yes," I say, then go back to cleaning with Jett. Snack wrappers, screwed up napkins, discarded food—which we *can* throw out if there is a bite missing—all goes in. Before long, Itch interrupts us again.

"Hey, look!" he says. I turn to find he's juggling three bright red balls.

"Where did you get those?" I ask, annoyed.

"They were under the table," he says, not taking his eyes off the balls in the air.

"Well, put them back. They must have been left there for a reason."

"They're for the monkeys," he says with a smile. "We use them in the show. I just learned how to juggle with them."

"Yeah, took you long enough," Oscar says. He looks at Jett and me. "Slow learner."

"I am not!" Itch snaps playfully. "I'm doing it now, aren't I?"

"Well, it's great," I say flatly. "Now put them back and help us."

"Yeah," Oscar says. "Stop monkeying around."

I roll my eyes. Itch doesn't listen to any of us, though. "Want to see me juggle them as a monkey? Wait here."

He dashes behind the curtain before any of us can say no. I look up at Jett. He shrugs, dropping the garbage bag next to his feet. Great.

Itch shifts behind the curtain and comes back into the ring as a fuzzy little monkey walking on two legs. He holds the three red balls in his hands—two in one and one in the other.

Itch stops in front of us and starts juggling the balls. Oscar watches him judgingly—arms crossed and head tilted to one side. "Hmm. You need to toss them quicker than that," he says. "You don't have the right stance. Here, pass them to me. I'll show you."

Itch messes up, missing one of the balls. It drops to the ground with a thud. He hesitates and the other two follow. *Thud. Thud.* Oscar laughs. "See, you're doing it all wrong. If you do that during a show you'll—"

"He'll what?" The four of us look around to see Nora standing by the benches, holding a bucket of cleaning products in her hand. She sets it down by her feet.

Jett picks the garbage bag up again and I continue filling it up, as if I have been doing all along. It's a pathetic attempt to cover up not working, but Jett goes with it, and Nora's too busy glaring at the monkeys to pay us much attention.

"Shift back," she snaps at Itch. "Then return the juggling equipment to exactly where you found it." Itch scurries off behind the curtain again. "Oscar. Don't let me hear you speaking to a performer like that again. We all have to learn. You should encourage him, not put him down."

Oscar looks at his feet. "Sorry."

"Flo and Jett." I freeze, then look up, Jett by my side. "You two should know better than to engage in the foolish activities of monkeys. I want this place finished by lunchtime. If not, you'll be coming back. Didn't I give you permission to visit the beach this afternoon, Flo?"

I nod. "You did."

"I'm sure you'd hate to miss that. Back to work, then. Make sure you wipe the benches down and get everything looking spotless." She kicks the bucket with her heel. "Use what's in here." She bends down and pulls out a small tube of red paint and a paintbrush. "Jett, you're repainting the sign outside. It's a mess."

Jett hands me the garbage bag with a sorry look on his face. He walks over to Nora and takes the paint and brush from her. Jett follows Nora out of the tent, leaving me alone with Itch, who's human again, and Oscar. They both look at me. I force a smile and get back to work.

"Spoil sport," Oscar mutters. I don't know if he's speaking to me or talking about Nora, but it brings back memories of when the triplets used to taunt me with that name and stings all the same.

12

WHEN THE SUN SETS

Jett comes to find me before lunch.

"All done?" I ask.

"Yep," he says, a streak of red paint beside his eyebrow.

"You have paint on your face, you know?"

He lifts his hand to his head. "Where?"

"Here," I say, licking my thumb and scrubbing the spot of red. I feel his eyes on me as he watches me work at it. I glance up and meet them with my own, offering a small smile.

He smiles back. "Crappy morning, huh?"

"The worst," I say, stepping back and wiping my thumb on my jeans. "At least we're done. Beach after lunch."

"Can't wait," Jett says, picking up the bucket of cleaning products. "Let's go eat."

Today's meal is hot stew with potatoes, carrots, and onions. I lift the spoon to my mouth. The stew burns my throat, but I eat it quickly anyway, anxious to finish and go down to the beach. Jett takes my bowl once I'm done. "I'll wash these, you go let Nora know we're going now."

Nora's standing by the newly painted sign with Ava and a toddler I don't recognize. "Good job in the tent," she says as I approach. "It's spotless."

I smile uncertainly and nod. "Jett and I are heading to the beach now."

Nora looks at the sky. "Two hours max. Then I want you back here. Stay where we can see you."

"Who's this?" I ask, gesturing to the toddler. She's cute—chubby cheeks and short curly hair. Her denim dress is too big for her, and her purple daisy-covered shoes are caked in mud. She needs cleaning up.

"She's new," Ava says. "Her name is Rain."

I crouch down. "Hi, Rain," I say. The toddler backs away, flinching at the sound of my voice. She clings on to Ava's leg then starts to cry. I stand up again. "What did I do?"

"Nothing," Ava says, hugging Rain. "She's very nervous."

"Was she . . . was she in a bad condition when you found her?" I ask, lowering my voice.

"Flo," Nora says sharply. "You know that isn't any of your concern. We don't discuss that."

"Right. Sorry. It's just, she's . . . ," I say, trailing off. "Well, I hope she's okay."

I dash back to the campfire where Jett's waiting for me. "Ready?" he says, linking his fingers through mine. We take the short walk to the beach and I tell him about Rain. She's the youngest to join the circus for a while and no doubt people will be gossiping about where she came from and what happened to her parents.

"How old is she?" Jett asks.

I shrug. "Two. Maybe three."

When we step from wet mud to soft sand, we take off our shoes and stash them behind a rock. We join hands again and walk toward the ocean.

The wind blows in from the water, sharp and fresh. I breathe in. My hair whips around my face and my feet sink into the cool sand. We walk right into the ocean, letting the small, rolling waves crash against our ankles. The water is freezing, though, and I have to back up out of it after a moment.

"Why is it called Violet Bay?" I ask. I've never thought about it in all the times we've been here. Perhaps I'm paying more attention to place names since visiting The Flaming Horse Inn—one I'd like to forget.

"Because the water turns a deep shade of violet when the sun sets," Jett says.

"Really? That's why?"

"I like to think so. I don't know for sure, that's just what I imagine."

"You mean you made it up?" I say with a grin. Jett shrugs. My smile widens. "It's beautiful. I'm sure that's the reason."

I stand in silence for a long time after that, watching the ocean stretch far, far out and meet the sky. Watching the lazy waves reaching for my toes.

I suck in a breath as Jett's arms circle my waist while I'm distracted. I angle my face toward him. He gives me a sideways glance, holds it, then looks back out at the ocean with a smile tugging at his lips.

"What?" I ask, causing him to look back at me. He shakes his head. "No, what?"

"It's just being here with you. It's nice," he says.

"Nice," I echo.

Jett's smile widens. "It's perfect, is what I meant to say."

I take in the empty beach, the stretch of water. Feel the wind in my hair, and the sand between my toes. "It is perfect," I say. Jett squeezes me to him. I close my eyes and take a deep breath of the salty air, too aware of how soon this will end. How soon we'll have to go back to the circus. Two hours isn't long enough. Two hours is no time at all. I wish I could stay here with him until the water turns violet.

13
COLD THORNS

The paying crowd files into the circus tent and takes their seats.

Numbers are low tonight. It's raining heavily outside. I imagine most will be at home, indoors, avoiding the cold wind and hail. The little frozen stones bounce off the big top, loud and disruptive. The stereo is going to have a hard time competing with that.

The usual row of kids holding balloons and snacks occupy the front seats with their parents on the benches beside or behind them. Someone taps my shoulder. I turn around to see Owen smiling at me. "What are you doing tonight?" I say.

"I'm with the lions again," he says. "But I'm here to give you a message."

"A message?" I ask, puzzled. "From who?"

"Ruby. She's calling in her favor," he says. "She wants you to work the door for the first half of the show so she can watch."

"Seriously?"

"Yes. And the weather is horrible outside."

I look up at the material roof above our heads. "I can hear. Right, fine. I'm coming." What choice do I have? I told her I'd return the favor and this is what she wants. Sighing, I follow Owen. He leads me out through the entrance to where Ruby sits, taking money from late arrivals.

"Flo," Ruby says after she hands a man his change. "You know how to count, don't you?"

I scowl at her. "Of course I do."

"I didn't mean it offensively. Here," she says, hopping down from a stool. "I'll be back before your turn. I never get to watch the show, and you said you owed me one so . . ."

"A little warning would have been nice," I say, hugging my arms to my chest. "Have the elders agreed to this? The customers like being greeted by you."

She scratches her beard. "They're busy inside—they won't notice."

I sigh. "Fine. Go on, then. But make sure you're back with plenty of time for me to get ready for my act."

"Will do," she says before dashing off.

I see headlights up ahead—more customers. I swivel around on the chair to face Owen. "It's freezing out here. Can you bring me something to put on my feet?"

"No can do. I have to go get ready. Good luck." He leaves before I can stop him. Wonderful.

The wind howls through the trees and the rain falls at an angle, slapping me in the face. Each drop feels like a cold thorn nicking my flesh. I hear seagulls in the distance, screeching, their caws drowned out by the wailing wind. The inside of the tent is filled with a soft glow, and the sound of music fights the sound of the weather as the show begins.

My stomach growls—dinner was small. We only had the party leftovers between all of us so they wouldn't be wasted. It wasn't enough.

I hug my arms to my chest and try to keep warm.

I don't know how long I've been sitting on the stool, hunched and shivering, when Ruby returns to her post. "The lions are on," she says.

I jump up and she squeezes past me to take her seat.

"The weather's calmed down, I see."

"Yep," I say. My robe is soaked. "Just in time for your return. Hasn't let up until now."

She giggles. "That's funny."

"For you, maybe," I mutter and enter the tent. Someone calls my name and tells me I'm up next almost the second I step back inside. I head straight for the stage entrance.

Jett's there, waiting for me. "Where have you been?" he asks.

"Working the door for Ruby," I reply.

I gesture for him to turn around so I can peel the wet robe off my skin and shift. "What for?" he asks, but I can't answer because I've already shifted and Nora is by my side, ready to lead me out into the ring.

Jett twists back around to face me. "Good luck," he says quickly.

I step out with Nora for the second time. The stage lights blind me for a moment until my eyes adjust. I'm led over to the audience, and I take the time to scan it. Four children step up to pet me. One boy is wearing a jumper with a horse print on the front. He beams up at me and strokes my side. I bend my head toward him, but the feather headpiece tips and covers one of my eyes. I shake my head, which scares the boy.

Nora rights the headpiece and we move away to get ready for the jump. I'm handed over to Ava again and taken outside. I actually feel excited to perform tonight. I think I'm finally beginning to understand why others are so desperate to turn sixteen and join in. Jumping, clearing the hurdle, the flames, is all such a thrill. The energy of the audience is infectious.

This time, when I run toward the tent, I do it with confidence. Galloping fast, I almost can't wait to get there and make the jump. I crave the sound of the flames crackling above the hurdle, the way the crowd gasps as I approach it, and the cheers when I clear it.

I burst into the tent, leap into the air, glide over the flames, and land cleanly once again. Nora rushes over to me while I relish in the sound of applause. It's thrilling. I can't get enough of it now that I've had a taste.

Too soon, Nora guides me backstage. I shift and slip my robe over my shoulders, tying it at the waist. It's still wet and cold against my skin, but I hardly notice the discomfort. "Good job, Flo!" Owen cheers, and Ursula squeezes my arm.

Jett's behind them. Once they step away, he comes forward and plucks a blue feather out of my hair, handing it to me. "You were great," he says. "Again."

I feel so happy here with my friends. I'm so much more grateful for the circus than I ever have been before.

I can't stop smiling.

14
OUTSIDERS

There are strangers in camp.

People I've never seen before. Two girls and a man. I see them talking to the triplets. I want to go over there, but I watch for a little longer first. *Who are they?* I wonder.

I study them, then decide to approach the group. I start walking but before I get there the elders intervene and send Lucas, Lance, and Logan away.

I backtrack and wait for Jett outside his tent. The triplets make their way over to us. "Who are they?" I ask as soon as they're close by.

Lucas looks concerned for once. "They want to join."

"*Join?*"

Jett crawls out of his tent, just in time to see the three strangers escorted off the grounds by the elders. "What's going on there?" he asks, nodding his head to the six retreating figures.

"Lucas said they want to join the circus. That's *never* happened. Where did they come from?"

"They said they'd left their pack," Lance says.

I frown. "They're from another pack. Do you think they were with the ones who—"

"This conversation ends now," someone says from behind me. I whirl to see Nora standing there, arms folded across her chest. "I don't appreciate gossip."

"But—" I start.

"One more word and it's double chores."

I keep my mouth shut, but my brain continues producing questions that are desperate to spill out.

"Did you practice yesterday, Flo?" Nora asks. I shake my head, lips clamped tight. "Don't you think you should have? Instead of spending a full two hours on the beach?"

I nod.

"Speak."

"Yes," I say quietly, even though she told me I could have that time on the beach. This is so like Nora—let me have something then use it against me later. Ava and Hari are coming over now, too.

"I'll set her up after breakfast," Ava says to Nora. Then she turns to me. "You can make it for everyone this morning. Go on."

I leave without another word, heading over to the campfire to make breakfast. The ingredients are in a bowl beside the plates and cutlery. It's just bread this morning. So I'll have to toast and butter more than thirty pieces until I get my own. I groan inwardly and get to work.

Jett crouches down beside me as the logs around the fire start filling up. He holds out plates and I drop the blackened bread onto them. Jett applies a thin layer of butter to each piece and hands out the portions.

When I've finished serving everyone else and swallowed down my own dry piece of toast, chasing it with water, I clean my plate in the bucket and head off to practice. Jett has washing chores this morning, so he can't come with me out to the field.

Ava's in the clearing, setting up the hurdle. "What are your jobs for this morning?" she asks.

"I have none until the afternoon," I tell her. "I'm setting up the tent for the show."

She nods once. "Spend as much time as you need then."

Ava leaves. I wait until she's completely out of sight before removing my clothes and shifting.

I do a few laps of the field to warm up and get used to my form. I jump the hurdle a few times after that, then I'm bored. I don't need to practice today. I've done the show perfectly twice now.

I decide to go help Jett with his washing in the hope he'll be done sooner and we can hang out. I shift back to my human form and get dressed quickly.

As I'm pulling my jeans back on, a movement in the bushes catches my eye. It comes from the side of the clearing, opposite camp. The figure seems to be wearing dark clothing and is only slightly covered by the bushes. My first thought is that the protestors are back, but the calm way the person watches me makes me call out. "Hello?"

Whoever it is takes a step back and disappears behind the trees. *That was odd*, I think. Then another, more urgent thought occurs to me: *Did they see me shift?*

I don't think so. Did they? I'll have to tell the elders, just in case. I didn't see the figure while I was a horse, but who knows how long they had been there. If it was a protestor—a human—what will they do? Who will they tell? They could get us into a lot of trouble.

I rush back to camp to look for Hari. I don't want to speak to Nora—she's already mad at me. Ava's out because she's with Nora and the tigers this morning. I haven't seen Hari much over the past few days, but he's usually the most understanding over things like this. I can't actually remember a time like this, though. Who's been caught shifting by a human before? I can't be the only one.

Jett waves to me from the laundry area as I walk through camp. I remember my original plan to go help him so he could get off earlier. He stands and drops a shirt into the water. The others curse him as he sprints over to me.

"I can't talk," I say. "I need to find Hari."

"Hari? What for?"

I hesitate. Should I tell him? I decide no. I don't want to share what I saw, don't want to panic anyone. Jett would likely flip out with the knowledge of someone seeing me shift. It's too soon to start worrying people over it. "Nothing much," I say. "I just need to speak to him."

"He's resting. At least, that's what I overheard," Jett says. "He didn't teach his class today."

"Oh."

"Nora's over there," Jett says, pointing to the other side of camp where Nora and Ava are sitting having their own breakfast while the tigers prepare for practice. I don't want to go over there.

I calm down a bit now that I'm no longer alone. I'm still worried that the protestor saw me shift, but should I really panic this much before anything's even happened? Because it might not. They might not have seen anything. I look back at Nora and Ava, wondering if I should just go over there and tell them. They'd be mad, though, and it could all be for nothing.

"No, that's okay," I finally say. "I'll wait until Hari's up and speak to him."

15
PANIC

Another show begins and I still haven't found Hari.

I knocked on his trailer after lunch, but there was no answer. I assumed he was still sleeping and left. But I haven't seen him this evening, either. He's usually in the tent over-seeing the performances before going out there himself.

I head to my usual spot, passing Nora and Ava to get there. "Flo, a word," Nora says. I stop in front of her, avoiding eye contact. She snaps her fingers in front of my face. "Look at me."

This is why I didn't want to tell her about the protestor in the field. I look at her. "Don't swap places with Ruby again," she says. "The door is her job. It's important that she's there."

I'm about to argue—tell her that it was her idea, that I owed Ruby a favor and that was her demand—but what would be the point? I am curious, though, as to why it's such an issue. "I won't, but I did well enough—I don't think the customers minded for just one night."

Nora narrows her eyes. "It's not about what the cus-tomers want; it's about what I want. And I'm telling you that it's important that it's Ruby. Only exception is Ava, Hari, or myself to take the door."

She turns away, but whips back around when I ask, "Where is Hari?"

"Around," Nora says unhelpfully then leaves without another word.

I glower at the back of her head then continue on to my usual spot behind the curtain to watch tonight's show. Jett's out there performing.

I scan the crowd. It's larger than last night's, but smaller than the first show here. Children take up most of the front row again, adults behind them holding coats and unwanted snacks and drinks. A family in the third row sport matching tie-dye T-shirts. Then something strikes me as odd—on the back row, three men and one woman dressed in black look completely out of place. Their faces are serious. They're watching carefully. They don't seem to be with anyone else, and they don't seem to be speaking to each other much. I suddenly feel uncomfortable with them here, wondering what they're thinking. What are they watching us for if it isn't entertaining them?

I make the link between the figure dressed in black in the field and the four dressed in black here. Is it possible one of them watched me from the tree line? Are they the protestors? Are they planning something for during the show? I have to tell one of the elders—even if it is Nora. Now it's urgent. Now is the right time to panic.

A hand lands on my shoulder and I jump a mile. "Hey, hey," Jett says soothingly. "It's just me. I thought I'd find you here."

"What—?" I look back through the curtains and see the lions performing. I was so absorbed in the four in black that I hadn't even noticed the switch in acts. Now I've missed my chance to speak to Hari.

I can only see Nora and Ava out there, though. That's strange. "Hari isn't out there," I say.

Jett frowns. He parts the curtain a little more and peers through. "I heard Pru gossiping about him with Maria and Lexi earlier. I didn't hear what she was saying, though."

"So he's not here? At all?"

Jett shrugs. "No idea."

I look back at the four in the back row. I need to speak to one of the elders. Now. "I better go get ready," I say.

"I'll be here," Jett says. "Good luck."

At the stage entrance, Owen comes through the curtain with a grin on his face. Nora appears next, rushing to change into her ringmaster costume. "Nora, I have something I need to tell you—"

"Shift," she snaps. "Quickly."

"Wait! It's important!" I protest.

"*Flo,*" she growls. "Shift. Now."

I throw off my robe and do as she says, anger coursing through me. Is it any wonder I waited for Hari? She doesn't take me seriously. She doesn't pay attention to any of us.

I perform my act on autopilot, not really concentrating on anything I'm doing. I just want it to be over tonight so I can tell Nora about the protestors—that is, if they haven't already done what they came here to do. After jumping the hurdle, I look up, but the strange group has gone.

Nora pulls on my reins and drags me backstage. I shift and she throws my robe at me. "What the hell was that? I didn't know watching a horse jump a flaming hurdle could be so boring. What is *wrong* with you tonight?"

"Easy, Nora," Ava says.

"I've had enough of the trouble she causes!" Nora says as though I'm not standing right here.

"I tried to tell you what was wrong before we went out there," I say. Nora glares at me.

"Is that true?" Ava asks Nora.

"She was whining about something," Nora admits. "I don't know. I was rushing to change for her act."

"What is it, Flo?" Ava asks.

"I-I saw someone watching me earlier," I tell them. "I think whoever it was saw me shift."

"Are you serious?" Jett says from behind me. His voice startles me. "Flo, why didn't you tell me? Why aren't you telling anyone until now?"

"I tried! I've been looking for Hari all day."

"I can't believe this! Someone was *watching* us. What if they know what we are? What if they did see Flo shift?" He's panicking, just like I knew he would. Then he gasps. "What if they're hunters?"

"Keep your voice down," Nora hisses.

"I . . ." I start in response to Jett, then close my mouth. What if they are hunters? And because of me, everyone is in danger and they don't even know it. "No," I breathe. "They're hunters, aren't they? They've finally caught up to us."

"We don't know that, Flo," Ava says.

"I've never seen one," I continue. "I-I've never seen a hunter. I thought the protestors were back. I'm sorry. I-I didn't know."

Ava steps forward. "Don't panic yet. Come through to the tent and we'll talk properly."

Jett and I follow Nora and Ava through to the benches where the audience usually sits. The two elders do a quick check of the tent to make sure it's empty while Jett and I wait. "Did you see them clearly?" Jett asks.

"Not really. I don't know. I wasn't really sure of anything—who they were, if they saw me. I didn't know if I should be panicking about it or not. Hunters didn't cross my mind. I know that's strange, seeing as we're always on the lookout for them, but it's just one of those things you don't think could *actually* happen to you, you know?"

"I know," Jett says.

"I'm always scared of them coming. But I never truly thought they actually would." I take a deep, shuddering breath and wait for Ava and Nora to rejoin us.

16
KEEP HER SAFE

The curtains are thrown apart and Ava and Nora make their way over to us.

I assumed Hari would be present for something like this. *Where is he?*

Ava and Nora pull one of the elephants' podiums over to the benches and sit down on it, facing us. "Everyone's gone. So, let's have it. From the top—what exactly have you seen?" Nora says.

I swallow. "I saw someone was watching me in the field this morning when I finished practicing. There's a chance they saw me shift." My robe falls off one shoulder and I tug it back up. Nora and Ava exchange a look. They don't seem all that worried—are Jett and I overreacting?

"And then?" Ava prompts.

"I don't know. I only saw them when I shifted back to human. When I shouted over, they stepped back and they were gone."

"I see." They both stare at me for a long moment.

Jett breaks the silence. "Do you think we need to get Flo away from here?" he asks. "In case a hunter really did see her shift."

"We don't know that they're hunters," Nora says.

"But it seems likely," Jett pushes.

"We don't know that they're hunters," Nora repeats. "We need to think about this, not make snap decisions that could draw further attention to us."

"There was a group in the audience tonight, too," I say. "They seemed *wrong*. They were alone—no kids, no family. They didn't laugh or cheer or clap. The four of them just sat watching like they were waiting for something."

Ava and Nora glance at each other again. I wish I knew what was going on in their heads.

"They are hunters," Jett says. "Aren't they?"

Ava closes her eyes. Nora nods. "Sounds like it."

"And they're here to kill us," I say. It's not a question. "How did they notice us? We're careful. Do you think it was the protestors stirring up trouble and focusing more attention on us?"

Ava shakes her head. "They moved on. Iris assured us."

"But before that?" I ask. "It's possible."

Jett nods. "We already thought hunters might be in the area, after the bear attacks. Our arrival wasn't exactly quiet."

"The reasons no longer matter," Nora says impatiently. "Not immediately, anyway. We need to take action to make the problem go away before looking closer at what exactly caused it."

"That's right," Ava says. "We'll look at how to prevent it happening again when it's no longer happening."

"So how do we solve this?" I ask, my voice calmer than I feel.

"We have to get Flo as far away as possible," Jett says. "It's not safe for her here if they know she's a shifter."

"They might not know," Nora says irritably. "I'm trying to think, Jett. Stop asking questions for a second, will you both?"

"No!" he snaps back, surprisingly. No one snaps back.

"What did you just say?" Nora says, eyes narrowed.

"I said no. I won't shut up. I'm not willing to take the chance that they 'might not know,'" Jett says, standing abruptly.

"Flo isn't going anywhere," Nora barks, rising to his level. "Sit down, Jett."

"No! I'll take her on my own if I have to. They're *not* going to catch her."

"Sit down, Jett," Nora says again, raising her voice.

Jett's breathing heavily, staring at Nora. She stares back. I tug on Jett's hand. When he looks at me, I nod, and he sits down.

"Okay," Ava says, taking a deep breath as Nora sits beside her again. "Here's what we're going to do: no one will let Flo out of their sight. She must be with someone every hour of every day."

Jett volunteers himself.

Ava nods. "Hari is away at the moment; he has been unwell and is with a doctor. You two can share his trailer until he returns. You'll be safer in there than in a tent."

"Is Hari okay?" I ask. "What happened?"

"That's really none of your, or anyone else's, business, Flo," Nora says.

Ava sighs. "He's all right, but he'll be absent for a while. You should have his home for as long as he's away. And we're trusting you to always stay with her, Jett."

Jett nods. "I will. But—"

"Then as long as that's settled, we'll continue here as normal," Nora interrupts.

"Packing up and fleeing, or taking Flo away, will only raise suspicion," Ava adds. "The hunters won't act until they have a confirmed number of shifters and know who to target. We'll sit tight and be cautious. Now you two go and gather your things and move into Hari's home immediately."

With that, Nora and Ava stand and head out of the tent, leaving Jett and I alone. "Are you okay with this?" Jett asks once they're out of earshot. "Because if you want to leave, you only have to say so."

I'm tempted to go, but Ava's right—if we run, it'll only confirm to the hunters that I have something to hide, and they'll track us both down. I can't do that to Jett. "I'm all right doing what Ava said. We'll sit tight and wait it out." I get to my feet.

Once I've gathered my backpack and sleeping bag from my tent, Jett and I head over to Hari's trailer. Jett pulls the door, which opens with a creak. He flicks on the lights and I follow him inside.

The small space smells like musk and herbs. Candles and dried wax line most of the surfaces. There are dirty dishes and cups in the sink and a small table covered with paperback books, a portable DVD player, and a small pile of movies. There's a cushioned chair on either side, heaped with props and costumes.

"It needs cleaning," I say with distaste.

Hari's bed is an unmade mess of blankets. Jett bundles them up and pushes them to the side, stripping the bed entirely. He finds a fresh sheet in a small cupboard above the bed and spreads it across the mattress. I tuck the corners under. We lay out our own sleeping bags over the top.

"This feels wrong," I say.

"I know," Jett says. "But it's safer than your tent. We'll clean up in the morning." He jumps down on the bed and a spring pops. "Oops."

I can't help but laugh. "Let's sleep and sort the rest out tomorrow." I pull my pajamas out of my backpack—an unmatched secondhand set. It's cold, so I put a sweater on over the top. Once ready, I shuffle into my sleeping bag and settle down beside Jett.

"Are you okay?" he asks.

"Yeah. I think so."

He switches out the light. Still, I can just make out his smile. "Good night, Flo," he whispers in the dark.

"Good night, Jett," I reply, closing my eyes, but I don't sleep. I don't know what this means for us, for the circus, and I'm terrified. I lie here, in the darkness, afraid of what tomorrow might bring. If they're hunters, I don't know how many more tomorrows I'll have.

17

WATCHING ME

I wake face to face with Jett.

I climb out of my sleeping bag, leaving Jett asleep. It's strange waking up beside him, since we don't typically spend the night together. Strange, but nice. If only the reason behind it were something other than mortal danger.

I open the door to Hari's trailer to see what's going on outside. Everyone's getting on with their chores, the fire is dying down, and the dishes from breakfast are laid out to dry. It must be late morning.

Pru spots me and heads over. "Hey," she says.

I raise my eyebrows. "Hey," I reply, my voice croaky from sleep.

"We heard what happened," Pru says.

"'We'? Who's 'we'?" I ask.

Pru looks over her shoulder. The other tigers are watching us talk but won't be able to hear from where they're sitting. "Everyone."

"You mean the elders told all of you what happened?" I ask, surprised the details were aired this way after I'd tried so hard to keep them quiet to prevent panic.

"Well, yes. Of course. We need a warning if hunters are watching us. There was a meeting about it this morning in the big tent."

"A meeting? What was said?"

Pru frowns. "No shifting. Stay in groups of two or more. There's a buddy system in place, effective immediately. We're on lockdown, basically. No more trips to the beach."

I swallow. "Until when?"

Pru shrugs. "Until they say otherwise, I guess. I assume Jett is your buddy. Lucky."

I rub the back of my neck. "About that. We are—"

"I know. The triplets told me. I'm over it. So, what did the hunters look like?"

"Mean," I say.

She crosses her arms, frustrated. "I'm serious, Flo."

"So am I. They look mean."

"What else?" she asks.

I sigh. "They were wearing black. They were watching the performances like—why does it matter now?"

"Because it's important. We all need to know in case we see one. Do you think they know you're a horse?" she pries.

"I don't *know*, Pru. Did you just come over here to interview me?"

Her face turns a deep shade of pink. "I was just making conversation," she snaps. *Yeah, right.* Without another word, she turns on her heel and stomps back to her group. When she reaches them, they lean in while she presumably recites the conversation to them. I sigh and step back inside.

I slam the door shut in frustration, forgetting that Jett is sleeping. He wakes up with a start. "Sorry," I say.

"Did you go out?" he asks, rubbing his eyes.

"I just stepped outside the door to see what everyone's doing," I say. "They had a meeting this morning without us."

Jett blinks. "What time is it?"

"Almost lunch, I think."

I turn my back to Jett and pull on my usual pair of black jeans, boots, an old band T-shirt (a band I've never heard of), and a black jacket. Jett gets dressed in dark jeans, too, a white T-shirt, and a brown coat. He gives me his scarf again, and I wrap it around my neck. Once the two of us are dressed, we head out of Hari's home.

Out of the stuffy, musky trailer and into the fresh, salty air, we make our way over to where everyone is sitting around the campfire, preparing for lunch. We pass my tent. "We should take that down after we've eaten," Jett says.

"I'll finish packing up and we'll collapse it," I say, running my fingertips across the material as I walk by it.

We reach the others and hover beside the logs. Most spaces are already taken. "Something smells good," Jett says.

I inhale, but nothing I smell appeals to me, my appetite gone. "I'm not sure that I want to eat," I say. "I feel sick."

"You shouldn't skip lunch, Flo. Especially when we missed breakfast this morning."

"I know," I say with a clipped voice. I sigh because he's right. I have to eat. *Carry on as normal.*

I pick up a bowl. My stomach growls when I see the bubbling soup and the steam carries the scent to me, but I still don't feel like eating it.

Instead of sitting on the packed logs by the fire, Jett and I head back over to Hari's trailer and sit on the steps outside the door. "Everyone is staring at me," I say, looking back to the campfire. Pru and the tigers are huddled close and whispering, casting glances my way. "This is so stupid!"

"Ignore them, Flo," Jett says, blowing on his soup. "What does it matter? They're not the ones we have to worry about."

"It makes me feel . . ." I trail off. I don't know how it makes me feel.

I force a spoonful of soup into my mouth. It's peppery again, and I miss Hari's cooking. I wonder where he is right now, if he's okay, if he's missing the circus.

The soup is too hot and burns on the way down my throat, but I hardly notice. I'm already scanning the trees for any dark figures, as well as looking back to camp and becoming increasingly paranoid that people are talking about me.

Jett, noticing what I'm doing, says, "I doubt they'll be watching us now. The hunters, I mean. I can see you looking at the trees. They won't watch us from where they can be seen."

"Well, if that's the case, they aren't doing a very good job. I saw them twice in one day."

Jett swallows a mouthful of soup. "Don't underestimate them, Flo."

"I'm not. I'm just saying . . ." I trail off again, making a habit of not finishing my sentences. I'm not sure what I'm saying; the whole thing is confusing. I look back across the camp and notice the triplets are making their way over to us. "I don't want to sit here. Can we go for a walk?"

"I don't think that's a good idea. We should stick with everyone."

"They're acting like it's my fault."

"No one thinks that, Flo," Jett says. "Everyone's scared, but I'm sure no one is blaming you."

"But if I'd just told someone sooner."

"Then we'd probably still be sitting here doing exactly what we're doing now. The situation wouldn't have changed, neither would the decisions that Nora and Ava made. I know it's hard, but we need to eat and rest before tonight's show. Everyone's on edge and if there are hunters in the audience we can't let anything slip."

"Why are you so calm about this?" I gently touch his side, tracing the scar from memory. "After everything you've suffered."

Jett looks down at my hand. "I'm not calm. At all. Inside, I'm freaking out. I'm just trying to keep it together for all our sakes." He meets my eyes. "I don't know what else I can do. Other than run away, which we decided wasn't a good idea. Unless you've changed your mind?"

I shake my head no. He's right. We need to keep it together. I take a deep breath and exhale slowly. Then the triplets reach us. "In cahoots with hunters now, are you, Flo? Double agent, helping them out?"

"Guys—" Jett starts, but I'm already up.

Trust them to say something. Something *nobody* needs to listen to. What's funny about this? Where's the humor in any of this?

I shove through the triplets and march toward the camp-fire. I hear Jett curse and come after me but I don't slow down.

I throw my bowl into the washing pot, splashing Itch, Oscar, and monkey number three, Maven. "Hey!" they all yell at once. I turn my back on them and walk away. Jett rushes over when they start shouting me back to do my own washing.

"I'm telling Nora, Flo," Maven shouts.

"You can't just do that," Itch adds. "It's not fair."

"Flo!" Oscar shouts when I ignore the other two. But I ignore him, too.

Fighting tears, I rip down my tent, tossing my belongings out onto the grass and pulling the pegs out with such force they scatter all over the place. Jett grabs my arm. "Flo," he hisses. "Stop."

It starts to rain as I start to cry. I look up. The clouds are a menacing color. They look black and dangerous, swollen with rain and thunder. I can't believe the hunters have finally caught up to us because some stupid shifters attacked a human nearby. I've spent my entire life fearing them, looking over my shoulder—we all have—and now they're here, and if anyone's at the forefront of their minds, it's me. The horse they watched shift into a girl.

I think of them sitting on the benches in the circus tent, watching us so intently. How did they get inside the show? Did they pay Ruby at the door like everyone else? And she didn't realize something was *off* about them?

My skin crawls as images of them fill my head. They blended into the darkness, wearing black pants tucked into black boots, black tops that stretched from their torsos to their chins and right down to the wrists of each hand where their sleeves met black gloves. Their faces were the only skin exposed. It seems so obvious now that they're hunters. How could I have mistaken them for anything but?

They know what they're doing. They've probably killed shifters before, and they'll kill shifters again. Starting with me, most likely.

I need to get away. Jett's words are just mumbled sounds breaking through the ringing in my ears hitting the back of my skull, making no impact. I need to get away from the noise, from the cold rain numbing my fingers, from the stares of the other shifters, from the fear of the hunters watching us right now—watching me.

I shrug out of Jett's grip and walk away from all of it.

"Flo?" Jett calls after me.

"Oh, leave her!" Pru shouts. "The elders said act normal, not have a tantrum."

I don't respond to either of them.

I don't go far or put myself in danger. I walk in a straight line to Hari's trailer and shut myself inside.

18

HERE WE GO AGAIN

I feel the tension in the air like a thick fog.

As everyone takes their places in the tent, readying themselves for tonight's show, I can see they're all nervous, on edge. Now they all know that hunters are watching the camp and will possibly be in the audience, too.

I watch the show from my usual spot behind the curtain. Logan sits on a foldout chair next to me as the lights dim and the show starts on time with no sign of the hunters. I relax a little, but don't forget that late-arrivals often hurry in during the first act. I continue to watch the benches.

Tonight's audience is fairly small—we don't often get a big crowd, and very rarely fill all the seats, so it's easy to take a moment to study each person. I spot the tiger shifters snaking between the wooden beams beneath the benches, reaching up and taking what they can from beside people's feet.

Owen trades places with Logan when it's the elephants' turn to perform. Instead of sitting on the chair and ignoring me as Logan did, Owen stands beside me and teases the curtain open a little more. "I'll help you keep lookout," he says. No one but Jett has spoken to me since my outburst earlier. I've spent most of the day with my thoughts. "Two pairs of eyes are better than one, right?"

I freeze mid-nod as the curtains at the back open and a group quietly makes their way over to the benches. My stomach churns. *They're here.* The hunters are here. The tigers see them, too. They scurry out from beneath the benches and duck under the curtain.

I grab Owen's arm. "Is that them?" he asks, eyes wide. I nod.

Jett's up, and the four hunters watch Nora as she introduces him to the stage in his bear form. I feel sick. I hate that they're watching him. They don't miss a movement. At times, they lean toward each other, their eyes still fixed on the ring, and mutter something quietly.

Just when I don't think I can take it anymore, Jett finishes and Nora introduces the next act to the stage. Even she seems tense—she must have noticed the hunters, too.

Jett comes running around the corner, his robe fanning out at the sides. "They're here," he whisper-shouts.

"I know."

"When did they get here?" he asks.

"Just before you went on." I turn and make sure the curtain is fully closed.

Owen stares at me, his face pale. "I'm performing with the lions."

"You'll be okay," I tell him. "Just act normal. We all have to. We can't stop the show. There's nothing we can do. Nothing at all."

He sits down, head in his hands. Seconds later, he's back on his feet. "I need to find Ursula." Then he's gone. I watch him leave, wanting to tell him not to panic, but what good would it do? We're all panicking in one way or another.

"What did they do?" Jett asks. "While I was performing?"

"They just watched you. Carefully. They whispered to each other now and again," I say, my head spinning.

Jett pales, too. "Oh, shit. Really? What do you think they were saying about me?"

"I don't know . . ."

Jett wipes his brow. "Oh, this is bad. This is really, really bad." He runs his fingers through his hair, leaving it stuck up.

"*Jett*, don't start. I haven't gone out there yet and you're getting me worked up."

"No . . . sorry . . . I don't mean to," he stutters. "Ignore me. I'm overreacting."

"I really don't know if I can do this with them watching again. Why have they come back? What do they know?"

Jett pulls me to him and crushes me in a hug. "We'll be fine. Ava and Nora said—"

"I know what Ava and Nora said!" I say, pulling back. "I *know* we have to act normal and ignore that they're here, but I don't think I can carry on if the hunters keep coming back."

"If you want to go, just say."

"But what if they follow us?"

"I don't know, Flo! This is all such a mess."

"I have to go get ready," I say, pushing past him.

"Wait! I'll come with you." He hurries after me. I get to the back just as I hear Nora introducing my act. I'm no longer the finale—that spot belongs to the lions again—so I'm on sooner than usual. It'll be good to get it out of the way, though.

I yank my robe off and shift quickly, trying to clear my mind of everything. *Don't think, just do.*

Nora comes to get me, my usual headpiece and reins forgotten. We dash out on to the stage. My eyes dart to the hunters. They sit up straighter, lean forward. *They know!*

The hurdle is already lit. Nora really is in a hurry to get through this. She doesn't take me to the audience tonight. I'm handed straight over to Ava, who takes me outside so I can get in a good run before my jump.

"Focus," Ava says to me once we're outside the tent. "Don't think about anyone watching, just make the jump, then it's over for another night, okay? They might be gone tomorrow . . ."

I nod my head and puff air out of my nostrils, hoping she realizes I mean yes.

"Right, go!" Ava says, patting my side.

I hesitate, finding it hard to focus. I don't want to go in there, but I have to swallow my fear. *Just make the jump then it's over for another night.*

I take off, running fast and gathering speed. I can't stop now.

Once inside the tent, I see the flames, feel the heat. But I can also feel the eyes of the four hunters crawling over me.

I glance up at them, and with that moment's distraction, I make the jump too late. I clear the hurdle, but the flames lick my stomach as I leap over them. The pain is instant, agonizing. I cry out.

And when I land, hard, on the ground, I am no longer a horse.

19
WITH FIRE

Stunned screams erupt from the audience.

Some clap, slowly and unsurely. I hear children crying and benches scraping against the floor. But I hardly notice what they're doing or where they're going. There's a rushing sound in my ears that makes it hard to work out what's really going on around me. My main focus is the singed flesh on my torso. I barely register that the pain caused me to shift back into human form in front of the audience—*in front of the hunters*—until Nora drags me, naked, off the floor and runs behind the curtain, pulling me along with her. I cry out again as the tender skin on my stomach stretches with each step.

I've never experienced being ripped from my shape without any control. The pain tore me from horse to girl in an instant. It hurt. Not only the burn to my stomach, but the sensation of leaving my shape so suddenly. It felt like I was being sucked backward through a tiny hole. Then the ground appeared in front of my eyes, and before I had a chance to do anything at all, to even understand what was happening, I hit it, and the screaming started.

My skin feels too tight, my head feels like it's going to explode. Another pair of arms takes me backstage. Gentler than Nora. I don't look up—my head's spinning and my vision is unfocused—but I know it's Jett. He wraps my robe around my shoulders and scoops me up in his arms. Then we're moving.

I can hear screaming and shouting coming from everywhere around us. Nora and Ava come into step on either side of Jett. "What are we going to do?" Ava says frantically.

"You're in charge, you tell me," Jett snaps.

"We didn't know that something like this was going to happen!" Ava replies, her tone high and frantic. The sound of her voice adds to the ringing in my ears. "We need to go. Immediately. All of those people have seen what we are. We need to lay low for a while—"

"Oh, shit. Hari," Nora cuts in, running a hand through her hair and ripping the bow tie off her neck.

Jett stops. "Where are the hunters now?" he asks.

"Gone," Nora says. "They left with the rest of the audience."

"We don't know where they went," Ava adds.

"Only pack what we need," Jett says, taking charge. "We can't spend a second longer here than we have to. Tell everyone."

"But they're all over the place—shifters and humans, they're all over the camp. There's no easy way to round them up," Nora says.

"*Try*," Jett hisses.

"We will," Ava says, grabbing hold of Nora's arm. The two of them stride ahead.

"I mean it," Jett calls after them, as if he's their superior rather than the other way around. "Five minutes, max. We might not have even that."

I bounce up and down in Jett's arms as he rushes us back to Hari's trailer to collect our things. The pain of my stomach is sickening. Black spots dance at the edges of my vision. I blink hard. I can't pass out, not now.

Jett places me down on the bed while he grabs our clothes and backpacks. "Put these on," he says, throwing the outfit I had on earlier to me.

I think about the material rubbing against the burned skin on my stomach and a wave of nausea rushes over me. "I don't think I can."

"Flo. There's no time," Jett says, dashing around the trailer, grabbing things and shoving them into our packs. He stops to pull his own jeans on under his robe. "Just grit your teeth and put them on. We're leaving in a second."

Tears pool in my eyes. I grab the clothes from where they're sprawled out beside me and do as he says. I cry quietly as I shimmy into my jeans, stretching the wound from side to side, and when I lift my hands into the air, pulling on the tight skin, to slip my T-shirt over my head. I can't make myself bend forward to put my boots on, so I shrug my jacket over my shoulders and hold the boots in my hand.

Jett's dressed now and searching through Hari's cupboards. "I'm ready," I croak.

He looks over his shoulder at me. "Grab the sleeping bags," he orders.

I roll them up as best I can and pass them to Jett. He shoulders our backpacks and tucks the sleeping bags under his arms then ushers me through the door.

"Can you run?" he asks.

"I . . . I . . . do I have a choice?"

"No, I guess not. Head straight for the car. Don't get separated, no matter what."

We start running. I wince, biting hard on my lip to stop myself from screaming, each time one of my feet thuds against the ground. The pain brings tears to my eyes again, but I don't let them fall. I taste blood on my tongue and mud squelches between my toes as I follow after Jett.

All around me is chaos—a rush of people zigzaging back and forth to vehicles with their belongings, piling things into the cars, crying, screaming, shouting. It's all down to me. This is entirely my fault. I put everyone here in danger.

I should be helping them, not running away. I stop and look around me. I can't see the triplets or the elders. Everyone's dashing around so fast that I can't focus properly on anyone's face. Where are Ursula and Owen? Star and Ruby and Itch and Oscar? What about Pru and her friends? *Where are the hunters?*

Ahead, Jett signals for me to hurry, to keep up with him. "Flo, come on!" He backs up and takes hold of my arm. "Keep moving. Stay with me."

"Where are the hunters?" I shout. They're certain of what I am now, so why aren't they here for me? I feel more frightened not knowing where they are or what they're planning. Where did they go?

As if in answer to my question, the circus tent goes up in flames.

I scream and cover my head as the fire suddenly bursts to life and claims the tent. Jett pulls my hands away from my face and weaves his fingers through mine. "Keep your head down," he shouts over the noise.

I glance to one side. I can see the hunters now, lit up by the fire's menacing glow. They're making their way into camp, throwing nets over shifters. The shifters cry out in agony as the chains connect with their bare skin. "Jett," I whimper, tearing my eyes away. "Silver."

"Keep moving," he says again. His gaze is set ahead. I don't know if he knows what's happening around us or if he just doesn't want to look.

"We should help them!"

"We can't," Jett says, more or less dragging me now. "I'm getting you out of here. We should have left before."

It's chaotic. The hunters were on us before we even had a chance to group together. The fight is fierce and fast. I can hardly follow what's going on, and Jett's pulling us along so fast that everything is happening too quickly to register.

We make it to the car. Jett yanks the door open and shoves me into the passenger seat. My body twists and a stab of pain makes me gag. Jett climbs into the driver's side and slams his door shut.

I yelp as something hits the glass of the front window, causing it to chip. The back door swings open and Jett rushes to start the engine. "It's us, it's us," we hear from behind. I turn to see Lance, Lucas, and Logan spilling into the back. Blood runs down Logan's face, coming from an unseen cut beneath his mess of blond hair. Pru clambers in after them, squeezing into what little space is left. There's a nasty red mark on her cheek.

Jett starts the car without a word and drives away before they've even closed the doors. We don't know who else is coming or where we are going. At first I felt angry at Jett for pulling me away, but now I realize he was right to do so. We're no match for the hunters. All we can do is go and hope the other shifters get themselves out of there, too.

20
A STRING OF BAD DECISIONS

My head slams against the car window as we bump over a pothole in the road.

"Ouch." I rub my head with one hand and protect my stomach with the other. I'm trying to keep the seat belt from going anywhere near the burned flesh. I grit my teeth and sit up, fresh tears springing to my eyes.

"Sorry," Jett says. "This is a bad road."

"Where are we?" I ask, settling back against the seat.

Jett glances out the side window then looks back at the road in front of him. "Well, I wasn't sure where to head for. I haven't seen another car following us, so I don't know who made it out. I'm just driving to the next location. I thought it might be where Nora and Ava will go after they get Hari from the doctor. I don't know . . ."

"We aren't due at the next site for almost two months, though. Do you really think that's where others will think to go?"

Jett shrugs. "Do you have a better idea?"

I think for a moment. "No. I guess not. It's a long way, isn't it? How long until we get there?"

"Another hour or so, maybe. How's your stomach?"

"Not great," I say as the skin throbs.

"I gathered what I could for you from Hari's trailer. I'll take a look at it when we stop. Unless you need me to pull over now?"

"No, I can wait. Thanks, though."

I try to look over my shoulder, twisting in my seat until the pain is too much. "They're asleep," Jett whispers, looking in the rearview mirror.

"I thought it was quiet," I say, wondering how the four of them were comfortable enough to sleep squished together back there.

The two of us sit in silence for a few long moments. All I can think about are the things I saw before escaping the circus site. Fire. Silver. Hunters.

"I can't believe what happened there. Back at camp."

Jett nods, his face pained. I wonder if he partly blames me like I blame myself. I shifted. I caused the chaos. How many shifters are dead or captured because of me? I think about Ursula and Owen. About Ruby. About little Star. I hope they got away. I hope they're safe.

"I hope everyone got out," I whisper.

"I don't think everyone did," Jett replies.

"No," I say, hanging my head. "I don't either."

I somehow sleep for the remainder of the journey, even with the images of the circus spiraling in my head. I can't stop seeing Star's face. She's one of the youngest. Where is she now?

Jett rolls to a stop at Newlake Park, the next circus location, at almost 11:00 p.m. The six of us climb out of the car. I stretch, then gasp when the skin pulls around my burn. I wonder how long it's going to take to heal. Shifters heal fast, but some injuries are worse than others and this burn is definitely bad.

Jett sends the triplets to collect wood for a fire. Pru is leaning against the rear of the car, crying, while Jett rounds up the spilled contents of our backpacks from inside the trunk. I hear him mumbling something to Pru. Something reassuring, most likely. He's good at that, at making people feel better, at grasping at the hope in any situation.

When he takes an armful of camping equipment over to the clearing, I walk around the car. "Pru?" I say cautiously.

She sniffs and rubs her nose. "What?"

"Are you all right?" I ask. *Stupid question.*

"Do I look all right, Flo?" she snaps, turning her back to me.

I walk around so I'm standing in front of her again. "There's no need to—"

"Isn't there?"

"You don't even know what I was going to say!"

"I do. You want me to forgive you and tell you none of it was your fault."

"I don't!" I exclaim. And it's true—I don't. I know it was my fault.

"But wasn't it *you* who attracted hunters to the circus in the first place?" she snarls, stepping closer to me. I want to take a step back, but I hold my ground. I won't let her intimidate me. She's cruel, everybody knows that, but I'm not standing for it now—not after what we've just been through. "Wasn't it *you* who took forever to tell somebody about it? And wasn't it *you* who shifted back to human in front of the circus audience, including the hunters, and caused them to attack all of us?"

"I . . ." I don't know what to say.

"Save it, Flo. I don't want to listen to your bullshit excuses. You did this."

I open my mouth and close it again. I will admit it was me, I do accept it's my fault, but she's making it sound like I did it all knowingly. Mistakes. That's what they were. Mistakes that mounted up. A string of bad decisions.

Tears burn in my eyes, threatening to fall, but I hold them back. It feels selfish to cry when everything she's said is true. "I know," I say.

"Good. Now answer me this." Pru steps even closer to me. She swats my stomach, right against the burn. I stagger backward. The pain makes me nauseous, but I stay standing, stay to answer her question. "Why is it that *you* get to live? That you come away with only a small burn on your stomach, while other shifters suffered back there—I mean *really* suffered. And some are probably still suffering right now."

I take another step back. I've already considered this. Asked myself the exact same question. Maybe if I'd stayed where I was and been captured by the hunters, maybe they'd have left the rest of the camp alone. But I didn't stay. I ran. I left. And now we'll never know.

"If they're still alive," Pru adds.

I swallow the lump in my throat. "I've admitted it was my fault. What more do you want me to say?"

She looks at me—a look filled with so much pain I almost can't stand it. "Just stay away from me," she barks.

"I will," I say, sounding braver than I feel. I walk away.

I make my way over to Jett, hoping to busy myself by helping him. My eyes sting, my breathing hard and shallow. *Don't cry.*

"What was that all about?" Jett asks as I get near. He's crouched down, rifling through his backpack.

"You saw?" I say, wondering why he didn't come over.

"I saw the two of you talking, what did she say?"

"She told me to stay away from her," I say.

"Oh," Jett says, looking at the ground. "I see."

"It's fine. You don't have to pretend like what happened isn't all on me. No one else is," I say, crossing my arms over my chest, then flinching when they brush the top of the burn.

"Oh, Flo." Jett jumps to his feet. He takes each of my hands, our conversation forgotten. "Come on."

The two of us go back to the car. I lie flat across the backseat. He lifts my T-shirt carefully. I watch him, his hands moving so cautiously, like I might break. I almost forget the pain, seeing him like this, feeling his fingertips

129

skim over my ribs. It's almost enough to distract me from the stinging, throbbing wound. Almost.

"I'm so sorry," Jett says, looking at the burn. I focus my attention on seeing it properly for the first time. It doesn't even look like it's begun to heal at all. The raw skin is melted and blistered—black and red and wet and weeping. I look away. "I should have pulled over to look at it the first chance I got. I don't even know how to treat a burn."

"It doesn't look like it's healing at all."

"I think it is," Jett says. "Slowly. It's so severe that it'll take longer than usual." He rubs his hand through his hair. "I don't know what to do."

I shake my head. "Neither do I."

"Water, do you think?" he asks.

"Maybe. I really don't know. What did you bring from camp for it?"

"Bandages and things, but I don't know if that's right, either."

"We could try . . ."

"No, Flo. I'm not guessing over something like this. I'm going to speak to Lucas. Stay put."

I remain lying over the backseat while Jett goes to find Lucas. I bunch my T-shirt up and tie it in a knot so it won't fall back over the burn. The light pattering of rain on the roof fills the silence. I close my eyes and listen to it, trying to relax and ignore my injury.

When Jett returns with Lucas, Lucas gently lifts my legs and climbs into the back, putting my legs back down over his lap once he's sitting inside. He has a bottle of water and a plastic bag in his hand. "What are you doing?" I ask, feeling both uncomfortable with him touching me like this and afraid of what he plans to do next.

Lucas shrugs. "Not sure."

Jett kneels on the front seat, watching over us.

"Seriously?" I say, looking from Jett to Lucas. "Don't touch it, please—"

Before I can stop Lucas, he tilts the bottle and lets some of the water splash onto the burn. I suck in air to stop myself screaming. I breathe heavily, the raging heat returning after less than a second of relief. "That's not working," I say through gritted teeth. The splash felt like a slap; the returning heat feels like a fire's been lit on my stomach. "Please stop."

Lucas ignores me and unfolds the plastic bag.

"What's that for?"

"If you burn your hand, you wrap it in a plastic bag until you get treatment," he says.

I shake my head and attempt to move away from him, but there's nowhere to go. "Well, just don't. We're not getting treatment. And it's not my hand. I don't want you to touch it. Please, Lucas," I beg.

"Are you sure about the plastic bag thing?" Jett asks. "Where did you learn that?"

"It'll heal on its own," I whimper.

"It's healing too slow," Lucas says.

"Just leave me alone."

Lucas drops the bag and the water bottle onto the seat beside him. "Whatever you say."

21
TAKE SHAPE

"They're not coming, are they?" I say.

Jett doesn't answer right away. Like me, he's hoping for the best and fearing the worst.

It rained for a bit, just a light and short shower.

Lance and Logan are setting up tents while Lucas starts a fire with the wood the three of them collected earlier. Pru is still by herself, leaning against the car.

"It hasn't been that long," Jett says. "Give them time."

I rub my face and step away from the group. Jett follows close behind, seeming to sense my restlessness. I turn to face him. Out of earshot from the others, I say, "After the . . . the accident, I wish I could have done something. I put everyone in danger, including you, and I did nothing to help anyone. We left Star behind, Rain, Ruby, our friends, some too young to understand. "

"Flo," Jett says softly. "You were badly injured. You only had to look at you to see how much you were hurting."

"There were people weaker than me there. Hurt or not, I wish I could have helped *someone*."

"I'm sorry, Flo. If I could've taken it for you, I would—all of it."

I shake my head. "That's the thing. I wouldn't want you to. I don't ever want to have to depend on you and everyone else like I did back there. I hate that you were trying to get me out, I hate that I didn't help you, and I hate that I could have cost you everything."

Jett guides me farther from the group, pain clear in his expression. "You *are* everything, Flo. Your life means more to me than my own."

A sob catches in my throat.

Jett reaches out, brushing away tears with his thumb. "Please don't be upset," he says. "I would never have done anything different. I would never leave you, if that's what you're suggesting—whatever the cost."

"No," I breathe. "I'm not. I'd never leave you either. I just hate that I felt so helpless. I never want to feel like that again."

"You're not helpless. You were hurt."

I nod. "I know. . . . Let's go back. It's cold out here."

Jett takes my hand and we join the others as the campfire crackles to life. He puts his arm around me, pulling me close to him. We huddle together, sharing each other's warmth. Pru watches us from the other side of the flames. When I make eye contact with her, she glares and turns away. I need to do something about that. If we're all in this together, we can't be fighting. I realize there doesn't seem to be any bad feeling between the triplets and me. It's just Pru.

I think about going over to speak to her again, then wonder if I should leave it until morning—give her some space. Before I can come to a decision, she speaks up. "What are the sleeping arrangements?"

We only have two tents between the six of us. That's all there was time to get in the rush after the show. The triplets and Pru brought next to nothing with them. Jett ransacked Hari's trailer, stuffing things into our backpacks, and had the good sense to pick up both of our tents from by the door before leaving. I guess he knew we wouldn't be going back. Whatever was left there feels lost to me now—clothes, tents, people.

I think about sleeping, squished up in one of the tents with two other people, and hover my hand over my stomach, my T-shirt still bunched up. Around the edges of the burn, the skin has gone pink. It's tight and wrinkly, sore to touch, but actually starting to heal. I just keep telling myself that it could have been worse. Much worse.

Before anyone has a chance to offer their suggestions, Pru offers her own: "I say I should sleep in the car on my own or have a tent to myself. I'm not sleeping with any of the boys."

"There aren't only boys here, Pru," I say, not that I want to share a tent with her either.

"Hmm?" she says, like she's noticing my presence for the first time. "Well, it goes without saying that I'm not sharing with *you*."

Jett's posture hardens and his eyes dart to Pru. "Pru, if you want to stay here, you're going to have to stop that."

"Stop what?" she says, all innocent.

"You know what."

"I don't!" she shrieks. "And even if I did, I'd have pretty good reason after everything she's done. It's her fault we're in this mess. I don't even know what happened to the other tigers." Pru's voice hitches, and for a second I feel sorry for her. I wonder how I'd feel if I'd lost Jett back there. I'd be heartbroken. It even hurts just thinking about it. Pru recovers and continues, "We got split up. So *excuse me* for being a little sensitive about it."

Silence follows her outburst. I swallow and step forward. "None of us know what happened to the rest of the camp, Pru. We're all worried."

"And no one here is blaming Flo," Jett adds. "She got hurt—badly hurt—which caused her to shift. She didn't plan it."

"Are you sure about that?" Pru says.

That's too far. I understand her anger, can relate to it even, but to outright accuse me of planning this? It's both hurtful and ridiculous. "Pru—" I begin.

"Okay. *Okay.* I'm not saying you shifted on purpose." She turns to address the rest of the group. "But she did other things, too. She didn't tell anyone about the hunters." Pru goes on as though I'm not standing right in front of her. "Who knows how much they knew by then."

"I'm not discussing this with you again," I tell her.

Lucas stands from his seat around the campfire. "Bury it and move on, or you can leave here alone."

He looks to Jett and me for confirmation. Jett nods once.

Pru gasps. I'm as surprised as she is. "You'd cast me out? You can't!"

135

"We're scared for our friends, too," Logan tells her.

"Like Itch and Oscar," Lance says.

"And Ursula and Owen," Jett adds.

"Star, too," I whisper.

Pru's eyes shine with tears. "You can't cast me out."

"Nobody here, including Flo, is to blame for this," Jett says. "The only people to be held responsible are the hunters themselves. So forget your grudge and move on or leave us. It's your choice." Pru wipes her eyes, and Jett's posture relaxes. "Look, Pru, I don't mean to be harsh. But we have to get along. This won't work otherwise. We have to trust each other and move forward."

The triplets remain silent now. I wonder if they're still picturing the missing like I am. All those faces. All those unknowns.

"Fine," Pru mumbles, pulling me from my thoughts.

"'Fine,' what?" I ask.

"Fine. I'll put it behind me."

"Good," Jett says. "You can sleep in the car. The triplets can have one tent, and Flo and I will share the other. Everyone okay with that?"

I nod, and so do the triplets. Pru mutters, "Fine," again, and we're all agreed. Then we move on to the next matter: food.

"I'm starving now," Lucas says, sitting back down beside his brothers.

I move closer to the campfire and settle down in front of it. Jett does the same. "Well, we have no food and very little money, which I'm saving for gas," Jett tells them.

"Then what are we going to do?" Pru asks, her attitude returning. "Escape the hunters then starve to death somewhere else?"

"We could always shift," Jett suggests.

"You're joking, right?" Pru says.

"No. Why not? We're hungry. We don't have food, but we can shift and eat as animals."

"That's disgusting!" Pru says. "I'd rather starve."

"Be our guest," Jett says, seeming frustrated.

"It's not actually that bad an idea," I say. Because it's not. It makes sense, even if it isn't appealing.

"For you guys it's not," Pru says. "You and the triplets get to eat . . . I don't know . . . leaves and grass. Even you, Jett, if you want to. But I'm a *tiger*. What am I meant to do? Hunt something and kill it by tearing its flesh with my teeth. I *can't* do that."

She has a point. I don't think I could do that either, if I were her. Tiger or not, we've spent our lives suppressing our animal natures.

"You'll feel differently if you allow your animal self to take over," Jett says.

He's met by five blank stares. "Jett?" I say. "We've been trained to fight our animal instincts and be more human when in our shapes. It's not as easy as it sounds. None of us know *how* to allow our shape to take over."

"It's in you, though. It's in all of us. You must have held on to some part of the horse, of the elephant, of the tiger. It can't be gone forever. Our animal selves are somewhere inside us still, deep down. We just have to find them again."

"And how do you propose we do that?" Pru asks.

"And isn't it dangerous?" I say. "What if we can't come back?"

Jett opens his mouth and closes it again. He rubs his face. "I don't know," he says in defeat.

"Have you done this before?" I ask.

"Yes. Once. It works," he replies.

"When?"

"Supply run. Hari took me with him and wouldn't let us take any food, just water, because we were only supposed to be gone a couple hours. The car broke down in the middle of nowhere and—"

"It took you two days to come back," I finish for him. "You left out some details of that trip then."

"I suppose I did," he says sheepishly.

I guess that'll have to be good enough for me. "I'll do it, then. If you do."

Pru and the triplets are quietly considering. Lance and Logan whisper between themselves while Lucas watches Jett. "What would you eat?" Pru asks.

Jett shrugs. "Probably a squirrel or something."

"Ew! Gross! I can't do this!" Pru squeals, shaking her hands out in front of her as if something is stuck to them.

"I'm not too crazy about eating grass," I say to Jett. "But a squirrel? Are you serious?"

"Why not? I'll be happy to eat it once I'm a bear, physically *and* mentally. Trust me, Flo, it'll be fine. I mean it."

"I just don't see how."

The triplets stand up and start taking their clothes off. "Let's give it a try, then," Lucas says. "I'm too hungry to care."

Pru shakes her head. "*Please!* If you like the idea so much, maybe I'll shift and eat one of you."

The triplets look at one another and roll their eyes. "I'd like to see you try," Logan says, and the other two laugh.

Pru stands up. "What am I supposed to do? I wouldn't even know what to look for, or how to . . . to . . . *catch* it."

"You will," Jett says simply. "Trust me, you'll know."

"But *how*?"

"Your tiger instincts will kick in if you can let them. So, let them. They're always there, fighting their way in. Look for the tiger, and let it out."

Pru doesn't look like she believes Jett, but agrees anyway. "Right. Fine. Let's just get this over with," she moans. She stomps off back to the car to stash her clothes and shift.

I watch her go. "Aren't you nervous that she might actually eat one of us if she gives the tiger control?"

Jett smirks. "I guess we'll find out."

"Jett! It's not funny. She hates me. I don't want to be eaten!"

"She won't eat you, Flo," he says, ruffling up my hair. "She'd have to munch through me first to get to you."

I tilt my head and smile back. "Thanks. Now turn around."

Jett turns his back to me so I can undress and shift. I take my necklace off carefully and put it in the pocket of my jeans.

It's the first time I've shifted after the accident. I'm afraid the horse won't let me back inside. When I close my eyes and concentrate, same as I always do before shifting, nothing happens. It takes longer than it should. "Is everything okay?" Jett says over his shoulder.

"I-I think so."

"Flo, what is it?" he asks, then starts to turn around.

"No! Don't!" I say, attempting to cover myself up, but he stops. "I just—I'm not sure if I can shift right now."

"What? Does it hurt or something? Your burn?"

"No. I don't know. I just can't find . . . that place."

"It's all right," Jett soothes. "Just close your eyes and listen to me."

"I'm not sure it's going to work."

"You're thinking about it too much," he says. "About what happened at the circus, about letting your animal instincts take over. Am I right?"

I nod, then realize he can't see me. "Yes. Maybe I'm trying too hard."

"Right. So close your eyes." I do. "Let out a long breath. Relax. Forget everything that's happened. None of that stuff exists right now. It's just you—you and the horse. Listen to your surroundings."

I do as he says, relaxing to the sound of night animals in the trees and rustling leaves on the ground. I start to feel my shape, tingling at the edges, pushing its way back to me. My arms, which are bunched up covering my chest, drop back to my sides. My legs, which are shaking, start to steady.

"Now think of where you want to go," Jett continues. "Think of the darkness, the cold. Think of the heat, your coat. It's all there, waiting for you, to awaken your shape. You just have to find it and let it take you."

And I do.

I open my eyes, just this once, because I want to shut out my human instincts entirely. Everything blurs out of focus. The tree trunks shudder to jagged lines, and their bare branches extend like cracking ice. I await the Blackout; I know I can stand it now, and I want to feel it. All of it.

The blurred colors that dance before my eyes fade to nothing. The ground beneath my feet disappears until all that's left around me is blackness. I feel like I'm floating, suspended in a place between worlds that's made only for me.

Then everything starts to feel *wrong*.

I'm suddenly dizzy and unsteady. I feel trapped. I feel as if I've been turned inside out and back again, and something's not been put back in the right place. My skull vibrates, threatening to crack in two. I want to hold my head but I can't move.

This isn't right. *This isn't right.*

Then the cold comes and soothes it all. It numbs the pain so I feel nothing but the chill biting my skin and the prickling in my bones.

My shape finally comes back to me, as agonizingly slow as it is, giving me another chance. My human form slips away and heat consumes me. The feeling reminds me of what happened at the circus, but I push past that; I know if

141

I give in to the feelings those thoughts bring, I'll be sucked right out of my shape again, and it'll hurt like hell.

My insides ignite and boil. My chestnut hair coats my body, making me hotter still, and the world comes back into focus through new eyes. The first thing that fully develops is Jett.

His dark eyes shine in the moonlight and he takes a step toward me. He puts his hand on my face and grounds me, then everything around him forms and comes rushing into focus. "Are you okay?" he asks.

I am now, I think. Why did it take so long to change? Why did it *hurt?* I can't tell Jett about it, not while I'm a horse, so I put it behind me, chalk it up to the accident, and nod my head in response to his question. He smiles. "Good."

Once we're all in our animal forms, Jett and Pru go into the surrounding bushes, and the triplets and I stay put to eat by camp. This is so weird.

The elephants are pulling branches from the trees with their trunks and lowering them into their mouths. The leaves are either yellowing or turning brown and crunchy with the season change. How can that possibly taste good? I look at the grass below my feet and ask myself the same question.

I lower my head and sniff the ground. It's still slightly wet from the light rain shower earlier. I smell dampness and soil, earthy and crisp. Nothing appetizing. Nothing in the slightest bit appealing.

I try to do what Jett said—try to let the horse take over. But I can't. I don't know how.

I nibble a little on the ends of the grass, deliberately trying not to get any of the soil beneath it in my mouth. It isn't too bad, so I take a bit more, this time pulling the grass from the roots and taking a huge clump of dirt into my mouth along with it. I stop myself from spitting it out and chew slowly, tasting, feeling. It's okay. Nice, even. My brain is telling me it's wrong, but I find that I still want more.

I concentrate on being a horse first, and a girl second. A sensation in the back of my mind flutters to life, bringing with it a sense of relief—the letting go of worries and thoughts and fears—and I focus only on the grass beneath my feet. The horse wants to eat. She wants the grass. I let her in a little more, giving in to that feeling, welcoming it and allowing it to edge forward. I eat the grass, soil and all. And I keep eating until my jaw aches.

Once I've had enough, I let my human side edge forward and take over once more. I don't know how I do it, but when I concentrate on it, and really think about those two separate sides of myself, it comes almost naturally.

I go behind the car to shift back. I close my eyes and feel myself being pulled back into my human skin. It's always worse going from horse to human, like trying to squeeze into a space that's too small. It's easier this time, though. Much easier than I thought it would be, given the effort it took to find my shape. Still, the burn on my stomach throbs as my body adjusts. Maybe I'm supposed to stay human for a while, to heal and recover.

I throw my clothes back on and come out from behind the car. Lance, Logan, and Lucas are already dressed and sitting around the fire. "Well?" Lance says when I approach and take a seat across from them.

"It wasn't that bad," I say.

"Yeah right!" Logan scoffs. "We watched you eating after we'd finished and shifted back. You were loving it!"

"I'm not even going to respond to that," I say.

I sigh and watch the fire. Images of the last night in the circus flash before my eyes, dancing in the flames. I can't look away.

Fire.

Fire caused all of this. Fire hurt me. Fire split the camp apart. Fire took the circus tent, burned it to the ground. Fire is the reason only six of us are here now.

"I'm going to bed," I mumble to nobody in particular. I stand and turn in the direction of the tent I'll be sharing with Jett.

"Whoa!" I hear one of the triplets shout and I look back to see why. Jett and Pru are coming out of the woods, their mouths and necks bloody. They are both naked. Even though it's dark out here, they don't seem to mind that we can see them. I wonder what that feels like—to not care, to be so free, so comfortable in your own skin. Some of the other shifters used to tease me, saying my embarrassment is "*so human.*"

Lucas glances back at me and smirks in his usual teasing way. Heat spreads across my face and neck. I turn and keep going to the tent.

I've never seen Jett naked before. Not properly, any-way. I always avoided *looking* if I was around him when he was shifting.

Once inside the tent, I zip it up tight. I crawl slowly into my sleeping bag, easing onto my back, and close my eyes. I don't sleep, though.

Before long, I hear the front of the tent unzipping. Jett crawls inside and zips it back up quietly. He must think I'm sleeping.

I think about telling him it's okay, that I'm awake. But something doesn't let me. I can't get the image of him out of my mind—naked and covered in blood, walking out of the woods.

I roll over to face the canvas wall beside me. "Flo?" Jett whispers. "Are you awake?"

With effort, I roll back over to face him, but keep my eyes closed. I don't know why this bothers me so much. Maybe because I've never allowed him to see me without my clothes on. Maybe because I thought the first time I saw him naked would be under different circumstances. Some time in the future . . . I don't know. But this is our life as shifters. If it's not a big deal to him, it shouldn't be a big deal to me. I open my eyes.

Jett's lying on top of his sleeping bag, propped up on one elbow and looking down at me with his hair falling over his deep, dark eyes. He's clean now and wearing clothes. "All good?" he asks.

"All good," I say.

He watches me for a second before I close my eyes again. He clears his throat and I can hear him shuffling around on top of his sleeping bag, unzipping it and wriggling inside. He sighs as he lies back. "Good night, Flo," he whispers.

I think again about seeing him naked, walking back to camp out in the open and covered in blood. It made me feel embarrassed, but why should I be when he's not? When nearly all the shifters in camp have never cared about being seen in their human skin without clothes on because it's who we are, what we are, one of two forms. We've always been encouraged to be comfortable in whatever skin we wear, and I've always had a hard time with that. It seems trivial now, though, worrying about that kind of thing.

Jett's stripped in front of me so many times and he doesn't even think twice about it. And though I've never *looked*, I'm probably the only person who's made a conscious effort not to. I shouldn't be embarrassed, though, not with him, not after all this time. I make the decision to put that behind me starting now.

"Good night, Jett."

22
NO MORE WAITING

The color of the sky matches my mood.

Gray and miserable. I wish it'd stop raining all the time. The campfire burned out in the early hours, now a heap of black logs in the dull morning light. The air smells of damp earth and wet leaves.

No one else from the circus has joined us.

Lucas, Logan, and Lance are huddled in their tent with the front panel open. They're watching the car. I look over to see it rocking, and Pru's foot is pressed up against the window as she struggles into her jeans and boots. Then she opens the door, staying inside for shelter (with the interior lights off, so the battery doesn't drain), and watches the rain fall. She looks sad. The triplets do, too. I think we're all losing hope that others will meet us here. I know I am.

We haven't slept much. We turned in late and woke up early, but if the others feel anything like I do, sleep isn't a priority right now.

The skin on my stomach itches as it heals. The center of the burn still looks no better, but the area around it seems to be recovering. I resist the urge to scratch around it, knowing if I start I won't be able to stop.

"Everyone else is up," I say to Jett. "We should figure out what to do next. No one has come, which means they could've gone elsewhere, been captured, or worse."

Jett rolls over, groaning. I'm not sure he heard a word I just said. "What time is it?" he asks.

"I don't know," I say. "Early."

"It doesn't even look like the sun is up yet."

"It's raining. Did you hear me? No one else is here. We need to make some kind of plan."

He rubs his eyes. "Okay. I'm up."

"Thank you," I say, looking back outside. "We should probably all discuss what we're going to do now. Maybe we should move on. Or go back."

Jett looks more alert now. "You want to go back there? What if the hunters are still around?"

"I don't think they would be. Do you?"

"I don't know," Jett says nervously. "It's not like them to make a big scene like that. Things must have gotten out of hand pretty quickly. Maybe they're sticking around for damage control. They might be watching the area."

I sigh. I don't want to stay here, waiting, wondering. I want to go out there and get some answers—find out what happened to our friends, to the elders. I can't help but feel like we're wasting time here even though it seemed like a good idea last night.

"Well, let's just get the others and figure it out together. I'm going to go over to the triplets' tent, so come when you're ready."

"Okay," Jett says. I crawl forward to leave but he holds me back. "Wait." He pulls himself up and slides his hand behind my neck. With his other hand, he reaches behind his head and pulls my necklace out from beneath his sleeping bag. "I woke with this jammed in my ear," he says with a grin. I smile back and lift my hair so he can clasp the necklace back in place. Then he lets me go, and I crawl out of the tent, my insides fluttering, despite the circumstances.

I dash through the heavy rain to the car, my boots squelching in the watery grass, mud splashing up my legs. Pru sees me coming. She crosses her arms over her chest. "What is it?" Her voice lacks the ferocity of yesterday, but is still hostile.

"Come over to the triplets' tent so we can decide what to do today?" I say. It's not meant to come out like a question, but it does.

"What do you mean?" she asks. "Aren't we staying here and waiting?"

"No one's here. We should think about what to do now."

"Well you haven't given anyone much chance," Pru says. It might seem that way, and I have considered that we could miss others arriving if we go rushing off again, but we're only a few hours away from the site. They've had time. I think something bad has happened to most of them, and it's killing me not knowing for sure.

"Pru, don't you want to find out what happened to the tigers? What happened to the camp? What if everyone's there, thinking *we've* been killed or captured, and we don't know because we're sitting here thinking the same thing?"

"This is the next location on the tour," she says stubbornly.

"In seven weeks. I'm not waiting that long to find out. And how do we know if the circus will carry on its run after what happened? I think we need to go back."

Pru stares at me. I take her silence to mean she's in some kind of agreement.

"So are you coming to speak to Jett and the triplets and figure this out?"

She shrugs.

"Have it your way." Frustrated, I turn away from her and head over to the triplets' tent. I'm soaked now, my clothes heavy and uncomfortable and sticking to me. "Can I come in?" I ask the three brothers. They need to scoot over to make room for me.

"You're soaked," Lance says. "You'll get everything wet."

"It'll dry," I say irritably. "But I won't unless I get out of the rain."

"You have your own tent with Jett," Logan says.

"I know. He's coming, too."

The triplets shuffle backward to make some room. I step inside, my soggy boots spreading mud all over the plastic sheeting on the floor. "Oh great," Lucas mumbles. "What's this about?"

"It's about what to do now. Staying here and waiting might not be the best idea."

"Flo suggested we go back to see what's happened to the camp," Jett says, appearing in the doorway and squeezing in beside me.

"Well that's stupid," Lucas says.

150

"That's exactly what I said," Pru says from outside, joining us. "Now, make room for me."

Jett and I shuffle to the side and Pru ducks and crawls in beside me. She shakes out her wet hair. Droplets of rainwater go flying everywhere and strands of hair whip me in the face. I'm certain she did it on purpose, but I ignore her and focus on convincing everyone to go back to the circus. "It's not stupid," I say. "We don't know what it's like there. What if everyone's fine and wondering what happened to us? What if the elders left a message? We have to check it out. I can't just sit here waiting. I hate not knowing."

"And what if we go back and the hunters are there, waiting for us to do exactly that?" Lucas asks.

"We'll be careful," I say. "Come on. We can do this if we prepare ourselves and take it one step at a time."

"So what do you suggest?" Lance asks, getting elbowed from both sides by Logan and Lucas. I smile. Now I have their attention.

Raindrops bounce off the tent and I speak up over the noise. "I think we should go back to camp. Park a little way away. Scope out the area first, like the hunters did. See who's there, what's left, any sign of where shifters might have been taken."

"And what if no one is there?"

I hesitate. "Then I guess we come back and carry on waiting."

"We could speak to Iris," Jett says.

"We're only meant to contact the area agent in an emergency. As a last resort," I say.

"I think the whole camp missing is an emergency situation," Pru says.

I frown. "Okay. But it might not come to that. Like I said, let's just take it one step at a time. We should probably get going soon if we want to get there and check out the area before it starts getting dark."

Pru sighs. The triplets shrug. Jett nods. I guess that means we're in agreement.

We're going back to Violet Bay.

23

BLUE EYES, BLUE LIPS

I don't sleep on the journey this time.

I'm too nervous to even think about closing my eyes. I have no idea what to expect when we get there. What if I'm making another mistake? What if I'm leading us into more danger? Haven't I hurt enough people already?

But I can't let myself think like that, because no matter where we are, we're in danger. And we can't abandon the circus, our friends, the elders. We have to do this. We have to go back.

I feel like I did on the car ride to my first show at Violet Bay—sick, anxious, dizzy. I glance at Jett, but he keeps his eyes on the road. No one has said a word so far. The only sounds come from the wheels rolling over the ground beneath, the purr of the engine as we drift along straight, flat roads, and Pru sighing in the back as she fights the triplets for legroom.

We park a short distance from the camp, making sure the car is relatively hidden by the trees. We thought of leaving the car in the beach parking lot, but we can't afford the fees.

The six of us continue on foot, staying away from the roads. Branches scratch at my body and face like clawed fingers pulling at my hair. The ground is damp and muddy, each footstep squelching and leaving a trail. Drops of rainwater fall from the trees, startling me each time one lands on my head. I hardly dare to breathe.

We're nearing the camp. There are noises in the distance—voices, car engines, static radios. My spirits lift instantly, even though I tell myself not to get my hopes up. I look at the others, who seem to all be listening just as carefully. "The circus?" I whisper. I hope more than anything the sounds I can hear mean that everyone's okay and that the hunters are gone. I motion us forward and the six of us edge closer.

Once we reach the tree line surrounding the circus, I can smell the leftover stench of burning—wood, grass, metal, plastic. Flesh. I can't help but picture the scene when we left—the circus tent of fire, the shifters screaming and running, the hunters coming out of nowhere. Chasing. Burning. Capturing. *Killing?*

Distracted by thoughts of what we might find, I walk straight into yellow tape that reads: POLICE LINE DO NOT CROSS. It's wrapped three times around a tree trunk in front of me and stretched across to the next, and then the next, flapping in the wind. My heart plummets to the bottom of my stomach. I don't know exactly what I expected, but it wasn't this. When I heard the sounds, I thought . . . I thought maybe everything was okay now. Maybe it wasn't as bad as I had envisioned. But it's worse.

Far ahead, I can just make out the police dotted between the tree trunks. We should leave.

I back up so the trees still hide me and look upon the aftermath of that night. The big tent is a sludgy mess on the ground, burned and blackened. The others are torn and tipped over, belongings strewn out all over the ground.

I did this.

I may as well have set the tent on fire myself. I may as well have hurt those shifters, wrapped them in silver and made them bleed, made their flesh burn.

I may as well have been the one to destroy this place.

In a sense, I did. I did destroy it.

I drop to my knees. Beside me, Jett places a hand on my shoulder. I look up at the others, wondering if they're thinking the same thing I am. Pru rolls her eyes and walks away, but before she does I see her tears escape. The triplets face the other way now, not involving themselves, not making jokes for the first time in forever. And still, I'm suffocating.

"Breathe," Jett commands.

I exhale. Inhale sharply. Repeat.

"What are you thinking?" he asks, rubbing my back.

I shake my head, at a loss for words.

He squeezes my shoulder, tells me it's not my fault. But it doesn't matter. It doesn't change anything.

I have to find the shifters, if there are any left. I have to find the hunters that did this. I have to find Hari, Ava, and Nora and put things right. I have to do *something* right. But where do I even start?

Iris. I realize now we really are going to have to go see the area agent. I've never spoken to her before. We're not meant to. They just get us set up and turn a blind eye. They keep our secret, as long as they get their cut. Iris might turn us away, but she's our best chance now at getting somewhere with all of this.

I draw a deep breath and get to my feet. "We can't stay here," I say, gesturing to the police beyond the trees. If we can see them, they might see us. "I think you're right about going to Iris, Jett. We need to find out whatever we can about—"

A scream.

I whip around, searching for which direction it came from. "Pru!" I yell, then cover my mouth and look back toward the camp. There's movement beyond the trees—are the police grouping together in reaction to the sudden sound? How quickly will they be able to pin our location?

"Flo, be quiet," Jett hisses, pulling me low to the ground. The triplets drop down beside us.

"She needs our help!" I say. I yank my arm from Jett's grip and stand again. Pru can't have gone far. I can still hear her, even though I can't see her. She's crying.

I run, following the sound. "Flo! Don't!" Jett calls after me, but I ignore him.

A million thoughts run through my mind. I think about getting there and finding her on the ground, her flesh burning under silver chains. I think about the hunters holding her. I think of her waiting for us to come and help her. She could have been attacked. It could be a trap. The police could get there before me and take us both away for questioning. And what would we ever say? I will myself to move faster.

And then I see her.

She isn't wrapped in silver. There are no hunters or police standing around her. She's kneeling on the ground, crying. As I get closer to her, I see the bodies.

The tigers.

She's holding one in her arms. It's Maria, I think. The other tiger girl, Lexi, is under a pile of dead leaves, moss, and dirt, like she's been hidden in a hurry. They died in their human forms. Neither of the girls are wearing clothes, so they must have shifted and put up a fight. The public must have arrived before the hunters did; the hunters never leave a mess like this. They don't make mistakes like this.

I take a step back, afraid to make a sound. A twig snaps under my foot, leaves crunch with the pressure of my boot, and Pru turns around. Her eyes are red and puffy, her cheeks wet. "You," she snarls between sobs. "You did this."

"Pru, please—"

"Get away. Get away, get away, get away." She leans forward, sobbing harder. "G-go."

I turn on my heel and run. Run from Pru, run from the bodies, run from the approaching police force. I go back the way I came, hurrying to Jett and the triplets.

I crash into Logan, meeting them partway. He steadies me. Beside him, the others stop, their feet slipping in the mud. "What is it? What's happened?" Jett says frantically. He isn't looking at me. He's looking over my shoulder, scanning the trees. The triplets are, too. "Is it hunters? Are they here?"

"No," I say, numb. "They aren't here. It's not them."

Jett relaxes a little. His shoulders drop, some of the tension leaving his body. "Then what?"

I shake my head. I can't say it.

Jett frowns and looks to the triplets. "Go ahead and bring Pru back," he tells them. "Flo, is it safe for them to go to her?"

I nod and they go. I don't want them to, though. I don't want them to see what I saw. I shake my head again. How do I tell him what's through those trees? I can't form the words. Shifter bodies dumped in the woods, scarred like he is by silver chains. Two of them are lying there with Pru, both tigers, both her friends. How many more bodies could be out here?

"I can't . . . I think . . . we should go back. Now." I want to get out of the woods. I want to get back to the car, drive away and never come back here. But I'll never be able to leave this place behind, will I? No matter how far I go.

"Let's go meet the triplets and Pru. Okay?"

"No. I shouldn't. I need to get back to the car." Pru blames me; it's not right that I should be there while she grieves.

"Then we'll go together. But I have to tell the others. We can't split up." I can tell Jett is losing patience with me. His voice tightens; his tone sharpens. Subtle changes, but there all the same.

"I'll wait here," I say.

Jett runs his hands over his face. "Flo, I don't want to leave anyone on their own out here."

I give up and mutter one word. "Tigers." My voice cracks, but Jett catches it.

He looks puzzled. "Tigers? Survivors?"

I hate the answer. "Not survivors."

Jett's face drops. His skin pales. "*Oh.* Oh, no. No. They're dead? The tigers are dead? You saw them?"

I nod, biting down hard on my lip. "Maria and Lexi."

"We have to go get Pru and the triplets away from the bodies. It's important, Flo. We can't stay here any longer."

I wipe my eyes with the heels of my hands, stopping tears from falling. My lips sting where I've bitten away the skin. I need to pull myself together. It's dangerous out here. I nod to Jett and he tugs me forward. Then, somehow, I'm running toward the tigers again.

I run faster than before. Back to the same place. I don't want to go back, don't want to see that again, don't want to hurt Pru. But more than any of that, I'm afraid. Afraid that the hunters could come back any time. Afraid that the police are already there.

Pru is still holding her friend when we find her. The triplets stand to one side, looking the other way, their faces pale. "I'm sorry, Pru," Jett says. He hesitates as he takes in the scene, then he adds, "But we have to go."

I stay silent.

"No," Pru says, sniffing loudly. "I'm not leaving them like this. Can't we bury them or something?"

"There's no time. I'm sorry. We have to leave now," Jett replies.

Pru is stubborn and staying put, making no attempt to get up and come with us. Every moment we spend here, we're closer to being caught.

"Pru," I whisper. She doesn't look at me. "Hunters don't just leave bodies lying around for anyone to find."

"Are you saying they didn't do this?" she asks, turning to face me now.

I swallow. "No. I'm saying they'll be coming back."

Her eyes widen. "To do *what?*"

"Get rid of them, I guess," I say quietly. I look to Jett for confirmation and he nods. Lucas closes his eyes and leans against Logan.

Pru squeals and hugs Maria's body tighter. I cringe. I've never seen a dead body before. I'd have thought Maria was sleeping were it not for the weird angle of her body, the way her arms hang limp from her shoulders as though they're really heavy, and the way her head lolls to the side each time Pru moves her. Twigs and leaves from the forest floor are tangled in the dead girl's hair. There's a red line around her neck, which I recognize as a silver burn.

I glance at the other girl. I can only see Lexi's legs sticking out from under the leaves and dirt. I haven't even confirmed it's her, but I can't make myself get close enough to check. Pru, Maria, and Lexi were always together. It has to be her. Her feet are bare and caked in mud, black beneath the nails. The soles are cut and bloody. I look away.

"We have to move them," Pru says. "Take them with us, bury them somewhere else."

"There isn't any time for that," Jett says while I'm staring at Lexi. "You drew the attention of the police with your screaming. They're looking for you."

"I'm not leaving them," Pru says.

"Pru, the police are searching the woods as we speak, and for all we know the hunters could already be around here, back for the bodies," I say. Pru turns her back to us and continues to sob. "Pru, please. We're all in danger. Maria and Lexi wouldn't want you to throw your life away like this."

"How do *you* know what they'd want?" she snarls.

I ignore her tone and step forward, putting my hand on her shoulder. She smacks it off. Maria's body drops to the floor when Pru lets go to hit me so I pull her away. "No!" she screams.

"Help me!" I shout, turning back to the others.

Pru's kicking and screaming, trying to break free of my hold on her. "I'm not coming with you! I'm not coming with you! Please! Just leave me, *please!*" Her elbow hits my stomach, breaking open the healing skin, and tears spring to my eyes. I bite down on my lip in agony, but I keep my hold on her.

"Shh," Jett hisses, but Pru continues to struggle and yell. She scratches at my hands, but I still don't let go.

"I'll shift! I'll shift and hurt you all!"

"Pru, stop! We're not leaving you here." I feel fur beneath my fingers and find I can't focus on Pru's body anymore. "No! Pru, *stop!*"

Lucas and Jett take an arm each, while mine are wrapped around Pru's waist. Lance is standing over Lexi's body. He grabs her legs and pulls her out from beneath the dirt. I see blue eyes, blue lips. An angry red line around her neck, just like Maria's.

Lance winces and throws something toward us. It catches the light in the air, winking silver. It hits Pru and starts to sizzle. She comes back into focus, screaming and thrashing. The smell of burning flesh is almost unbearable—too many bad memories attached to it—and I struggle to keep hold of Pru.

Lance approaches us, shaking out his hand where the silver briefly burned him before he threw it. Logan helps him wrap the chain once around Pru's stomach. She screams again. I cover her mouth and, with the help of the others, drag her backward through the woods.

It feels so wrong, hurting her like this. But she can't shift with the silver chain around her, and she was deadly serious about doing so. I've no doubt she'd have hurt us. I push away concerns and focus on getting out of the woods by any means necessary.

The walk back is clumsy and slow. Pru stops fighting and lets us carry her, weakened by the silver around her middle. My stomach still throbs where the new skin tore and I do everything I can to block the pain out of my mind and focus on getting away from the circus.

When we reach the car, we set her down beside it. I kneel in front of her and, using my sleeves to cover my hands, lift her T-shirt and peel the silver off her stomach. "I'm sorry," I whisper. "I'm so sorry."

Her eyes are vacant and her face is sticky with tears. She gives no indication she's heard me. Lucas and Lance lift her and put her on the backseat, then the triplets squash in beside her. Jett and I sit up front again. A few moments of silence pass before Jett starts the engine, backs out onto the road, and sets off for Iris's house. I hope she can help us.

24
WITHERED TO DUST

We drive past the entrance to the site.

We pass police cars and officers standing along the side of the road. There are people in regular clothes, too—wearing woolly hats, gloves, and scarves to protect themselves against the cold weather. Some are holding microphones to their mouths and talking into the lenses of large cameras that balance on the shoulders of others. The ground and car rooftops are littered with disposable coffee cups.

"What the hell?" Jett says, but I'm too busy staring out the windows to respond.

Heavy black cameras stand on tripods, facing the camp, placed right along the edge of the yellow police tape cordoning off the area. The cameras are as close as they can be without crossing the line. Men and women, with various passes and information cards hanging from their necks, lean forward, stand on tiptoes, hold out microphones, ask questions.

Jett slows the car, but not too much. The last thing we need is to draw attention to ourselves and be stopped. I watch as a policeman raises his hands, palms forward, in an attempt to back up the mob of news reporters leaning against the police tape that blocks the way into camp.

I tune the car radio until I find a local news station. It's crackly and static, but I can make out the words—just about. They're discussing what happened at the circus, when I changed in front of the audience, the chaos that followed, and the fire that destroyed the camp. They are still speculating over what happened, but no one really knows. I flick the radio off and let out a deep breath.

Jett glances at me then back at the road. "Flo," he whispers. "You've got to stop feeling guilty over this. You shouldn't have to carry the weight of that around with you when it's crucial that we stay strong and focused right now. Your shift was an accident. You got hurt, badly." He looks over his shoulder. "Pru was just lashing out. Nobody should be blaming you. And you especially shouldn't be blaming yourself."

I keep my eyes trained on the road ahead. Looking at street signs, digesting his words. He's right, in a way, but it's hard. I just hope Iris knows where the elders are. And I hope they know what to do. And I hope someone can tell me how to make all of this right again.

It hits me, then, that things will probably never go back to normal. The circus members are scattered, the hunters know who/what we are, the elders have disappeared and aren't likely to set up again for a long, long time. If ever. Where will we go? What will we do?

I shake my head, flinging away negative thoughts. I shouldn't focus on what comes next; I should focus on what's happening now. One thing at a time.

It takes us a while to find Iris's house. On a normal day, seeing the area agent is always the last option, and right now Iris is the *only* option. I can't think of anywhere else to turn. And that scares me, because if this doesn't work out, I have no idea what we'll do.

Jett pulls up against the curb and cuts the engine. It's getting dark now. There's one light on in the front room of Iris's two-story townhouse. The building is very *blue*. Sky-blue exterior and white window frames. A stone path leads to the front porch behind a waist-high gate. There are dead flowers in a pot by the door. "Are you sure about this?" I ask.

"What other choice do we have?" Jett says.

Lucas leans forward. "There's nowhere else to go."

I unbuckle my seat belt, careful not to let it touch my burn. It's been weeping ever since Pru hit me there. My T-shirt is sticky with it. It needs cleaning. It needs resting. It needs time to heal. I hope again that Iris can help us. We're desperate. *I'm* desperate.

Pru and the triplets wait in the car. There's no point in all of us hovering around Iris's front door if she's not going to let us in. We don't want to draw attention to our group and we don't want to scare her off. The gate opens with a creak. Overgrown grass chokes the front lawn. Weeds grow between the stones on the path. It's not a bad house or a bad area; Iris is just obviously not so great at the upkeep. Close up, the paint on the door is peeling, and the dead flowers must have been there a while—their crisp petals withered to dust.

Jett knocks softly. When no one answers, he tries again, harder. The hallway light turns on and I see a figure behind the netted curtain covering the front window. There's the sound of several locks turning, then the door opens slightly and Iris peers out, her red hair tumbling around her face. "What do you want?" she asks.

"I'm Flo," I say. "And this is Jett. We're from the circus."

"Sorry, not interested," she says shortly. Iris tries to close the door, but I stop it with my hand.

"Wait! We're in danger!" I say quickly.

She scowls at me. "Move your hand."

I shove the door open a little more. Jett leans against it, too. "We need your help," I say. "We don't know who else to ask."

Iris shakes her head. "No. I'm sorry. There's nothing I can do." She pushes the door again, but it doesn't budge now that both Jett and I are holding it open. "I will call the police. I'm sure you wouldn't want that."

"Why won't you—" The sound of a child crying cuts me off. I frown. "Who's that?"

"That? That's my daughter," Iris answers.

"You don't have a family," I say.

"How do you know?" she snaps.

I step forward and see little shoes in the hallway—purple with daisies, muddy and scuffed. Rain.

I shove the door open now, knocking Iris back, and then follow the sound of the child. I step into the front room and there's Rain, sitting on the floor in a mess of blankets and pillows, holding a stuffed bear in one hand. Her face is red and scrunched up as she cries. Iris runs in behind me. She dashes over to Rain and scoops her up. "Shh. Shh," Iris soothes.

"What is Rain doing here?"

"Rain? As in the new toddler at the circus?" Jett asks, looking from me to them. I nod.

"Nora and Ava gave her to me for a short while," Iris says, bouncing Rain in her arms. "Why are you here? What do you want from me?"

"We need to know where the elders are now. We need to know what happened to everyone at the circus."

Iris shakes her head. "I don't know anything about that. You *have* to leave." A car horn sounds outside. Iris hurries to look out the window. "Is that your car? Who's beeping the horn like that? Tell them to stop!"

I sigh. The triplets. "I'll sort it," Jett says. "Will you be okay?"

"Yes," I say, hurrying him out as one of the triplets presses on the horn again.

Iris continues to watch out of the window. "I'm serious," she says. "I don't want you here. I said the same to the others, but they didn't force their way inside like you—"

"Others?" I gasp. "*Who?*"

Iris shrugs. "I don't know! I told you. I don't know anything!"

"Describe them," I press. "*Please.*"

"Twins. Or at least they looked it. Black hair. A boy and a girl."

"Owen and Ursula," I breathe. Not twins, but they do look alike. "Just the two of them?"

Iris shakes her head. "Two more were with them, but they stayed at the end of the path. I didn't see them properly. They were girls. One was young, I think. Small, anyway."

"Star, maybe," I think aloud. Iris stays silent. I hope it was Star; I've been worried about her ever since the hunters attacked. "Where did you send them?"

"I told them to get lost, just like I told you. They were stubborn, so I told them about a pack around here they could seek out. That's it. They left with that information. They didn't barge their way into the house."

"I'm injured," I say. "Quite badly. I need time before I go back out there."

Iris shakes her head again. "I can't help."

"Where's Hari? I know he was with the doctor. Can't you put me in touch with him so I can get some treatment?"

"You're supposed to heal on your own! Hari was there for broken bones."

"What? *Broken bones*! What did he break? How did that happen? Nora and Ava wouldn't tell us anything."

"How do you think it happened?"

I swallow and look away.

"He's lucky. I'd take broken bones over being killed. But I'd rather not be faced with that decision, which is why I don't want you here."

"The hunters wouldn't kill you—you're human."

She shakes her head. "I'm not talking about me." She glances at Rain and I realize what she means. I wouldn't want anything to happen to her either.

I unzip my jacket and lift my stained shirt. Iris gasps. "It's not healing properly," I tell her.

She sets Rain down on the sofa and presses the heel of her hand against her forehead. "Tell them to move the car away from here and walk back. Not in a big group. And don't leave it anywhere that's too out in the open."

Jett comes inside. "Sorry, they wanted to know—"

"Bring Pru inside. Then move the car away from here," I say hurriedly. "Somewhere out of sight. Iris is letting us stay."

"One night. That's it," she says.

Jett beams at her. "Thank you. *Thank you!*"

She waves him away. "Hurry up."

Once he's gone, Iris draws the drapes and dims the lights. "I'll take you to Hari tomorrow. Then you're on your own. I can't get caught up in something like this."

Jett and Lucas carry Pru inside, putting her on the sofa next to Rain. Rain watches her curiously, but is more interested in the stuffed bear. I wonder, not for the first time, what Rain's shape is, where she came from, under what circumstances she was found.

Iris leaves the room, coming back moments later with a bowl of water and a cloth. She wets it and dabs Pru's head with it. "What happened to her?"

"She found her friends."

Iris looks at me for a long moment. "You mean . . . ?"

I nod. "Yes. They were dead."

Iris swallows and turns her attention back to Pru. "You can shower upstairs," she tells me. "There are towels in the cupboard in the bathroom. First door on the right. Don't turn on any lights. I'll leave a change of clothes out for you."

"Thank you." I head upstairs, following Iris's instructions. There's another door open at the top of the stairs—a bedroom. Inside, there's a small TV set on top of a dresser.

I look behind me. The boys aren't back yet and Iris is tending to Pru and Rain, so I step into the bedroom and gently close the door. Switching the TV on, I immediately press the MUTE button, then flick through the channels until I find the news.

I stop clicking when I see a news reporter standing in front of the circus camp with two body bags behind her. My stomach flips. I turn the sound to low volume and lean in to listen.

"... *two bodies found by police in the woods. It is not yet clear ...*"

The crawl along the bottom of the screen reads: HUMAN BODIES FOUND IN CIRCUS FIRE. I increase the volume a little more, missing some of the words.

"... *following the circus scandal where a performing horse somehow transformed into a young girl ...*"

They're talking about me. The crawl changes to: NO ANIMALS APPEAR TO HAVE BEEN HARMED IN CIRCUS FIRE.

"*No animals were found on site,*" the reporter continues. "*A spokesperson for the circus has not returned our call or offered to comment.*"

I'm about to turn it up when the shot changes to a prerecorded clip from the night of the accident. A man stands with his arm around his young daughter, holding her close. Her face-paint is streaked with tear tracks. Black soot patches cover both their faces, and their eyes are rimmed red like they've been crying.

Smoke billows up from the trees behind them. It's dark. Red and blue lights flash in the background. "*There was a horse, jumping over flames. The next thing I knew, the horse had vanished and a girl was lying on the floor. Only I think something must've caught on the tent because after that, the whole place went up."*

"*So it was a magic trick gone wrong?*" the reporter asks.

The man hesitates then nods. "*Seems that way.*"

So I guess that's one theory. One explanation for what happened. The most reasonable, I suppose. The hunters won't be happy with this kind of attention. They've made a mess. They'll be working overtime to clean it up. And we're part of that mess. No wonder Iris didn't want to let us in.

25

BLOOD AND MUD

I feel better as soon as the water hits my skin.

I have the shower set to cold, and I'm awkwardly holding the showerhead to avoid touching the burn on my stomach, but it's *still* good. I can't remember a time when I showered indoors. I want to stand here for hours, letting it wash the past few days from existence. I remind myself all of this isn't in the past yet. We're still in danger, and once I'm done, I have to go back downstairs and make plans with the others.

I wash my hair, combing out the tangles with my fingers, glad to be rid of the smell of smoke. I wash my body with Iris's lavender shower gel, scrubbing away the blood and mud, watching it twirl around the drain and disappear. I'm careful to keep away from my burn—it hurts every time the water even splashes near it. I can't carry on like this. *When* will it heal?

I wash the suds from my hair and body then reach around the shower curtain for a towel. I wrap one around me before stepping out onto the cold black and white tiles. The bathroom is small. The shower takes up most of the space. Squeezed next to it is a tiny sink cluttered with products and a toilet beside the door.

The toilet lid is down, and there is a pile of clothes waiting. Sitting on top of the clothes is a tub of antiseptic cream. Iris must have put them there while I showered.

I open the pot of cream and carefully apply it to the healing burn, steering clear of the raw bits.

Iris left out a pair of black leggings and a short black and white dress with long sleeves and a little rip on the hem. The leggings fit well, but the dress is a little big. Iris is taller than I am. There's also a thick pair of socks, which, teamed with my boots, will keep my feet warm. The long sleeves of the dress and my jacket will have to do.

I towel-dry my hair and leave the bathroom. Downstairs, Iris is cleaning a cut on Lucas's leg. She tells me to sit down quickly. There's one lamp on in the room; the rest of the house in darkness. "Who's showering next?" she asks.

Pru sits up, startling me. I didn't know she was awake. "Me," she says quietly. Without looking at anyone, she stands and makes her way upstairs.

"No lights," Iris whisper-shouts. "And be quick." She looks at me now. "You took your time."

"Sorry, I—"

She waves her hand, shushing me. "Just help me with this."

I take over cleaning Lucas's cut while Iris moves onto inspecting a lump on the side of Logan's head. I didn't realize everyone else had been hurt, too, my main focus being my own injuries. I look at Jett, his leg propped up on the coffee table, and mouth, "You okay?"

He nods at his leg and says, "It's nothing."

Once everyone's cleaned up, Iris makes *a lot* of toast and puts a big plate in the middle of the room for us. She hands out some glasses and tells us to help ourselves to tap water. "Remember. No lights. No noise. You're gone in the morning." Then she takes Rain and goes upstairs, leaving us alone in the dark.

"Is that it?" Jett whispers. "I wanted to ask her more about Hari."

"She said she'd take us to the doctor to see him tomorrow," I whisper back.

"Where is this doctor?"

"Backstreet?" I shrug. "I haven't been. But Star did once when we were performing at Violet Bay. She wouldn't stop talking about it." We have a doctor in most of the circus locations. They know who we are, *what* we are, just like the agents.

"So that's tomorrow's plan?" Lucas asks. "Visit a backstreet doctor's office and hope Hari's still there?"

I bite the inside of my cheek. "Maybe there's a chance he is. He'd be safer there, I think, than out on the run with any of us. . . . Do you have a better idea?"

Lucas leans back against the sofa. "All our ideas are based on not having a better one lately."

I stand and go into the kitchen to get some water.

Jett comes into the small kitchen, too, making as little noise as possible. I turn and his closeness makes me jump. "Sorry," he whispers.

"What's up?" I ask.

"I never got the chance to tell you how glad I am you're alive."

I know exactly what he's thinking and how he's feeling. Silently, I wrap my arms around him and press my face into his chest.

"I wish we'd left when we had the chance," he says. "We could be somewhere far away, together and safe. If I could go back and do it all again, I would. I would pack up our things and get the hell out of the circus, then maybe we wouldn't be in this mess."

I flash back to my first show night and think of how I had wondered about life outside, about how I'd been convinced that the circus was our only option, our only life, even if I wasn't sure I had wanted it to be.

"You can't protect me from everything, Jett. Bad things are always going to happen—to me, to you, to the people around us. If it wasn't this it'd be something else, eventually. It's how we deal with it afterward that counts. There is no going back and redoing life. There's only now. And right now you're standing here, and I'm standing here, and I would say things could be a lot worse than that."

I step away from him to meet his eyes. "I would say so, too," he says.

"*Shh*," someone hisses from the hallway. I look past Jett to see Iris on the stairs, peering through the banister with her finger on her lips. She shushes us again then goes back upstairs.

26
PARANOIA

I don't sleep, I can't.

I'm on the floor, lying on a sofa cushion and some of Rain's blankets, when Iris kicks me in the thigh. "What the—?"

"Wake up," she says.

"I was awake!"

Iris peers between the drapes, letting light into the room. "Time to go," she says. "Where did you park your car?"

"A few streets away," Jett says, his voice croaky.

"I'll have to take Rain with me. You pull up in view of the house. Follow me, but don't be obvious about it."

I rub my eyes. "You don't think someone's watching you, do you?"

"I don't know, Flo. I don't want to know. Go out the back way, through the garage. I'll leave in about ten minutes, so be ready in your vehicle and please be careful. I don't want to be mixed up in any of this. I've already got Rain to look out for and I don't want anyone coming after either of us, do you understand?"

I nod. "We'll be careful. Don't worry."

We pack up what little we brought in with us and Iris leads us into the kitchen and shows us out through the garage. The pale morning light pours in through the frosted-glass garage window, highlighting a thick spider's web that sways with the breeze coming from under the main door. Iris's car is parked in the center and shelves piled high with all sorts of junk line the brick walls.

"The side door leads out onto a small alley between my house and next door," Iris says. "Stay out of sight."

Outside, the six of us walk quickly to the car in two separate groups, Lucas in the lead. I'm jumpy. Every little sound has me whipping my head around, searching for the source. My breath clouds in front of my face, coming fast. We reach the car without any trouble, though, and I know it's just Iris's paranoia rubbing off on me.

Jett starts the engine when we're all in and drives slowly through the neighborhood until we can see Iris's house. She opens the garage door, backing the car out moments later, then goes back to close it again. Once she pulls out of the drive, we follow behind at a good distance.

We pass fewer houses, replaced by office buildings, stores, and cafés, as we near the main town. The buildings get taller; the streets get busier.

On the other side of town, away from the crowded main streets, Iris weaves through narrow back roads then pulls over. Jett stops the car behind her. She indicates left. I look at the building to our left. The bricks are painted black. There's a tattoo shop with neon signs in the window and designs displayed on boards. Beside it is a glass door with simple black lettering printed on the front. It reads: VIOLET BAY MEDICAL SOCIETY. Is this the place? It looks so . . . *ordinary*.

Iris drives away, leaving us on our own again. I spend a half-second feeling bad that I didn't get to thank her for putting us up and then I ask, "Should we all go in?"

Jett looks around. The street is almost empty, except for a couple sitting outside a small coffee shop at the corner. "Logan and Pru can stay here. Keep watch. Is that okay?" he asks.

Logan nods. Pru doesn't respond. She's hardly said a word since we left the woods. "I'll stay, too," Lance says. "The building's small. You three go in. Come out and let us know what's happening when you can."

Jett, Lucas, and I get out of the car and head for the glass door. It smells so clean inside the office that it stings my nostrils. "Can I help you?" a woman sitting behind a large black desk asks. The walls are white and bare. There are two black sofas with a coffee table between them and a fake potted plant in the corner.

I clear my throat and approach the desk, Jett and Lucas close behind me. "Yes. We're looking for a patient."

The receptionist taps her stubby fingers against a computer keyboard. I focus on her chewed nails and too-tight wedding ring instead of how fast my heart is beating. "Name, please?"

"Flo," I say.

She looks at me. Dark red lipstick, recently applied, sticks to her front teeth. "Surname?"

I shake my head. "I don't have one."

She frowns, then squints at the screen. "Sorry. No one called Flo on the files."

I swallow. "No, sorry, I mean . . . I'm not looking for Flo. *I'm* Flo. I'm looking for Hari—H-A-R-I," I say, spelling it out for her. "No surname."

Her eyes widen briefly and she looks back at the screen. "Hari. Yes," she says, without typing his name in. "He left two nights ago."

My stomach drops through the floor. He's gone. *Now what?*

"You didn't even look," I say, pointing to the computer. "Is there no information on there about him?"

She looks at the screen again. "No. Anyway, he checked out. His sisters came for him."

"His sisters? Ava and Nora? Are they okay? Can we speak to his doctor?"

She regards us. "Not usually. But I think I know why you're here. Ava said someone might come. Hold on for one moment." She picks up the phone and presses a button.

I stand in silence, tapping my foot on the tiled floor. I don't want to look at Jett and Lucas, don't want to see the hope drain out of them. *Hari's not here.* None of the elders are. I'd been relying on them to tell us what to do next. We've hit *another* dead end. I'm not sure how speaking to the doctor will even help us, unless he knows where they went.

"Three kids here for Hari," the receptionist says. She waits. "Okay." She hangs up. "Go through to Greg. Down there." She points.

We go down a set of stairs into the basement of the building. It's brighter than I expected. Lights line the ceiling and shine off the bare white-painted walls.

Metal tables, some on wheels, some against the walls, hold all kinds of documents and instruments. In a separate room, door open, there's an examination table and a bright light shining down on it.

Greg's gray hair is slicked back. He's wearing a white coat over his clothes. There's a pen in his front pocket, and his glasses sit on the tip of his nose as he studies a clipboard. He looks up as we reach the bottom of the staircase. "This is about Hari? Ava said someone might come. Here," he says, gesturing to a small leather sofa by the stairs. "Take a seat."

"We can't stay long," I tell him, sitting down.

"We just need to know where the elders went," Jett says, taking a seat beside me. Lucas perches on the armrest. "And Flo's injured pretty bad. Can you take a look at the burn on her stomach?" Jett adds, surprising me. I don't think there's time for a checkup if we're going to catch up to the elders.

Greg looks at my stomach as if he can see through the layers of clothing covering the burn. "I strictly can't treat anything without Hari's say so. I can look, though. If you'd like me to."

Jett turns to me and I nod unsurely. "Okay."

"This way, Flo."

I follow Greg to the next room and climb up on the table under the spotlight. I lie back while he inspects the burn and catch sight of Jett and Lucas hovering in the doorway, watching us.

"And did Ava tell you where to send us?" I ask.

"Iris's," he says as he rummages around in drawers, pulling out a pair of blue gloves. "The agent in the—"

"We know who Iris is," I say, maddened by his response even though I know it's not his fault. "She brought us here. To find Hari."

Greg looks puzzled. "Well . . ." He pauses. "Well. I don't know what to suggest, kids. I'm sorry. Hold still." He lifts my dress up over the burn. I grit my teeth and accidently bite my tongue. The taste of blood in my mouth is bitter and metallic.

Greg inspects the area without touching me. "This is healing well," he tells me. "The skin is broken in the middle, which will take the longest to fix itself, but the rest is looking fine. Lucky you lot heal fast."

"It's been slow," I tell him. "It's healing really slow. A normal injury would be gone by now."

"This isn't a normal injury," Greg says. "But you're almost there."

"Okay. Good," I say, somewhat glad. If I'm on the run, I could do without a serious injury.

"You'll be all right in a day or two, I predict. There's no infection." He removes his gloves. "Sorry, kid, that's all I can do. We have a specialist who could perhaps help you more but . . . well, secrets are secrets."

"The receptionist seemed to know more than she should," I comment.

"She's my wife," Greg says. "She's the only other person who knows about all of this, and I'd like to keep it that way. Besides, without Hari, I can't go ahead with anything even if I wanted to. I'm up to my neck in this mess as it is."

"How do you know Hari?" I ask. "How did you meet him and come to this 'arrangement'?"

Greg pulls at a thread on his sleeve. "I don't really have time. . . . It's a a long story."

"Shorten it," I say, surprised at my own aggressiveness. I'm so tired of not knowing what's happening around us.

Greg sighs. "Years back, and I mean *years*, a friend and I were in . . . shall we say, the wrong place at the wrong time. Hari helped us out of a dangerous situation involving another pack, at risk of exposing himself. I found out what he was and I owed him after that. I could have lost my life that night. Still, I was shaken from that and from what I'd just discovered—that Hari is, you know, a lion.

"I spent a long time looking over my shoulder, worrying about when he'd come back, thinking I'd maybe lost my mind and a lion man didn't actually save me. Then I saw him again. When I'd qualified and set up my practice here, he walked right through the door. Iris showed up a few days after that to work something out. And now here we are."

"So what now?" Jett asks. "We have to go back to her? To Iris?"

"That is what I advise. I can't have you stay here— I've had this deal with Hari, Ava, and Nora for years, but it's been dangerous in more ways than one, and I don't want attention drawn on the practice. I'm going to have to ask you to leave now. Iris's—that's where you need to be. That's all I know, I'm sorry."

Greg walks toward the exit, expecting us to follow. I look at Jett. He sighs and helps me off the table. Lucas joins us at the bottom of the staircase.

Iris is not going to help us. I know that, Jett and Lucas know that, Greg probably knows that. He and Iris are the same. They're involved, getting their cut for their work, then things get a little sticky and they back off. I can't say I blame them, but you can't be in one minute and out the next. We're supposed to be able to rely on them. They're all we've got in the outside world.

I guess we've got some convincing to do when we get back to Iris's house. I can just see the look on her face when we knock on her door again. . . .

I wonder if all the area agents owe the elders in some way like Greg does. It'd be too much of a coincidence for the elders to have rescued so many people that are useful to our cause though, which makes me think they must have set something up. I can only assume they tricked these humans in some way to get what they want, to have them forever in their debt. But how? What did they do to Iris? I could ask her, but I doubt she'd tell me.

"Well, thanks anyway," I say. "If anything happens, if you find anything out or remember anything at all, can you get a message to Iris?"

Greg nods once and gestures to the stairs. Conversation over, and we're no closer to understanding what's happening. In fact, we've gone backward, because we have to go back to Iris's now and convince her to let us back in and tell us what she knows.

It's clear Iris has been in contact with the elders, because they gave Rain to her. She's seen Owen, Ursula, and two others, one of which could be Star, and sent them off to join a pack. Is that what we should do? Give up the search—stop looking for the elders, stop looking for answers—and join a pack? What is a pack without the protection of the circus? I'm not sure I want to find out anymore.

Outside the building, I let out a long breath. "That didn't go as I'd hoped," I say.

"No," Jett agrees. "I guess we head back to Iris's and see what else we can find out. She's not going to be happy to see us."

We walk slowly back toward the car, all the urgency from earlier draining away. I feel defeated already. The car is parked illegally on the side of the empty backstreet. The doors are open. Pru stands to the side, leaning on the car and looking up at the sky. I look up, too, to see what she's seeing, but I'm not sure that's possible. Pru is not the Pru I'm used to.

A screeching sound draws my attention back from the clouds. A car comes from nowhere, skidding around the corner. It's going way too fast. And it doesn't slow down—

A scream catches in my throat as it plows straight into our car, sending it tumbling into a building with the force of the hit.

Jett puts himself in front of me and I skid to a stop. Something sharp catches my cheek. It all happened before

I could even blink. I lift my hand to my face and stumble back as the alley fills with smoke.

I stand, watching as if time has slowed down to almost a stop. Black smoke and acrid fumes fill the air, choking me, cutting my screams short.

I rub my eyes, trying to see what's happening. The car is on its side, smashed up against the wall, crushed and smoking. Something cracks beneath my boot and I look down to see the red plastic of a brake light in pieces. My eyes follow the trail of destruction along the ground, taking in the scene like I'm looking at a photograph.

A group of four, dressed in black, jump out of the other car. My knees buckle, and I grab hold of Jett's arm to steady myself, to stay standing. "The hunters," I try to say, but the words lodge in my throat.

Two of them go for the car, the other two head toward us.

Lucas charges at the hunters, yelling something I don't catch. The whole scene is like something from a dream. No, not a dream, a *nightmare*—one I hope to wake from any second.

"*Jett,*" I breathe when I see them dragging Pru from the car wreck. They drop her on the road—facedown on the floor and surrounded by broken glass. Her clothing is shredded and bloody and she isn't moving.

Someone comes out of the tattoo shop, which distracts one of the hunters. He goes to speak to the tattooed woman, to explain I assume. *A tragic accident. We're helping. The police are on their way.* Lies. The couple from the coffee shop on the corner are gone—did they witness the crash first? Did they hear? Are they close?

Lance crawls out of the car. He tries to sit up. His face is cut and smeared with black. Logan's on his back beside him, and I'm relieved to see he's moving, if only slightly. Lucas scrambles toward his brothers.

I make my way toward Pru, but a hunter cuts me off. He reaches for me, grabbing my sleeve and pulling me toward him. He holds a net in his other hand. Pru's face is still pressed into the road, her arm twisted at a weird angle. She looks so small among the wreckage. A hunter is pulling a now-unconscious Logan off the floor. Two hunters are holding a struggling Lucas, dragging him back to their car. Lance is upright now, dazed and rubbing his head. He can't get his balance. Then a net of silver lands on top of him, sending him back to the ground. His skin sizzles beneath the chains.

I yank my arm free and stumble backward, crashing into Jett. The hunter advances. "Come on!" Jett yells.

We run. I turn back and see the hunter is following. "Hurry!" I shout to Jett.

With the triplets and Pru captured, Jett and I are out-numbered. We'd never win a fight us versus them. Not like this.

We hurry on until we're out of sight, and keep running until we're hidden and the hunter isn't following us anymore. At least I hope he isn't. We managed to lose him, but he could still be close.

I make myself as small as possible in an alley behind a row of stores, squeezed between garbage bags and an old office chair with two of its wheels missing. It might seem like the most obvious hiding place in the world right now, but it's the best I can do, and when there are so many other alleyways that look exactly like this one, the chance of him finding us with ease narrows. They made a scene back there. Another scene. And they've now got the choice between hanging around and searching for two teenagers or leaving. I'm hoping they'll leave if they can't locate us quickly.

I press my back against the brick wall and try to catch my breath again. Jett's breathing heavily, too. The sound is ragged and wheezy. "I don't . . . know what to do . . . Flo. What do we do?" he says, his eyes red.

"I don't know. We can't go up against them on our own, though. Can we?"

Jett shakes his head. "No."

I lean my head back against the cold brick. "Follow them," I say.

Jett looks at me and frowns. "How? Our car is a wreck."

I scrunch my fists up and let out a frustrated groan. I don't know what to do! If they leave now we might never see our friends again. The car's ruined and I don't know how to steal one. It's too risky anyway, if we get caught by the police—we don't technically exist.

"Let's go back," I suggest. "To the crash site. See what we find."

I stand and slowly retrace our steps back to Greg's office. Jett follows without a word. I don't know what we'll find, or what I'm hoping we'll find, but I have no idea what else to do.

When we get back to the car, Jett inspects it while I search through the pieces on the floor. I don't really know what I'm looking for either—some kind of clue? Some indication of where they might have gone?

I stand, sighing. It's all metal and glass, useless. Then . . .

"Oil," I say.

"What?"

"Oil. Their car must have sprung an oil leak. You can follow the smell!"

"I don't know, Flo . . ."

"You're the one who told us to let in our animal selves. Bears have incredible noses—you should be able to do this, in or out of your bear form."

"You think?"

"Yes! Even I can help, kind of. My nose isn't bad either."

Excited by the possibility of finding our friends, I let Jett lead the way and we follow our noses.

27

CROOKED LINE

Following the hunters' car takes a long, *long* time.

We find splashes and streaks of oil that tell us we're heading in the right direction as Jett continues to lead. The journey, on foot, is tiring. Still, we press on after our friends.

Eventually, we come to a dirt track road that the car must have turned onto. The road is under the shadow of trees. It's so tiny, surrounded by overgrown bushes and sheltered by trees, that I'd never have noticed it if the trail hadn't led here. The track seems to continue into the distance for a while in a crooked line.

Jett takes my hand in his and we step forward together. We walk slowly, cautiously, side by side, along the dusty road, kicking up filthy clouds of earth around us. I know we need to hurry, but my legs won't let me. We're walking into danger, a danger with potentially deadly results if we're captured. Somehow, I can't walk quickly into that.

Up ahead, surrounded by dead grass, is a wooden cabin. It looks as though it could blow away with the slightest gust of wind. "Surely that can't be it," I whisper, slowing even more. Its roof sags in the middle like it's about to cave in on itself.

Jett frowns. "I wouldn't have thought so. Be careful, anyway. Just in case."

We approach the cabin cautiously. It's sitting on dead earth and rotting. The mismatched planks of wood look damp and fragile, covered in mold. We hide behind a pile of firewood. To get to the cabin, we have to come out of hiding and run across an open space, completely exposed.

We wait and wait behind the logs, scanning the area for anyone who may be around. If our friends are in there, the hunters probably are, too.

There's no noise or movement, though. The car we followed isn't parked outside, and it seems too quiet to be occupied. After a while, I whisper, "I think it's abandoned. This must be the wrong place."

"Something really doesn't seem right," Jett says, which unnerves me more.

"Should we go back? Do you think there was another road off the one we followed? Or maybe we need to keep going."

"The tire tracks lead to this cabin."

"Then where's the car? Maybe it carried on."

Jett frowns. "I think we should check it out. I'll go and you can wait here."

"No," I hiss.

"But if anyone's watching, it's better they see only one of us, don't you think?"

"I think it's better that they see neither of us," I reply.

"Well, yeah, of course," Jett says, sighing. "I don't know what to do. I hate all of this. . . . I'm going to look in the windows. Please stay here. I'll be just a second."

He starts to stand but I grab his arm and pull him back down. "Not happening. We both go to the cabin, or we both stay here and wait. I'm part of this, too."

Jett rubs his face. "Fine. We'll go together and if we get caught, we get caught."

I cross my arms over my chest. "Well, I'm not looking to get caught."

Together we emerge from behind the logs and crouch low to the ground, making our way over to the cabin. Once beside the exterior wall, I can smell the rotting wood and I wrinkle my nose. Surely they can't be in here.

Jett holds a finger to his lips then points to his ear. I listen. There are voices coming from inside. The hunters?

My heart rate picks up, beating so loud in my ears I have trouble concentrating on what's being said.

"What are they saying?" I whisper.

"I don't know," Jett whispers back.

I strain to hear, will my heart to slow, but I can't make out any individual words. Jett ducks down below one of the dirty windows and peers through the corner. I look as well, but the glass is too smeared for me to see anything.

I turn to Jett. "How many?"

He holds up two fingers.

"Do you see Pru and the triplets?"

He shakes his head.

"Any shifters?"

Blackness fills my vision. I shake my head from side to side, close my eyes then open them again. My nose swipes against material. My breath is hot in front of my face. I suck in air, but it's warm and thick. I lift my hands to my head.

Then I start to burn.

28

UP IN FLAMES

Screaming.

The sound erupts from my throat before I even have time to think about what is happening to me.

The pain is so intense that I can't stop—

Even though I can hear Jett calling my name.

"Flo! *Flo!*"

I can't stop screaming to answer him.

The sound explodes from inside me, spilling from my lips in waves of agony. My hands are on fire. *They must be on fire.*

Burning.

The silver wrapped around my wrists, which stops me from reaching the canvas bag over my head, sinks into my skin. It melts layer after layer, gripping tighter and tighter.

Pain.

The earth shatters and I fall to my knees. The metallic scent of the silver mixing with my blood, sizzling and blistering, has finally reached my nostrils through the tiny holes in the material covering my face. I gag.

"That isn't necessary," a woman says. "Don't hurt them like that."

193

The hunter holding me sighs. "You broke your end of the deal, consider this us breaking ours. Get them inside."

"*Please*," the woman says. "We can fix this."

I'm hauled to my feet and shoved from one set of arms to another. "Take them inside, I said," the hunter says.

His words take a moment to register. Inside? Inside where? The cabin? It looked as if it could collapse any second. Are they holding the others in there, too? We came to save them, not join them.

The hunter clasps his gloved hands around my wrists, where the silver is still scorching my skin, and causes it to sink deeper. I scream, which must startle him for a moment because his grip loosens, then he holds on tight again, pressing down harder on the fresh wounds. "Come on," he says, tugging on my arms. I move my legs shakily.

I call out for Jett now, but he doesn't respond. I beg him to answer me over and over and over until the hunter holding me shakes me and tells me to stop screaming. I ignore him and cry out again. The hunter shoves me forward, marching me along, still with my eyes covered. I won't comply, though. I drag my feet along the floor, kick out at the walls, try to get a grip on anything I possibly can. It slows us, but it doesn't stop us. And when the hunter tires of pulling me along, he scoops me up in his arms and carries me the rest of the way.

After a while, I'm dropped to the ground and untied. I touch the wounds carefully. I can feel the dents all the way around my wrists, so deep they almost reach the bone. The hunter pulls the material off my head and a bright light blinds me temporarily. I hold my hand over my face until my eyes adjust and hear the sound of a door close. Then all is silent.

29

PROMISING SCARS

Once my eyes adjust to the brightness of the room, I take in my surroundings.

I'm locked in a square room. Four white tiled walls, one white tiled floor, and one white tiled ceiling with two bright lights that fill my vision with pink spots if I look directly at them. No windows apart from a tiny one on the door. It smells sterile, chemical, like Greg's medical clinic.

There's a toilet in one corner with a sink beside it. I turn the tap and the water comes out murky and the color of rust.

A flat bed with a thin mattress (no pillow) looks as if it's hovering in mid-air. Though, on further inspection, I can see that two sides are attached to the wall. I sit on the edge of it and examine my wrists. A bloody red ring circles each, promising scars.

Am I inside the cabin? There was no other building around that I could see, but the cabin looked as though it was crumbling in on itself. This is the last thing I'd expect the interior to look like.

I stand and go over to the door, looking out the tiny window. The thick glass distorts the view beyond and I can't see anyone outside the room or any indication of where I'm being held.

I go back to the bed and lie down, aching and exhausted, and think of Jett. We promised we'd stay together. We were ripped apart not long after making that promise. I think about him not answering me—or not being able to answer me—when I was calling out his name, pleading with him to tell me that he was there. Have they taken him some-where else? Killed him? Are they torturing him? Or is he in a room just like this one, lying on a bed with red rings around his wrists, wondering the same thing about me?

I rest my arms by my side. Keep my hands still, let the skin around my wrists calm and start to heal. I'm relieved that the burn on my stomach isn't causing me much trou-ble at all anymore either. I haven't looked at it since leaving Greg's office, but I can tell the skin has been repairing itself, I can feel it, the pain subsiding bit by bit.

My eyelids weigh a ton. I close my eyes, just for a sec-ond, then force them back open, knowing any longer and I'll fall asleep. And how can I sleep in a place like this when I don't know what's coming next? I blink, then press the heels of my hands into my eyes. *Wake up, wake up, wake up.* The pain left behind by the silver cuffs throbs and stings, but it's healing—I can feel the prickling sensation as the skin slowly knits itself back together.

I try to focus on something else, try to busy my mind and think about Jett, the triplets, Pru, the hunters, how to get out of here. But my exhausted brain has shut itself off and won't start back up again. My inability to focus on a plan to get us all out of here makes me realize how much I'm hurting. And even though the bed is uncomfortable, sleep is pulling at me. Sleep will help me heal.

My throat is dry and my tongue sticks to the roof of my mouth. I glance at the sink, remembering the undrinkable water that trickled out of its taps. I don't bother hoping for anything better.

My lips feel cracked. I rub them and dried blood crumbles away. I don't know whether my lips have split and bled or whether I've bitten them in pain. I can taste it, though—the blood. I can't stand the coppery flavor. I use my sleeve to wipe my lips and tongue, but the taste won't go away. Before long, I don't even have the energy to be bothered by it.

My eyes want to close. Every second is a battle against the stinging desperation of sleep. *How am I going to get out of here if I can't even keep my eyes open?* I ask myself, but I know I'm just making excuses, trying to convince myself it'd be okay to let go.

I turn on my side and hug my arms to my chest. I look at my wrists and I want to cry. I so badly want to cry. In pain, in anger, in fear. I want to mourn the shifters we've lost, but I don't even know if they're alive or dead. The lump in my throat is almost painful. But no tears come. My eyes are hurting too much; my body is too weak. I'm dehydrated, drowsy, worn down.

Finally, I give in and close my eyes, reveling in the relief. Without trying, I fall asleep.

30

STRONGER AS A HORSE

Someone's been in here.

There's food and water on the floor by the door. But that doesn't make any sense. The hunters set our camp on fire, murdered shifters, burned me with silver. I know what they're capable of. Why are they feeding me?

My arm itches in the crease of my elbow, and I notice a needle mark. They've either taken my blood or injected me with something. I don't feel any different, but *still*. They did this to me while I slept. I don't know what to think about that. I don't know what to think about anything. None of this feels right.

I move to sit on the floor and investigate my meal—a full glass of clear water, and something pale and lumpy in a bowl. First, I pick up the glass of water, noticing the cup is actually plastic. I lift it to my nose and sniff.

I stare at the water, all the while desperate to drink it, checking there's nothing else in there. They've had plenty of chances to kill me, though, so surely it won't be poisoned. I dip a finger in and taste it. It's warm, but seems clean, so I take a sip. Then another and another and another, until the entire cup is empty, and even then I wish for more.

Next is the food. I'm starving, however unappetizing it looks. I hold it to my nose as I did with the water. From the way it smells and looks, I assume oats. I take the spoon and start eating. It's cold, tasteless, and hard to swallow. But I'm too hungry to care. Once I finish, I lick the bowl clean.

I sit back on the bed, facing the door. Someone has to come back for those things and I'm getting out of here when they do. Only, I haven't quite worked out how. I sit in silence, staring at the white walls, thinking.

I think of Jett and I lift my hand to my neck, feeling for my chain, but it's gone. *It's gone!* It's been Jett's only gift to me. Did they take it? When? *Why?*

I'm so angry I can't think straight. That necklace is the only comfort I have in here—in the world, really. I have to get it back. Or better—get Jett back.

All I can come up with is the idea to shift. I'm stronger as a horse—bigger, faster, tougher. So I remove my clothes, stuff them under the bed, then wrap the white sheet around my shoulders and wait.

31
VOICES

Someone's coming.

There's a sound at the other side of the door. I throw the sheet off my back and move away from the bed. I squeeze my eyes shut and try to shift, but it's hard to concentrate while I'm panicking.

I picture myself back at Newlake with Jett, when he talked me through my shift, helped me find my shape. My breathing slows, my heart rate calms. The memories take some of the pressure off. I let out a long breath and shift.

I instantly feel more powerful with the strength of my legs, heightened senses, and intoxicating energy. I'm getting out of this cell.

Someone enters the room. I don't see who. I turn as soon as the door opens and kick out with my back legs. My hooves connect with a body, then I spin around and gallop out the door, trampling whoever's on the floor.

I think I'm learning to embrace this side of me, to control it better than the elders taught us to. They wanted us to push everything back, so only our human sides remained. But at Newlake, Jett encouraged us to get in touch with our animal and that felt good. There's a balance to be had, and I'm not sure we ever got the opportunity at the circus. Our animals were only ever for performing and nothing more. Maybe we can be more.

I run around a small corridor, passing more rooms like the one I was just in. I look in the windows, searching for Jett, for my friends from the circus. For the elders, if the hunters have them, too.

Empty.

Empty.

Empty.

Maybe they are all already dead. But if that's true, then why aren't I?

I start to lose hope of finding them, knowing that I will have to get out of the building soon if I have any wish for escape. Then I see him in the next cell. *Jett.*

He's alive.

He's lying on a bed just like mine, in a room just like mine. I shift back to human and bang on the door with my fist. Jett stirs and looks at the window. I try the handle. I knew it would be locked, but I had to try. I have no clue how to get him out. There's a red blinking light beside a swipe card device, which must be the lock. I run my finger along the thin strip. It's way more advanced than I'd have thought. What *is* this place?

Jett's up now, coming toward the door. "Go," he mouths through the tiny window. I shake my head and bang on the door again in frustration. I can't leave him here.

I press my hand against the glass. Jett's expression is pained, desperate. I watch him, wanting so badly to touch him. Then I hear someone coming. I tell Jett I'll be back, but he can't hear me through the thick door. I hope he doesn't think I'm leaving him behind.

I start running again, my bare feet slapping against the cold white tiles of the corridor. I look back to see if they're leaving a trail behind me and I'm glad to see they're not. My footprints disappear as quickly as they appear, like I was never there.

I hear faint voices ahead and crouch low as I approach a corner. Moving slowly, shoulder brushing against the wall, I see a hunter leaning against the large window of a room that looks out onto the corridor. His back is pressed up against the glass, and there is a woman's hand on his shoulder. I see a flash of blond hair in front of him. When I inch closer I can hear their hands moving, their lips touching.

For a moment I'm frozen, afraid to move in case I disturb them, in case they see me. But this is something I don't want to witness, so I duck beneath the window and move on, trying not to make a sound.

And that's when I hear her speak.

32

NET OF SILVER

This time, her voice is unmistakable.

I remember now—hearing it outside when the hunters captured me. Too wrapped up in silver and too worried about Jett to take any real notice. But there is absolutely no doubt it is Ava in that room.

I struggle to keep steady. Ava's here—*with* the hunters. Not captured, just . . . with them. How is that possible?

She's still wrapped around the hunter, but they are no longer kissing. "What are you going to do with Flo and the others?" she says. My heart beats faster in response to hearing my name.

"*That's* what you were thinking about just now?" the hunter replies.

Ava's laugh is strained. "We have a deal, Dale. You can't kill them."

"You owe us five shifters. I can't control what the others do. Orders are orders. Right now, they're here for testing. After that, I don't know. Maybe they'll be moved to a bigger lab facility. Maybe we'll be ordered to execute them. It's out of my hands now that they're here."

My head aches trying to process the information. She *owes* the hunters shifters—what does that mean?

"Just try and keep them comfortable while I look for replacements. Please. I've never asked you for a favor like this before."

The hunter—Dale—snorts. "You've asked for plenty. Remember asking us to keep the child shifters alive and out of the labs for your circus? Do you know how hard it was for me to convince the others to do that for you, *and* to keep it between the four of us? They called me a sympathizer. I was this close"—he holds his finger and his thumb an inch apart up to Ava's face—"to losing my job."

"And don't you just love reminding me of that, Dale? That was—"

"A long time ago. I know. But look at what's happened now! I got them to agree to letting you keep the children and one of them exposes herself in front of the audience. Have you seen the news? Head Office wants her dead. They know we have her. They gave the order. I had to convince them to let me run tests on her. I can't just swap her if you bring another shifter to me."

"That was a mistake," Ava argues. "She's new to performing."

"She shouldn't have been performing if she's that unstable."

"I don't want her to die, Dale. I don't want any of them to die. They're too young to be in here and you know it. It's not right."

"You can bring me four shifters and I'll try to let the bear and the elephants go," Dale says, his voice softening. "But not the horse. I'm sorry. I'm in enough trouble with Ethan as it is."

"I'm trying. I know there are two parrots in this area, but I can't find them. There's a pack, they recently split from another. The parrots run it. I'm looking for them. I saw a white tiger, too."

"I'm not interested in what you saw or what you think you might find. Find them, and we'll exchange. All but the horse, I won't budge on that. I *can't* budge on that."

Dale's radio crackles to life and the two of them stop talking. The voice on the other end informs Dale of my escape. The two of them start for the door and I take off down the corridor again.

Questions swirl and battle inside my head, desperate for answers, but I push them aside and concentrate on the now. I slow to a jog when I pass the open door of my cell. I must be running in circles—what did I miss? Where's the exit?

I stop outside Jett's door again. He's pacing inside his cell. I knock on the window. He comes toward the door immediately. But before he reaches the glass, a sharp pain in my side startles me and my knees buckle. My forehead smacks against the window as I fall forward and grip the wall to keep myself standing.

I glance through the window and see Jett shouting, panicking, banging his palm against the door, but I can hardly hear him. And he can't do anything.

I try to shift again, but something's wrong. Something's stopping me.

I look down and see a silver dart sticking out of my thigh. Gritting my teeth, I pull it out. It burns my hand and I drop it. It lands with a clang on the ground. Then I push through the pain and shift back into a horse, ready to fight my way out of here.

Two hunters are coming toward me. I turn and kick, just like before. I hit one, but the other hunter moves to the side and throws a net of silver over me. My skin sizzles. He runs around me and brings the net down on the other side so I'm fully covered. Slashes of searing pain whip across my entire body. I fall to the ground, human again.

I gasp for air, but my lungs feel too tight. *Everything* feels too tight. Ripped out of my shape again, this time by a net of silver. A horse squashed into a human body. My head feels like it's going to burst. My ribs feel like they're going to snap.

The hunters pull the net off and lift me.

I can still hear Jett banging on his cell door, but I'm at the wrong angle to be able to see him and my vision dances out of focus.

Seconds later, I'm dropped back into my cell. The hunter I kicked as a horse kicks me in the face while I lie on the ground, helpless. Blood explodes from my nose. I press my forehead against the cold tiles.

The hunters leave me and I sit up, naked and hurting. The lines on my skin caused by the net are pink and sore. I'm just grateful the wounds aren't deep like the ones on my wrists, which still haven't healed fully.

My hands tremble. And I just sit and watch them shake.

Then the door opens again and a single hunter enters. A woman with sharp eyes, angular features, and dark-brown, almost black, hair. I try to move away when she crouches down beside me, but she grabs my arm and pulls me to her. "What's that?" I manage, spying a syringe in her hand. She's about to inject me with something and I have no energy left to fight her off.

She doesn't answer me. She shoves the thick needle into my arm and presses down on the end. I bite down hard on my lip, drawing more blood. Something solid is deposited under my skin. She pulls the needle out and I start to scream. "Silver!" I cry, my voice hoarse. I can feel it bubbling in my arm, rubbing against bone.

"Yes," she says simply. "That will stop you from shifting again." Her voice is cruel, cold. She bends down again and takes a sample of blood from the other arm.

I hardly even notice the sting of the needle there, compared to the melting sensation inside my other arm. She leaves without another word.

I muster the energy needed to push myself up off the floor and struggle back into my clothes. I wonder what Jett's thinking now. I don't want him to worry about me.

I lie on the bed. My arm's constant throbbing brings fresh tears to my eyes but I'm quick to bite them back. The silver is inside my arm, so I need to learn to put up with the feeling of it, however impossible that seems.

I swallow and squeeze my eyes shut, thinking back to the conversation between Ava and Dale. They're in a relationship—or at least it seemed that way. A hunter and a shifter. I can't get the image out of my head—of their bodies rubbing against each other and her pressing him against the glass and kissing him. I can't believe this is happening. Ava. She's . . . she's betrayed us. How long has this been going on? How long has she been pretending?

And what did Dale mean when he said she'd asked for plenty of favors, like keeping the children for the circus? Did she deliver my parents to the hunters and keep me? Is that their deal?

Sometimes, when I think about my parents, I'm sure I can hear them in my mind. The sound of their voices—speaking to me, singing to me. But I can't, not really. I try to picture them, but there's nothing there. When I think of my parents, my head is empty, my heart is empty, and they both ache with the effort to remember long-forgotten moments.

I rub my eyes. My vision blurs at the edges, dizzy with anger and pain. Why would Ava do something like this? "Five more shifters," Dale said to her. He told her he'd swap Jett and the triplets if she found some in exchange. But not me. My terms are nonnegotiable. At least the others stand a chance. If Ava stands by her word and helps them. I don't even know what to believe anymore. And no one mentioned Pru.

More anger is bubbling up inside me with so many unanswered questions. Another part of me is confused, in denial. And I'm sad, breaking into pieces and trying to fit everything back together.

I focus on the anger rather than the sadness. For now, anyway. Anger might get me through this, drive me on. Sadness could stop me.

All I've learned points to Ava potentially killing my parents and lying to me my entire life. And with that knowledge, my head throbs and my heart bleeds and I want nothing more than to rip hers right out of her chest so she knows how it feels. I've never felt like this before. I want to hurt her for what she's done.

33
RED TEARS

I open my eyes.

I'm afraid of sleeping. I fight it but it keeps happening. My body's telling me it's had enough of pushing on, pushing on.

When I untangle myself from the thin white sheet and roll over, I see Ava sitting on a stool by the door. I freeze. She startles me for a moment, but then the memories of the conversation I overheard yesterday come flooding back.

I push the covers off my legs and launch myself from the bed. Ava doesn't have time to blink before I'm on her. The anger I felt last night sizzles as much as the silver under my skin, pushing out of me, pushing me to hurt her somehow, in some way. For my parents. For my friends.

I dig my nails into her cheeks. "Did you kill my parents? *Did you?*"

Ava shrieks in surprise and tries to bat my hands off her. I let go, satisfied to see crescent marks on her face, some of them bleeding. I grab her hair in one of my fists as she tries to move toward the door. We do not treat our elders this way. A week ago, I wouldn't have dared touch her like this. But that was before the circus was destroyed, before I saw her kissing a hunter, before I discovered her betrayal. I pull her back. "Tell me!"

"I-I didn't personally kill—" I tug harder. "Okay! All right. Just let go and I'll tell you."

"Just say it," I snarl.

"Yes," she whispers, so quietly I almost don't hear. But it's there. The word that changes everything. That confirms my suspicions. That makes my life one big fat lie. Was anything the elders told us true? And what does this mean for my parents? Their deaths were at Ava's hands, then she stole me for the circus.

I let go of her hair and she gasps, bringing her hand up to the back of her head and rubbing her scalp. I shake off the white-blond hairs I've pulled out then bring my palm down on her face, sharp and fast. I slap her so hard the sound rings in my ears and my palm rings with it.

Ava yelps and cups her face in her hands, protecting herself against further attack. She sobs, says my name, "*Flo. Please.*" But I'm not going to hit her again. I'm not going to hurt her anymore. Because I want answers.

"Sit up," I say in a flat voice. I don't want her to know how sad or how angry I am. I want to remain neutral now. No more screaming at her, no more hitting her. I want her to think she can tell me anything and everything. And she better do exactly that.

Ava uses her hands to pull herself across the floor and into the corner, ending up exactly where I want her—out of sight from the little window in the door.

"How did this start?" I ask, taking her stool for myself and sitting down in front of her. "This deal you have with the hunters."

She looks alarmed. "D-deal?" she stutters.

"Don't even try to deny it. I heard you, right after you took your tongue out of that hunter's mouth."

She cringes. Good. "Flo, I—" She buries her face in her hands, but I lean forward and bat them out of the way. She's crying now, shaking her head. "W-we were discovered. You don't understand," she mumbles between sobs. "The four hunters here, Dale included, they *found* us. They were going to kill Nora and Hari. They only needed one of us—three lions are too much for the labs. Three lions released back into society are too dangerous. We made a . . . a deal with them in a bid for our freedom, for our lives. I never imagined they'd accept."

"You agreed to kill shifters for them to save your own skins." My hands are shaking. I press them flat against my thighs to steady them.

Ava cries harder. "Not kill. Not all of them. It sounds horrible when you put it like that, but you have to understand we were frightened at the time, moments from death at their hands. We'd have said anything to save each other— *done* anything."

"No, Ava. I don't understand. I will never understand why you did what you did."

"They were going to kill my family!" she cries.

"So you killed mine instead! And Jett's, and the triplets', and Pru's, and the families of everyone else at the circus.

Hari and Nora should have died that day. What you did . . . it's . . . it's unthinkable. It's evil."

"I know," Ava whispers, reaching out for me.

"Don't touch me," I snarl and scoot back.

"We were at a loss. We were frightened. The decision was fast, in such an extreme situation. I've regretted it ever since." She wipes her eyes with the back of her hand. "Hari, Nora, and I were part of a small pack. We lived up in the mountains half the year, and out in wild, unkempt lands for the other half. We never went near civilization. We never caused any trouble. Piper, another lion, she was Hari's partner, and she went missing on a hunt.

"We searched for her for months, all the while getting closer and closer to humans. We met other packs the closer we got, learned more about the human world. Hari didn't want to go back without Piper. He suggested the circus, getting the idea from a guy we met on the road whose brother set one up somewhere. He had given us some basic details, and after that Hari was obsessed with the idea. I think it took his mind off Piper. He knew as much as we did that we weren't likely to find her."

"And did you?" I ask.

Ava shakes her head. "Never. And the other members of our pack didn't want anything to do with Hari's plans. I didn't either, truthfully. The others went back, but we stayed. Nora and I stayed for Hari. We helped him set up the circus. It took a while to get going, never really lifted off the ground until we started recruiting and finding locations and working with the agents. Hari disappeared a lot, spending time on his own. He wanted to shift, to lose himself in the lion and forget. He was so torn up about Piper. We warned him how dangerous that was, but he wouldn't listen and he kept leaving, coming back days later. And one day he was followed back, and the hunters seized us. Hari made the deal. He got the circus off the ground. Nora and I agreed to the terms. We kept the children to perform, and we delivered the adults to the hunters."

I bunch my hands into fists by my sides.

"I'm sorry," Ava continues quickly. "I never wanted this for you, Flo. Or Jett and the triplets. I never wanted this for any of the circus shifters. Things just got so out of hand that night."

"Don't lie to me. You kept Jett and me at the circus when we told you what we'd seen. You kept us there when we could have escaped all of this, prevented all of this. So don't tell me you wish things were different. You had the chance to make it so."

Ava puts her hand to her chest. "Is that what you think? Nora and I didn't keep you for the hunters. I hoped we could keep you safe. If you ran away, you'd have been out of our protection and fair game to the hunters. They'd have tracked you down, Flo. Both of you. Please believe me."

"I don't know what to believe anymore."

Ava stares at the floor. "Just know how sorry I am, Flo. I know that probably doesn't mean much to you, but I want you to know."

"You're right. Your apology means nothing to me," I say coldly. I'm numb.

"May I leave?" Ava asks quietly, attempting to get to her feet. I don't answer, but I don't stop her. I don't know if I want her to stay or go. There's so much more I want to ask her, but I can hardly make sense of what little she's told me so far.

The tears that fill my eyes blur the whole room. I stand suddenly, and Ava stops in her tracks. "Where are we?" I ask.

Ava glances to the door. "We're inside the cabin."

"It doesn't look like it."

"It's below ground," she tells me. "Please don't try to escape again. It's completely locked. They'll kill you if you try it again."

"They'll kill me anyway," I say. "Thanks to you. I know I don't have any chance of leaving. I heard what Dale said."

"Then they'll kill Jett or the triplets. There's still hope for the four of them."

"I know," I say. I swallow my feelings—Ava might be the only hope of saving the others now. "I heard that, too. Do whatever you can to get them out."

Ava nods and starts for the door again. "And my necklace," I say. "Do they have it?"

"Yes."

"Jett gave it to me on my first show night. I want it back."

She shakes her head. "They won't return it to you, I'm sorry."

"*Why?*"

"You could use it as a weapon."

"The chain would snap before it did any damage!"

"Even so. The answer will be no, I'm sorry."

She reaches for the door, but I grab her arm. "Pru. You didn't mention her. Where have they taken her?"

Ava doesn't look at me. She puts her hand on the door handle and knocks three times, hard. Her hands are shaking. Blood has run from the cuts on her face like red tears. Her cheek is still a startling red from when I hit her.

"Ava, where is she?" I ask again, worried now.

"She didn't make it, Flo," Ava says, almost a whisper. It still has the power to knock me back.

"The crash," I breathe. "How did they find us?"

"Greg's wife called Hari."

"And he told the hunters! Then you hit us with your car and you *killed* her."

"Not me!"

"Stop saying it wasn't you!" I scream. "You're just as bad as the hunters!"

The door opens. Ava rips her arm from my grip and she slips out without another word or another look in my direction.

They killed Pru. She's dead. *She's really dead.* I know we were never real friends, but she was still one of us. And now she's gone. Another to add to the ever-growing list of dead and missing circus shifters. I think of little Star again, of Ursula and Owen, and hope for the hundredth time that they're okay. I think of Lexi and Maria, dead in the woods, wrapped in silver and left to burn. I think of Pru.

This can't be happening. It can't be.

Pru shouldn't be dead. None of them should be. Bile rises in my throat and I swallow it back down.

The door opens again, startling me. Dale steps inside. His eyes are burning, fierce and piercing, and they're locked right on me. He's bigger than the other three, strong, muscular.

Dale crosses the room in a second. The back of his hand connects with the side of my head so hard I hear a snap, and the room goes black for a split second before coming back blurred and filled with blue spots. "You're lucky I don't kill you now, shifter," he hisses.

I spit blood from my mouth and look back at Dale.

Ava scurries into the room after him, drags him out. She thinks she's saving me, helping me. Perhaps she thinks she's making up for all the wrong she's done. She doesn't realize that I don't care, because it takes my focus from everything I've just discovered. For almost my entire life, I've been brought up by the people responsible for the death of my parents. How do I even process that? It's too much to wrap my head around. Before I had suspicions—fragments of an overheard conversation. Now Ava's confirmed them, admitted to what she, Nora, and Hari have done.

My head throbs—and not just from Dale's slap.

I want to get my hands on them, all of them—the elders, the hunters. I want to hurt them for what they did. I want them to suffer. But how am I supposed to do anything at all trapped in this cell with the ache of silver in my arm to stop me from shifting? I feel weaker by the second with it lodged in there. Its presence makes me feel constantly sick, always hurting.

I curl up on the bed and think about what Ava said until I have no energy left at all. Until the darkness finally takes me and the nightmares start.

34
TOO DEEP

My sheets are wet with sweat.

I dreamt about the hunters, about my parents. About the hunters killing my parents. I can't stop thinking about them, and Jett and the triplets and Pru. *We're good.* We don't hurt people. We aren't a threat. It's the bears in the news the hunters should be holding down here like this. It's them they should be targeting. Not us.

Hari, Nora, and Ava's situation is odd, to say the least. Not that I approve in any way of what they did, but they are lucky to have come out of it the way they have. Once they were discovered that should have been it for them. Though I can't ever forgive or understand their actions, it's kept them alive. Death or testing, they're the only two outcomes of getting caught.

The door opens. Ava comes back into the room, surprising me. After what happened yesterday, I didn't expect to see her again.

I glare at her and hold it as she closes the door softly behind her, as if it'll make me feel better. It doesn't.

"Flo, please," she says. "I'm trying to make things right."

"And where are Hari and Nora? Are they trying to make things right?" I ask.

Ava hesitates. "Well, no. I suppose not. They're here, too. They come and go a lot."

I think back to when we were captured outside the cabin. "That was your voice," I say. "When Jett and I were caught. You told the hunters not to hurt us, but they wouldn't listen to you. They said you'd broken your side of the deal."

Eyes to the ground, Ava nods. "I don't want you to suffer, Flo. You're only sixteen, you shouldn't be *here*."

I shake my head. "The tigers were fourteen and fifteen," I say. "And what exactly is *here*?"

"Sometimes hunters bring shifters to small facilities like this one. Perhaps a shifter who is hiding others, or has information the hunters want, or sometimes for testing. Then the shifters are moved on to bigger labs and locked-down facilities if they're still useful."

I shudder. "What do they do to get the information? What goes on in the labs?" I ask, then regret it instantly. Ava looks at my wrists, which says it all. "They keep taking my blood," I tell her.

"They're experimenting. The hunters are a government-funded secretive operation to remove a potential threat to society—*us*. They're studying the properties of your blood, and Jett's and the triplets'."

"But *why*?" I ask, dumbfounded. "You always taught us hunters kill or capture. But you never told us much about why they kill us, or why they capture us. I know how it began, but I don't know why it *carried on*. And I don't understand all of this"—I gesture to the room around me, the four white walls—"that's going on right now with us. What do they want my blood for?"

"Many, many purposes. I'm not as knowledgeable as I'd like to be. There are certain things not even Dale will disclose. There are tests for military purposes—using our abilities to the country's advantage. Then there are our healing abilities and how those could be used in medical care. The organization wants to better understand why we are what we are, and what they can take from it for themselves."

"If that's what they want then why do they hunt us the way they do?"

"Because we're different. Because they can't explain us. Because they're scared of us. Because of things we've done in the past, things we will do in the future. We're a threat, Flo. They don't filter, they don't show mercy—they hunt, they contain, they kill. It works for them."

"So where do you come in?"

Ava swallows, takes a deep breath. "You already know."

"I want to hear it. All of it."

She can't meet my eyes. "We find a certain number of shifters each year—that's the deal. The agreed number is more than they locate alone. The hunters kill those who are not needed or those who are unruly and cause problems. The rest are taken to the labs."

"My parents?" I ask, hopeful. *Could they still be alive?*

Ava shakes her head. "I don't know. We don't know what happens once we inform the hunters. We just get the child. And we don't even keep all the children, just the ones we need to make a living. The ones that don't come with us are either killed with their parents or taken away for testing."

Bile stings the back of my throat, bitter and gritty. That could have been me. That could have been Jett. "So my parents could be alive? In one of the labs?"

"It is highly unlikely, Flo."

I feel like my heart is splitting in two all over again. Soon there won't be much left to break. I can't believe what I'm hearing. That they *could* be alive—trapped in a cage and experimented on since they were captured. But is that what I'd want if it meant they were still in this world? For them to be suffering somewhere for all this time?

As if Ava can hear my thoughts, she adds, "Please don't get your hopes up that they are still out there. If your parents weren't dealt with at the scene, they were taken thirteen years ago. Anything could have happened in that time."

I blink away tears before looking back at Ava, taking in her swollen face and the bruise on her cheekbone. I did that. "Would I have ended up here anyway? Is that what happened to the older shifters?"

Ava looks away and I know the answer.

"All the shifters that grew up and decided to leave, they didn't join new packs or another circus, did they? You gave them to the hunters, didn't you?"

"I'm sorry," she whispers.

"So this was my future? No matter what."

"Not unless you chose to leave us," she says. "You would never have been forced out. The ones who left made that choice on their own."

"How could you raise them then do that to them? Hari always acted like he cared, I *always* thought we mattered to him."

"You do—"

"DON'T LIE!"

Ava stands. I do, too. She holds a hand out. "Flo, stop."

"What did you come back for?"

"Because this," she says, pointing to my burned wrists, "is not what I want. It isn't supposed to be like this . . . this mess we're in. The hunters had been putting pressure on us for weeks. That's why they were coming to the shows, to intimidate us. And they hurt Hari, badly. That's why he was sent to Greg. It was a warning to us, but we were struggling to find more shifters. We still are. We know there are some in this area but . . ."

The room falls silent. I watch Ava as she sits again, quietly, looking at her hands. She looks frightened, exhausted, like she's in too deep and doesn't know how she'll ever make it back out. "I wasn't the one who located your parents if it makes you feel any better."

"It doesn't," I say. "What I can't understand is why you've kept up your end of the deal for all this time. Why didn't you try to get away?"

Ava runs her hand through her hair. "They kept tabs on us and the circus. We never thought we'd get far. It was safer for all of us if we carried on. We couldn't exactly run with all the circus members, which would leave all of you in danger."

I roll my eyes. "Don't."

"Don't what?"

"Act like you care about anyone but Hari, Nora, and yourself."

"But, Flo, I do! I'm trying so hard to get you out of here. I'm coming to visit you to give you answers, to help you understand."

"Well, I don't! I can't! Why do the hunters even need your help? Aren't they supposed to be able to do this on their own?"

"It's not that easy," Ava says. "Most shifters are careful. There are the odd packs that strike out and draw the attention of hunters, but most keep to themselves. They aren't so easy to find anymore."

"Unless they know another shifter who they think they can trust," I say.

Ava lowers her gaze and doesn't respond.

"So what happens now?" I ask. "If you give them the five of us, they'll let you go, right?"

"Yes."

I swallow. "Well, why haven't you?"

"I'm trying to find other shifters instead."

I'm not sure I'm comfortable knowing she's searching for someone else's life to take to spare Jett's, to spare Lucas, Lance, and Logan's. But they're my friends. I'd do anything to save them. And that makes me wonder if I really am all that different from Ava—to take the lives of strangers to save those I care about. I push the thought away. I have to push it away. I'm not getting out of here, and I'm all for Jett and the triplets escaping, whatever the cost. I don't want to think about what that says about me.

"I know what you're thinking," Ava says. "But it's not your decision. It's mine, and I've made it. I know I can't make up for what I've done, what I've been involved in, what I'm still involved in, but I promise I am doing everything I can to get Jett and the triplets out. You, too, if I can." She looks to one side and a small smile touches her lips. "The triplets were two-year-olds when they came to us, Jett a bit older. They came in at the same time, you a little later. Jett took such good care of the four of you. It might be hard to believe, but I do care about you, Flo. I care about all of the shifters at the circus. I'm heartbroken over everything that's happened. None of this has ever been easy. I've always tried to keep some distance, not get too attached, but I can't help it."

I try not to let her words sink in too deep. Try not to think too much about all the orphaned babies and toddlers whose parents were murdered. About the teenagers and children who ran for their lives that night at the circus. Some of them making it to safety, others dying in the woods.

"Do you know what happened that night? Did you see?"

Ava nods slowly. "They killed the ones who ran," she whispers. "If they caught them. We saw the tigers go into the woods. They are . . . ," she trails off.

"I know about the tigers," I tell her. "We went back. We saw them. Pru found them." Ava covers her mouth. She looks like she's about to speak, apologize maybe, but I stop her. "What about everyone else? Star? Ruby? Owen and Ursula? Itch and Oscar?"

Ava shakes her head. "I don't know for sure. I know the hunters don't have them. The monkeys . . . some escaped. I think. I don't know if the seals got away. Star did. She's with Ruby, Owen, and Ursula. They went to see Iris and she sent them to join another pack. I don't know if they made it that far, though."

So it was Star and Ruby at the end of Iris's drive when she gave Owen and Ursula instruction of where to go. I'm filled with relief, but it doesn't last long. "I don't really know what to think anymore," I say, thinking out loud. I don't expect Ava to respond, and she doesn't. "How do I even know if Jett and the triplets are still alive?"

"I'm telling you that they are," Ava says. She stands to leave, obviously having had enough of me for one day. She takes the stool with her.

"Prove it," I call after her. She doesn't turn around. "Let me see Jett," I add.

I'm using her. I know she wants to make up for what she's done, and even though she never can—ever—she's really trying and she might just do this for me. It would be nice to get the chance to say good-bye to him.

Ava sighs. "I'll try," is all she says before banging on the door. It opens and she's gone, leaving me alone with my thoughts, which is the worst place for me to be right now.

35

COME HERE

Ava visits me every day.

I wait for her every day.

At least, I think days are passing. I can't tell properly down here. There's nothing to do, so I sleep a lot. Partly to escape my thoughts, partly to escape the constant pain in my arm. The rest has helped the burn on my stomach almost fully heal. The burns on my wrists are now nothing more than pink lines. I'm recovering, but never fully. The silver under my skin slows everything down, makes me weak. I've come to the conclusion that I'll die here . . . eventually.

I drum my fingers on the edge of the lumpy mattress and watch the door, waiting for Ava to come. I hope it'll open and Jett will walk through it, but I doubt things will be that simple.

When the door finally unlocks and opens, I stand. Ava comes in balancing a plate on one hand and holding a drink in the other. She doesn't bring a stool to sit on today.

She hands me the plate. On it is plain white buttered bread and some grapes. I pick up a piece of the bread and it feels stale. I take a bite. It's dry but I shouldn't expect anything more, really. The drink is warm water again. But it's better than nothing.

I finish the lot. And I don't thank her.

Ava sits on the edge of my bed in silence while I wash down the last of the bread. Then she takes the empty plate and sets it to one side. I wipe my mouth with the back of my hand. The movement sends a fresh jolt of pain through my arm where the silver is embedded. I wonder, not for the first time, if it'll be left in there forever. Forever might not be that long for me, anyway.

"Do I get to see Jett now?" I ask.

Ava shakes her head and my heart sinks. "They won't let me bring him to you. I'm sorry, Flo."

"No," I say, fighting to keep my voice level. "No. That's not good enough. Try again. I want to see him one last time. Surely you understand that."

"I do understand. Absolutely. And I tried. Dale said it's too dangerous. Jett could try to break free. He could hurt someone."

I can't deny that he'd probably try, taking as many hunters down with him as he could. "What about if I went to him?" Ava starts to shake her head again, so I hurry and add, "I have the silver in my arm. I can't shift."

Ava frowns. Her gaze darts to my arm. "Show me."

I turn my arm over and roll up the sleeve of my jacket. I point to the red patch on my skin. Without a word, Ava stands and walks to the door. She knocks, waits. The door opens a crack and she slips out, pulling it closed behind her. Faint muttering floats through the gap in the door, but I can't hear what she's saying. I assume she's speaking to Dale. My heart beats frantically in my chest. *Please let me see Jett. Please let me see Jett. Please let me see Jett.*

After a couple excruciating minutes, the door opens again and Ava comes back inside with Dale.

"She can have a few minutes, Ava," he says. "No more than that. If the others find out—"

"They won't," Ava says, cutting him off. She turns to me and winks, but I ignore it. This doesn't mean we're friends. Not even close.

My blood is pumping. Every second since Jett and I were caught I have been desperate to be close to him again. To speak to him again. Especially now that I know he could possibly leave and I can't. Most of all, I want him to know that I'm all right. He hasn't seen me since the day I tried to escape and was attacked and captured outside his cell. He needs to know that when he leaves and I don't, that I will be okay. That I care for his safety more than I care for my own.

Dale holds up his gun. "I have silver bullets, shifter," he snarls, pointing the gun at me. "Imagine someone piercing your skin all the way through with a red-hot poker. That's how it'll feel if I use this on you. If you try anything—"

"That's enough, Dale," Ava snaps. "She knows."

I stare at the gun and wonder how many of my friends he's used it on. How many of my friends have felt what he just described?

Dale grabs me by the arm and shoves me out the door. Ava follows and overtakes us, leading me to Jett's cell. Once at the door, Dale hands her the swipe key and she opens it, gesturing for me to go on inside.

"You only have a couple minutes, Flo," Ava says. "Dale and I will be right outside the whole time."

I step inside, shaking. Jett is on the bed in the corner of a room with the same layout at mine. He has his back to me, lying on his side and facing the wall. His food is on the floor in front of the bed, untouched. "Why aren't you eating?" I say.

The muscles in Jett's back stiffen. He turns around slowly. His face is sunken and he has dark-purple shadows below his eyes. One eye is swollen and bruised. They must have hit him. Hard, by the looks of it. And recently, or it'd have begun to heal. "Flo?" he whispers. "Is that really you?"

"It's me, Jett," I say. My eyes fill with tears and I struggle to keep my voice steady.

"Come here," he says, stretching out an arm. I look back to the door to check if Ava and Dale are watching, but I can't see them. And the door is only open the smallest crack. We have as much privacy as I can hope for. "Please," Jett adds, mistaking my actions for hesitation.

I take his hand and approach the bed. I lie down beside him and bury my face between his neck and shoulder. "Are you okay?" I ask him.

"I am now," he says. "I thought you were dead."

Not yet, I think. "I'm sorry," I tell him. "I'm all right, though. You don't need to worry about me."

"All I do is worry about you. I want to save us, Flo, but I don't know how." His voice is so weak. Tears escape and

I think carefully of how to say what I need to. To tell him he might live, but I will not.

I pull back so I can see his face. "Looks to me like you're giving up."

He stares at me. "Aren't you?"

I shake my head. "Never. And don't you dare."

"Flo—"

"We don't have long," I say. "I have to go back to my cell soon."

"I don't want you to leave," he says, holding me tighter.

"I don't want to leave, either. But we'll be okay. We've seen each other now. I know you're okay, and you know I'm okay. That's good, right?" Jett nods slowly. "Good. But there's something else I need to tell you . . ." Jett wipes away my tears. "If you get the chance to go, *go*. Even if it's without me. Can you do that?"

Jett frowns, shakes his head. "Never."

I squeeze my eyes shut. That's what I was afraid of. "Well you might not have a choice. I don't know if I'm getting out of here. But you and the triplets might have a chance. When—*if*—the chance does come, I need you to take it. I need you to promise."

He sits up now. I do, too. "Flo, I don't understand. We're talking about leaving you. There's no way—"

The door bursts open and Dale lifts me off the bed and sets me on my feet. There's a voice coming from the radio on his hip. "Out," he says, shoving me toward the door.

"No!" Jett cries, scrambling to his feet and hurrying after us.

Ava is waiting outside the door and takes my arm when I get to her. I turn back to Jett just as the door is closing. "Eat," is all I have time to say before the door closes in his face and I'm marched back down the corridor to my own cell.

"They're on their way back," Dale says. "*Hurry up.*"

Ava comes inside the room with me. I throw myself onto the bed, ignoring her presence. Dale pokes his head around the door. "We need to be done now."

"One moment," Ava replies. Dale sighs and steps back outside.

"Why does he do whatever you want all the time? He's a hunter and you're a shifter."

Ava glances back at the door and lowers her voice. "Dale's a sympathizer. He joined the EOS twenty-three years ago, when his father felt he was ready to learn the secrets of the world and follow in his footsteps. He's never been committed to the cause, though, not the way his father wanted him to be."

I frown. "He seemed pretty committed when he beat me and threatened to shoot me," I say.

"You hurt *me*, Flo. That's why. Not because of what you are."

"It was extreme," I grumble.

"Yes. Well. We're past that now."

We're not, I think. I hate that she believes I trust her, that she thinks I've forgiven her for everything she's done. I swallow the feeling; I need her right now. Ava's my only chance of getting out of here alive, of getting Jett and the triplets out alive. "Why doesn't Dale do something to stop all of this?"

"One man against an entire organization?"

I shrug. "He could try."

"Dale does try, Flo. Quietly. His sister is part of the EOS, too. She joined younger than he did. She's very ambitious, and Dale's father is very proud of her."

"But not of Dale," I say.

Ava shakes her head. "Not so much. Dale just does what he has to. If there's another way, he takes it."

I frown. That doesn't sound like much help to anybody. He's not making a difference, no matter what he tells himself. "Are there others like him?"

"None I've met. There's no way Hari, Nora, and I would be alive, let alone running the circus, without Dale. The other three hunters are strong believers in what they do. Ethan in particular. I try to stay away when he's here. I only have ties with Dale, and he assures me there are other sympathizers in the organization. That's all I know."

I shudder, remembering their kiss again.

"I should leave," Ava says. "I've spent too much time down here today."

"I've spent too much time down here for a lifetime," I mumble.

Ava touches my hair, delicately runs her fingers through the greasy strands. I force myself not to pull away. "I'm trying, Flo," she whispers. She turns to leave.

"Wait!" I say, standing up. "You said the EOS? Is that what they're really called? The 'official' name? You've never called them that before."

"The EOS, yes. Shifters call them hunters but they don't call themselves that. They're EOS employees—the department of the Elimination of the Supernatural."

Fear stabs at my heart. "The Elimination of the Super-natural," I breathe. "And people are fine with that?"

"It's top secret, Flo. The general public doesn't need to be okay with it. The special agents are committed to the cause. Since the number of shifter incidents spiked three years ago, they've really come down hard, putting extra effort into hunting. You must remember that most shifters aren't like us—they aren't trained to contain their animal selves. So the world is kept 'safe' from us and its inhabitants will never need to know. It's been this way for a long time—since before you were born—and it will stay this way for a long time to come. This is very serious."

"I know it is," I say, still trying to process just how much trouble I'm really in here.

"Get some rest, Flo."

Anger rises. "In preparation for my death?"

Ava lingers in the doorway. "I don't know what else I can say. I told you I'd try to help you."

I grab her sleeve. She looks down in surprise, flinching at my touch. "You have to convince Jett," I say. "Please visit him. Tell him to leave if he gets the chance. Convince him it's what I want."

"I'll try, Flo. It's not even certain I can make the exchange. I haven't found traces of the shifters around here for days now," she says, tugging her sleeve from my grip.

I shake my head. "Just do what you can," I plead.

I turn my back on her and wait for her to leave. She doesn't right away. She steps farther into the room and lowers her voice so only I can hear. "The same goes for you. I can't exchange you, but I can still try and get you out of here. It just needs time and planning."

I don't turn around. I don't respond. I don't know how.

36
REALLY HURT

Another meal comes soon after the last one, which is unusual.

I've started to assume that the times when my meals come is sometime late morning or early afternoon.

On the plate is the same as I received just hours ago— stale bread and butter. I lift a piece of bread to my lips, then catch sight of something else poking out from underneath the other slice. I push the bread aside, almost knocking it off the plate, to reveal a knife.

I hold the knife in my hand, slowly wrapping my fingers around its handle. Am I supposed to attack the hunters with this little thing and get myself out of here? I doubt I'd get very far, and if this is Ava's plan then it's not giving me much hope that she will ever get me out.

I hide the knife under the mattress and sit on top of it. I suddenly lose my appetite, so I leave the rest of the bread but finish off the water. I know I should make the most of the extra meal, but I can't think straight, never mind eat. I need to work out how to use the knife most effectively and when to make my move.

I'm sitting on the bed with my back against the wall when the door opens.

Ava steps inside and closes the door softly behind her. I sit up and open my mouth to ask what the knife is for, when she plans for me to use it, who I'll be using it on, where to go if I get past the hunters, what about Jett and the others . . . but Ava holds her finger to her lips.

She's pale. I close my mouth and stay still on the bed, watching her make her way over to me. "Where is it?" she whispers.

I tap my hand on the mattress above the knife. "What is it for?" I ask first. She reaches out and takes my hand, turning it palm up. Then she gently runs her finger over the red mark where the silver is beneath my skin. My eyes widen. "No!"

Ava holds her fingers to her lips again. "I don't have long," she says softly. "Dale's waiting outside. He won't come in, I don't think. But I'm only supposed to be collecting your cup and plate. And he might come check on me if I take too long. You did attack me recently . . ."

I frown. She deserved that.

I look back down at the place where the knife lies waiting for me to use it, to cut *my own* arm open. "I can't."

"You can, Flo," Ava says.

I shake my head. "I'm not doing that. I really can't."

"Flo—"

"No, Ava! I can't *do* that," I argue, my voice climbing with each word.

Ava covers my mouth with her hand. I shake my head more, but she holds it in place. "I'll do it," she says quietly. "I'll do it."

I stop struggling.

"We have to. It's the only way," Ava says. She takes her hand away from my mouth and I take a deep breath. "Let me get rid of Dale."

She gathers up my cup and plate, returning to the door and handing them over to Dale. "I'll be a few more minutes," she tells him. "Will you take these?"

I assume he does, because she steps back with no trouble and closes the door again. I take another deep breath. I know Ava's right—I can't shift with silver lodged in my arm. But what she's planning makes my blood run cold. I've got to let her dig the silver out of me with the tip of a knife. You'd think I'd be used to pain by now, but this is different—this is expected pain, *slow* pain, deep pain. My mouth fills with a bitter taste and I swallow it back. I know what I have to do, and my hands are shaking like mad thinking about what it's going to feel like, how much it's going to hurt. I swallow again, try to breathe steadily.

Ava sits down beside me again. "Are you ready?"

I nod—I have to—and pull the knife out from beneath the mattress, handing it to her. My hands shake furiously and I feel sick in anticipation. This is going to hurt, *really* hurt. The room sways.

"Don't scream," Ava says and hands me a small piece of bundled material. "Bite."

Ava puts my bed sheet over her lap, then pulls my arm on top of it. I stuff the material in my mouth and bite down. Then I squeeze my eyes shut.

I start to sweat before the knife even touches me. A drop runs down my spine and makes me shiver. I breathe heavily through my nose, waiting for Ava to begin.

When I feel the cool blade slice slowly across my skin, my eyes fly open and I gag on the material in my mouth. Instinctively, I try to pull away, but Ava seems prepared for that as she clamps down harder, holding my arm in place. She speaks, as if to distract me. "I found two more," she says. "Shifters, I mean. So only two more to find and the others can go."

I ignore her. Nothing can distract me from what she's doing, especially when it's something I don't want to hear about in any detail. Pain shoots up my arm and I try again to pull away. Ava presses down and carries on. I'm glad, really—I don't want her to stop because I don't think I'd be able to let her start again.

I dig my nails into the palms of my hands. I can feel the warmth of my blood flowing down my arm. I make the mistake of looking at it, seeing it pool out around the knife and Ava's fingers. My eyes grow wide. The material in my mouth helps mute my screams.

Ava sucks in a breath, and then there's a *clink* as the silver hits the floor. She puts pressure on my arm. I feel like I've swallowed the rag in my mouth, feel like it's lodged in my throat, cutting off my air supply. My hair sticks to my forehead and neck with sweat.

"It's done," Ava says, pulling the material out of my mouth with her free hand. "It's over." She passes me a few square pads. "Hide these under your bed and use them to stop the bleeding while it prepares to heal." She hands me a bandage, too, for when it's calmed down and ready to be wrapped up. I stuff it all under the mattress, then take over holding the pad on the cut.

Ava leans closer to me. "I'm going to try and get you out tomorrow if I can distract the hunters with the two shifters I caught. Be ready to shift." She stands and wipes her hands on the sheet, using some of the rust-colored water from the sink to wash away the blood. "Do I look okay?" she asks, turning to me. "No blood or anything, I mean."

"No," I say weakly. "There's no blood."

"I'm proud of you, Flo," she says. "That was very brave."

Ava leaves the room and I collapse on the bed, tangled in blood-stained sheets.

37

BEARS HAVE A TENDENCY TO BE VICIOUS

There's movement outside the small window in the door.

Shadows flit across the empty floor of my cell. I sit up, expecting Ava.

Is it time?

I pull my jacket sleeve down to hide my arm in case it isn't her and do a quick scan of the room to check that nothing's where it shouldn't be. My bed sheets are bloody, but the hunters have beaten me and burned me so often that it doesn't look out of place. I pull the knife from beneath the mattress and slide it down the side of my boot. Then I lie back down on the bed with my back to the door.

The lock beeps and someone steps inside. Ava usually announces herself, but whoever is here remains silent. Panic flares inside me but I tell myself to keep calm. It's not unusual for a hunter to come in here. The heavy footsteps are unlike Ava's and I decide for sure it isn't her. I decide to stay facing the wall until they go.

But they don't. .

They come closer and closer, before stopping right by the side of my bed. I stay still and keep my eyes closed. I can feel them next to me. A hunter. I'm sure of it. Again, I tell myself not to worry, that it's likely he—

He takes a handful of my hair and pulls my head up off the mattress. I cry out and grab his arm, but he swats my hand away easily.

I reach for my boot, pull out the knife, and take a swing at him with it. I slice his hand and the blade comes away bloody. He doesn't seem afraid, though. And he keeps coming at me.

The hunter kicks my legs out from under me and I fall, landing on my back with a *crack*. I drop the knife. He kicks it out of my reach. My head is covered with a burlap sack again, like the one they used on the day I was captured. I'm pulled off the floor and forced to my feet.

I close my eyes and conjure the energy to shift and get myself out of this, whatever this is. Silver cuffs are clamped around my wrists again, cutting the connection. *No!* I bite down hard on my bottom lip and it trembles with the scream I won't let free.

The hunter leads me out of the room. I keep stumbling and falling, but that barely slows us down.

Then there's a voice, right by me. "Ethan, put her down!"

Ava.

"And there's no need for those cuffs—she has silver in her arm," Ava says. She shouldn't draw attention to it— what if he checks and finds the wound? I see what she's trying to do, though. She's trying to make him take the cuffs off so I have the ability to shift if I need to. And I think I'm going to need to.

"I don't take orders from you," Ethan snarls.

"What's going on?" Dale. I'm sure that's him.

"Your *girlfriend* gave the horse shifter a knife. She shredded my damn hand with it."

I'm pushed through a door, which opens as I crash into it. Fresh air hits me and I feel a breeze as I stumble forward and try to keep on my feet. I take a deep breath, but it's unsatisfying with the bag over my head. The air around my face is thick and warm.

I'm walked a little farther. I can hear dead leaves crunching under my feet, and I can feel the uneven ground beneath them. We stop and I'm forced to my knees on the damp ground.

"Round them up," Ethan, I assume, says. "Over here."

"And bring the car around," a woman says. "Just the horse and one elephant, right?"

I shake my head, wishing I could see where I am, who is in front of me, what they are planning. *Just the horse and one elephant*—what does that mean?

When the bag is whipped off my head, I frown and blink. I look to my left and see Jett, kneeling down beside me. Ava's behind him, and she pulls the bag off his head, too.

"*Ava*," Dale growls. So she's not meant to be doing this. She's going to get herself killed. I try to tell myself I don't care, that I even want it, but I can't help but worry for her.

"There's no need for any of this. Uncuff them, too!"

"Not a chance," Ethan says, grabbing Ava roughly by the arm and pulling her away from us. The silver cuffs sink into my skin, melting away the layers for a second time. I'm almost used to the touch of silver now.

"You can't do this!" she yells. "I've found others!"

I look to my right. The triplets are kneeling alongside each other, too. Lucas's head is still covered but Lance and Logan are bag-free. Their faces are bruised, their hair thick with grease.

We're in a line. In front of us are the four hunters, holding back a struggling Ava. Nora and Hari stand slightly behind them. Hari's arm is in a sling and one of his eyes is swollen shut. "Stop it, Ava," Nora says. "Now."

"It's not right!" Ava argues. "I got two shifters. Let Jett and the triplets go."

Nora clucks her tongue. She turns to Ethan and the female hunter. "You may as well take the girl and the elephant while I speak to Ava." Nora calls me "the girl" like she doesn't know my name. Like she hasn't raised me. Like she didn't teach me to shift. Is she too ashamed to call us by our names? Or does she really not care at all?

Two hunters haul Lucas to his feet and march him around the cabin toward the car. Ethan keeps hold of Ava while they go. Nora steps forward. "Ava, you need to stop this right now," she says in a hushed tone. "It's decided."

"They can't just kill them," she cries. "I found others."

"We don't need the ones you found," Ethan says, close to Ava's ear. He's behind her, with her arms locked in his.

"We have the horse and the elephant for testing and no need for the others. You know how it works."

Ava starts to cry. "Not the circus children, though. You promised! You always promised. Just let the others go at least."

Nora slaps her sister. "*Shut up.*"

"Bears have a tendency to be vicious. We can't allow him back into the human world, and we don't need him in the labs," Ethan says. "Simple. It's decided. Now let it go unless you want to join them."

Nora gives Ava a look that says *I told you so* and pulls her away from Ethan and over to Hari. "We don't have to stay and watch," Nora says.

My heart is in my mouth. I realize now that they were never going to let Jett go, regardless of Ava's plans to exchange him. *Bears have a tendency to be vicious.* I struggle against the silver cuffs, slicing the skin on my wrists.

"What is she doing?" Ethan mutters, looking my way as I wriggle around. I can't let him kill Jett. There's no way. One hand slips out, the skin burned from wrist to fingertips. I swallow my screams and my vision blurs with tears.

I'm working on the other hand when gunshots ring out from the other side of the cabin. Ethan, Dale, and the elders whip around to face the direction of the sound. I keep wiggling my hand through the silver cuff, ignoring everything that's going on around me. But when a flash of white streaks between the tree trunks and Ethan aims his gun and starts firing, I realize something big is happening. Is this part of Ava's plan?

The creature in the trees darts by again. I get a better look at it this time. It's a white tiger. I remember Ava telling Dale there were white tigers in the area. But what are they doing here? Are they helping us for Ava? Or have they just wound up in the wrong place at the wrong time?

A bird caws overhead, loud and deliberate. Two of them circle in the sky, too far away for me to see them properly. More shifters? The parrots, maybe.

I stand while the hunters and elders are distracted. There's a growl from the tree trunks, followed by another. Bullets pepper the sky. If we're going to get away, it needs to be now.

Ava rushes at Ethan while he's scanning the trees, gun aimed. She side tackles him and the two of them wrestle on the ground. Nora and Hari back up, watching the fight. I can see in their eyes that they're torn between helping and running. I stare at Ava and think back to our conversation underground, "*Flo, please,*" she said. "*I'm trying to make things right.*" This is Ava keeping her word.

Eventually, Nora decides to help. She steps forward and kicks Ethan in the head. I cringe at the sound when her boot connects with his skull. Ethan goes still and Ava climbs off him. Nora tugs her sister's arm. "We're going," she says. "Now."

"Wait!" Ava cries, but Nora keeps dragging her away.

Ava's eyes find mine and she throws something in my direction. It catches the light as it falls to the ground. I crawl forward and grab for it. I want to go after them, but I want to leave more.

I find the tiny keys among the dry leaves. They are silver and burn my raw hand, but I keep hold of them, undoing the cuff on my other wrist. Then I hurry to free Jett, Logan, and Lance from theirs. The brothers take the keys from me and hurry to the car to find Lucas.

I stand, pulling Jett up with me. "Flo," he breathes, his eyes closing. The silver's weakened him too much. He can hardly stand. "Go," he whispers into my ear. "Go."

I loop his arm over my shoulder and we stumble into the trees together. "Not without you," I tell him. "Never without you."

38
SO WE RUN

The triplets catch up to us in the woods.

Jett comes around more, and the rings on his wrists begin to heal. My hand is taking longer—the burn is more severe—but it's getting there, too. I don't have time to worry about it anyway.

"What do we do now?" Lucas says, holding Jett up on his other side. I wonder if Jett started eating again when I told him to, or whether that's the reason he's so weak now.

"There were other shifters," I say. "I saw them—in the trees, in the sky."

"We should follow them," Lucas says.

I shake my head. "The hunters are following them."

I look behind me at the cabin. I won't be satisfied until it's completely out of sight. I won't feel safe until we're out of the woods. Probably not even then.

I hear a shot. Lucas flinches at the sound. It's close. "We should run," Lucas says.

"But Jett—"

"I'm fine," Jett says, stumbling back without our support. "I can run if we need to run."

I nod, even though he isn't fine. "We need to run."

So we run. Dead leaves flutter around my feet and legs, kicked up from the ground with each step I take. A bird flies from a tree as I pass it, startling me. I look for the parrots but can no longer see them. I need to focus on the path ahead, though—the tree roots sticking out of the ground, the burrows in the soil big enough to cause a twisted ankle.

One look back, and I see Jett and Logan lagging behind. I shout for Lucas and Lance to slow down, but they don't hear me.

I stop and wait for Logan and Jett to catch up. "I'm going to shift," I tell them. "I'll be faster if I shift, and I'll be able to carry both of you." Jett starts to shake his head, but I hold up my hand. "It's decided."

I hurry removing my clothes. Logan keeps lookout while I hand everything to Jett. I can see the roof of the cabin in the distance. I hate that I can still see it.

Lucas and Lance have stopped now. I can hear them calling over to us. It takes me a little longer to shift, having had contact with so much silver. I close my eyes and concentrate until my shape comes.

When it does, Jett hoists himself up onto my back. Logan hurries after him, sitting behind and holding on tight. We start to run again and soon pick up speed. I match Lucas and Lance's pace and keep it, though I could easily outrun them. I feel stronger already.

I quickly get used to the extra weight I'm carrying, but my steps falter when I hear another gunshot. This time the bullet whizzes by me, hitting a tree trunk and shattering the bark. The hunters are coming for us. And I'm faster now, but I'm also a bigger target.

Another shot. Jett and Logan hold on. Their bodies tense, and their legs squeeze tighter around my middle. I keep running without looking back. I can feel Jett and Logan twisting around, shifting their weight as they position themselves. It's frustrating that I can't speak and tell them to stop moving so much.

Two shots. I can still see Lance and Lucas running a little ahead now, their figures flashing in and out of sight as they weave between tree trunks. I fight the urge to overtake them. I want to keep them in sight.

Another crack. That one was close. I felt the bullet zip by my side and heard it lodge itself into another tree. Jett lets out a breath and pats my side.

I don't know how many are following, how many are shooting. Another gunshot rings out, but I can't tell where it lands.

We don't stop, not for one second, but no more silver bullets come. No more footsteps follow behind. Perhaps we'll outrun the hunters and get away after all. The tree trunks get thicker and closer together, providing cover, and I slow to a trot before stopping completely. Jett drops my clothes, climbs down, then helps Logan.

I shift back and pull on my dress, leggings, socks, and boots, but my jacket is missing. I turn and find Logan lying on his side. Jett's hovering over him, my jacket bundled up in his hand and pressed down on Logan's back. I drop to my knees beside them. "W-what happened to him?" I stutter, though the answer is obvious.

"They shot him. Their final shot. They got him, Flo."

Their final shot. Logan isn't moving, isn't making a sound. "Will he be—?"

Jett shakes his head. "Silver bullet," he says. His eyes shine and he looks away. "Where are the others?"

I stand just as Lucas and Lance duck under a bush and join us. Lucas sees us first. He stops. "What happened?"

Lance runs the extra distance and skids to his knees on the other side of Logan. He takes over holding my jacket as Jett stands and backs away. The two of us move back to give the brothers some space. I remember Dale telling me how it feels to be shot by one of the hunters' guns: *Imagine someone piercing your skin all the way through with a red-hot poker.* Logan was feeling that and I didn't even know it'd happened.

Jett puts his arm around me and the two of us move farther away. Neither of us says a word. We stay together now, holding each other, and that's enough.

And we wait. We wait for one of the triplets to come and tell us that Logan is dead.

39

FOOTSTEPS

I don't know how much time has passed when Lucas and Lance come to us.

It seems like seconds.

It seems like hours.

Lucas has his arm draped over Lance's shoulder. He opens his mouth to speak but no words come out. Turning, he presses his forehead to Lance's. They both close their eyes. It feels wrong to watch them and wrong to look away.

A sound distracts me. Footsteps. Coming closer.

Closer.

I hear them first. Then Jett. He grasps my arm. Lance and Lucas realize something's wrong. They stand straighter and listen, too. Someone's coming.

I catch movement in the trees close by. I'm torn between warning them off and staying still and quiet. They turn, then, and look right at us. And I recognize them. Before I know what I'm doing, I'm running straight for them.

"Owen!" I shout. "Ursula!"

The others follow me. Owen and Ursula run to meet us, too. The two of them crash into me and wrap their

arms around me, gathering me into a hug. I'm both star-
tled and comforted, and I hug them back, holding tight.

"We knew it was you when we saw you by that cabin,"
Ursula stays, stepping back. She goes around me to hug
Jett, then the triplets. She freezes when she realizes there
aren't three of them. What are you supposed to call triplets
who have lost a sibling? Twins? Or do they remain triplets?
I think of Logan, lying in the woods, a bullet hole in his
back. I can't imagine what Lance and Lucas must be feeling right now.

"We panicked when we saw the hunters," Owen says
after a long stretch of silence. "We were searching for
friends who are missing from our group and wound up
outside the cabin. We ran as soon as the hunters spotted us,
but not before we saw you five." He falters. "Um . . . four."

Ursula looks at her brother, eyes wide. "He didn't mean
that insensitively," she tells us.

Owen shakes his head. "No. I didn't. Really. I'm sorry.
It's just . . . what happened?"

"I'll tell you later," I say, to save the brothers from
explaining Logan's death. Owen and Ursula nod at the
same time. "Will you take us back to your new pack? Can
you do that?"

They nod again, like they've forgotten how to speak. I
sigh with relief. We could actually find a new home with
this pack. Running into Ursula and Owen is the first good
thing that's happened to us in days.

"Lead the way," Jett says. He gestures for Lance and
Lucas to go first, then we follow. I'm finally following

someone I trust. I finally feel like I'm going in the right direction.

I hope to be reunited with Star and Ruby and any other circus shifters who joined this new pack. I can't help thinking of Logan and Pru, though. The tigers in the woods. The shifters we've lost. Where we were. Where we are.

The air is cold as we weave between the trees. I wrap my arms around myself. I'm shivering without my jacket. Noticing, Jett shrugs his off and wraps it around my shoulders.

"What's the bandage on your arm for?" he asks. I look down at my hands. One is pink and shiny, and my wrists are still scabby and sore. The white material over the wound on my arm is speckled with red. "The hunters injected me with silver after I shifted and tried to free you."

Jett stops. He looks suddenly furious. "*Where?*" he demands.

I wiggle the bandage down and show him the inside of my arm. The bandage really does need changing, but the wound is healing well. "Ava cut it out."

Jett holds my arm gently, keeping his grip away from the cut. He rubs his thumb over unmarked skin and frowns. "Why did she cut it out for you?"

"She was trying to help me," I say. "The silver was stopping me from shifting. She planned to get the five of us out this morning and needed us to be able to shift. But I guess things didn't quite go as planned when the hunters came for us."

I don't say what I'm thinking: that Jett almost died. I never want to think about that again.

"She still saved us, though," Jett says, walking again. I match his pace. "I just don't understand what Ava was doing there in the first place. She wasn't captured, Flo. I saw her in the cabin talking to the hunters right before we were caught. I think she was in on it."

I don't want to tell him about our parents.

I don't want to tell him that Hari, Nora, and Ava found us, told the hunters where we were, let them kill our parents, then kept us for the circus.

I don't want to tell him that the people who raised him are the people who're responsible for the death of his family. For that horrible night he remembers parts of. For the scars that line his stomach. And the new ones on the rest of his body.

I don't want to tell him about their deal and the whole reason we were being held inside the cabin.

I don't want to tell him any of it, but he has a right to know.

So I take a deep breath and start from the beginning.

40
AN ABANDONED
WAREHOUSE

"We joined a new pack after everything went to hell," Ursula says.

She walks beside Jett and me while Owen talks to Lance and Lucas. "I worried about you," I tell her. "And Owen. I've been thinking about all of you. Then when we visited Iris and she tried to send us away, she told us you'd called on her and she'd sent you to a new pack. We were so relieved to hear you were alive, weren't we?" I say, looking up at Jett.

He nods. "More than." He's been quiet since I told him the elders' secret, and I've given him the space to think.

"Who else is with you?" I ask Ursula.

"Star and Ruby. That's all. We saw others escape, though. Itch and Oscar got out. The rest of Star's group went with the baboons. We tried to catch up with them but it never happened. We don't know where they are."

"And where are you?" I ask. "Staying, I mean."

"In an abandoned warehouse for now. We're almost there," Ursula says and then walks ahead to speak to her brother.

A short walk and we arrive at the warehouse. It is perfect. There's a chain-link fence running around the entire perimeter, for keeping people out—or at least making it more difficult for them to get in. The building itself is a six-story block with wide windows and a flat roof, ideal for keeping lookout.

Ursula opens the gate and ushers us through. "Don't worry," she says. "The guard dogs won't come near us. They got one whiff and ran the other way the first night we came here. We hear them barking, but we haven't seen them. Think of them as our own personal alarm system—if anyone comes snooping around, it'll set them off and we'll know right away." She wiggles her eyebrows.

"Perfect," I say. "No actual guards?"

"I'm just getting to that. This place is set to come down in three weeks, so our stay here will be tragically short. Tragic because, as you said, it's perfect for what we need right now. There are guards who come to see to the dogs and check the warehouse. They're absolutely useless. But they'll start setting up for demolition soon, so once the equipment and office buildings start coming in, I doubt they'll be as easy to fool. We need to be gone by then."

I nod. "I'm glad you found your way here, to this group. I'm just sorry you're mixed up with hunters again so soon."

Ursula shrugs. "What can you do?"

Stepping onto the grounds, I feel the safest I have in days. We follow Ursula and Owen to a heavy metal door. She bangs on it three times, reminding me of my underground cell. I shake my head, refusing to think about it.

The door opens with a groan and Star stands in the doorway. She looks past Ursula and Owen, spots Lance and Lucas. Her eyes grow wide. Her mouth opens in surprise when her gaze finds Jett and me. She rushes out of the building and throws herself at me. I pick her up, even though she's a bit too big to be picked up now. She wraps her long legs around my waist. Everything hurts—my hand, my arm, my legs, my stomach—but I hold her anyway, squeezing her tight.

Star leans back and touches my cheek. "It's really you," she whispers.

Jett takes her from me and spins her around. She squeals in delight. "Are you going to show us your new house?" he asks her.

She grins up at us. "Right this way," she says formally, and we follow her inside.

The building smells of old leather, metal, and mildew. I wrinkle my nose. "Shoe factory," Owen says, picking up an old boot and tossing it behind him.

There's an elevator with an OUT OF ORDER notice on it and a set of stairs beside it. "Fifth floor," Star says, and we start to climb.

"Why fifth?" I ask.

"There are rats on sixth, and it's mostly controls and machines up there. Fifth is more . . . officey," Star says.

Owen laughs. "What she means is, fifth is more comfortable."

Star nods. "That's what I said."

The fifth floor is a huge open space. Wooden floorboards, old leather sofas, upturned boxes serving as tables, a fire inside a metal trash can. There are familiar and unfamiliar faces sitting in a circle around the fire. All of them turn to look at us. I count eleven, which includes Star, Owen, and Ursula.

One girl stands and makes her way over to us. Recognition sparks at the back of my mind, but I don't know where I've seen her.

"I remember you," Lucas says. "You came to the circus."

Lola nods. "My sister Kanna and I came looking for a new pack to join. Your elders turned us away."

Kanna and Lola are beautiful. Both with dark skin and golden-brown hair, their eyes framed by thick lashes. I remember seeing them both talking to the triplets at the camp. The elders broke up the chat and sent the triplets away, sending Lola and Kanna away shortly after. There was a man with them, too. A quick glance behind Lola and I spot him sitting in front of one of the sofas.

I look back at Lola. "Hi," I say. "I'm Flo. A horse."

Lola nods. "Impressive. I've never met a horse. Kanna and I are parrots."

"Impressive," I repeat. "I've never met a parrot. I saw you in the sky."

"And I saw you on the ground," she says with a grin. "I'm glad to know you made it out. But not all of you are here . . . ?"

Lucas and Lance stiffen beside me. "No," I say. "We lost someone. I don't think we're ready to talk about that." I glance at the brothers, wondering if what I said was right. Lucas catches my eye and nods.

"Very well," Lola says. "I'm sorry for your loss."

Ruby stands up by the fire. She waves shyly and I wave back. "Nice to see you, Flo," she says.

"You, too."

"Let me introduce you to everyone else," Lola says, leading us over. "This is Kanna." They look almost identical and I wonder if they're twins when Lola adds, "I'm two years older." I nod to Kanna, remembering their parrot shapes—beautiful exotic birds with feathers of shimmering color.

Lola perches on the arm of one of the sofas. "You know Ruby, Star, Owen, and Ursula. This is Jax and Hugo. White tigers." I take a moment to study the two of them. Both look like they're in their twenties and have blond hair and startling blue eyes. Jax has a scar on his jaw.

Lola points at two women, and a girl who looks around my age, pulling my attention away from the tigers. "Tia and Dee are cheetahs," she says. Both have sleek black hair that reaches their hips in shiny waves. "And Ebony is a bear." Ebony has lots of freckles and big brown eyes. She smiles at me and I return it. Her red hair is jagged and messy like she cut it herself.

"And that's everyone," Lola says. "Except Rowena and Chase. They're lions, but they're not here. We don't know where they are. We were looking for them when we found you."

"What if the hunters come here looking for the horse?" Kanna says so abruptly that all anyone can do is stare at her. "What if they've led the hunters here? Ursula, you should have never—"

"*Kanna*," Lola hisses. "They haven't. It's okay. And her name is Flo, not 'the horse.'" She turns to me. "I'm sorry, Flo. Please excuse Kanna's—"

"I want them to go," Kanna cuts in.

"They aren't going anywhere," Lola snaps. She turns to us again. "Please, excuse my sister. Take a seat anywhere you like."

Lucas and Lance sit on the floor in the corner, leaning back against the wall. Their position is out of the light and warmth of the fire and I understand that they want to be left alone. Jett and I sit on one of the old sofas, Star between us. Owen perches on the armrest beside me.

"You should know, the hunters are already aware you're in the area," I say. "The elders—the leaders of our circus— were working alongside them, and I overheard Ava telling one of the hunters she'd spotted a white tiger and a parrot in the area. Then they saw you in the woods. They were looking for you, but I don't think they know where you're staying. I never heard anything about the warehouse . . . but I was locked up and alone most of the time."

Fourteen people sit staring back at me. "The elders were . . ." Lucas starts but doesn't finish. Owen and Ursula whisper between themselves. Star stares up at me, but I'm not sure she fully understands. I'm not sure any of them do.

"Looks like we had a lucky escape, then," Kanna says. "More than once. Let's hope our luck lasts now the newbies are here, and the hunters are probably not far behind them."

"The hunters could have followed any one of us, Kanna," Lola says. "Most of us were spotted tonight by the cabin. Many of us chased. We have the fence and the dogs. If they come, we'll know." Lola looks from Kanna to me. "Carry on, Flo. And don't leave anything out."

I wonder how many times I'll have to tell this story. I take a deep breath and start from the beginning. Again.

41

DREAM OF THEM

"So no cheetahs were mentioned?" Lola asks.

I rub my eyes. "Not that I heard, but that doesn't mean they weren't."

"But you definitely heard them talking about parrots and white tigers?"

I nod. "Definitely."

"This is bad. I'm certain they took Ro and Chase. We had no idea we were so close to them. A hunter facility a stone's throw away. We're going to have to move sooner than we wanted to."

"We can't go without Chase and Ro!" Hugo exclaims. "We can't abandon them."

"I think you're right—they do have your friends. And if they don't yet, the elders have them held somewhere. Ava said she had found two shifters. She planned to exchange them to free some of us," I say.

"Ro is my ex," Tia says. "I'm not abandoning the search. If you all leave, I'm staying. I care too much about her to do that."

Lola holds her hands up. "Let's just have a time-out. Nothing's been decided. We'll work something out, Tia, don't worry."

I turn my hands over and over until the skin feels raw. I lean back, sinking into the sofa. "You look tired," Owen says.

"I am," I reply.

"Are you all right, though?"

"Better," I say. "Thanks."

"The triplets . . ." He breaks off. "I mean, um, Lance and Lucas—what happened? Is there anything we can do?"

I shake my head no. "Logan's gone, Owen," I say, lowering my voice.

Owen rubs a hand over his face. "And Lance and Lucas—is there anything we can do for them?"

I look over at the brothers, sitting together on the other side of the room. "I don't think so," I reply. "Not yet."

"Okay," Lola says, clapping her hands together and calling us back to attention. "There's nothing we can do right now—not without seriously thinking things over *without* arguing. That cabin is dangerous, and if that's where Ro and Chase are, then we need to plan a rescue attempt if there's going to be one. Let's allow our new friends to rest. We'll talk more when they've regained some of their energy and see what we come up with. Sound good?"

Half-hearted nods and mumbles respond.

"Good," Lola says. "I think we all need to recuperate." She turns to Jett and me. "Are you hungry? We've had dinner, but we can scrape together something else for you."

I shake my head, curling up on my side to rest. Star helps make something for Jett, though. I'm glad he's eating—he needs to.

I wonder where the elders are now. *Does* Ava know about this place, know who's here? And just how long will it take either the elders or the hunters to track us down? I'm worried for my new friends. I'm worried for the old ones, too.

I look around the room—two parrots, two cheetahs, two white tigers, two elephants, two bears, two zebras, a seal, a half-shifter, and a horse. Seeing so many with brothers and sisters and cousins makes me envious that I've never had that—I've never known any family of my own. Up until recently, I thought they were dead, and now I don't even know. I'm trying not to think too much about them, or about the people we've lost. I don't think my brain can handle it right now. But when I close my eyes, I can't help but picture them. And I dream of them when I finally fall asleep.

I dream about Logan, about Pru, about my faceless parents. We're at Violet Bay beach, sitting on the sand, watching the waves, all of us. Jett, Lucas, and Lance included. Logan, too. We watch the sky turn purple. How I wish dreams could become reality. I wish I could erase the past week, the past year, my whole lifetime, and start over. But then I wouldn't have Jett. I wouldn't know him.

I open my eyes. He's there. Beside me. His head back, his eyes closed.

The fire burns down, its orange glow fading. Shifters settle around it, around me, in this safe place they're calling home. For now.

Owen moves and I press my forehead into the arm of the sofa and stretch my legs out over Jett's lap. He stirs, and I feel bad for disturbing his sleep. But he looks down and smiles, running a hand over my calf. He leaves it there and leans back, closing his eyes again. I close mine, and this time I don't dream.

42
ANYTHING FOR YOU

I wake to the sound of a debate.

"Nowhere around here is safe for us now," Hugo says. "Not if the hunters know who we are. *Especially* not if they know where we are."

"I've already told you I'm not going anywhere without Chase and Ro," Tia says.

"Then what do you suggest?" Lola asks, her voice strained. I wonder how long this has been going on for—how much have I slept through and missed?

"We stay and carry on as normal," Dee suggests. "We don't know how much information they have on us. If we're extra cautious in continuing our search for Chase and Ro, who's to say the hunters will ever find out who and where we are?"

I sit up. "And what if they do? What if they already know?" I say.

"What do you mean?" Dee asks.

"I'm sorry," I say. "But Jett and I were careful and we still got caught. We're too close to the hunters here. All right for a couple of days, a week at most, but I'd start looking for other places, even while you keep looking for Rowena and Chase."

Dee narrows her eyes and turns away from me.

"Who made you the boss?" Kanna snaps, breaking a heavy silence.

"It's just a suggestion," I say with a sigh, already growing tired of Kanna's attitude.

"Well, thanks for the *suggestion*," she says. "But I say we should go after them now. We've got people who've been on the inside. We could end this *tonight*. We could find our friends and get rid of the hunters who took them."

"They'd never expect it," Tia says.

"I'm not doing that!" Lola argues. "There's no way. We don't even know for sure that the hunters have them yet!"

Kanna snaps at Lola. Jax and Tia begin to argue, too. Hugo leans his head back against the wall and closes his eyes. Ruby comes and sits by me. "You okay?" she asks.

I nod. "Fine. You?"

"I'm doing okay. It's just a lot to take in, you know? And I'm not even really a shifter," she says sadly.

"Yes you are," I say. "Ruby, you are."

She tilts her head. "Really, Flo? Am I? I don't transform into anything."

"You still change. You still have that ability. And it doesn't matter how much, because you *are* one of us."

She gives me a small smile. "Thanks, Flo."

I put my hand on hers. All I've been thinking about is how *I* don't belong, how *I'm* different and have no family. But what must Ruby be feeling?

"My parents were horses," Ruby says.

I look at her. "What? *Really?*"

She nods. "I was four when I joined the circus. Nora was disgusted, said I was useless, but Ava thought up the job for me and, when I was old enough, they trained me on the entrance. They taught me all about hunters, about what to look for and take note of. I reported to them every time I was suspicious of someone. It was always a false alarm at first. I suspected everyone," she says with a short laugh. "The elders said my job was important. In return I asked them not to share any of my history. I just wanted to be the half-shifter, the bearded lady, not someone everyone would compare to you."

I swallow. "Would that be so bad?"

"Your shape is beautiful, Flo. I'd give anything to be able to transform."

Tears prick my eyes. "Ruby, I—"

"It's okay," she says. "I don't want anyone feeling sorry for me. And I still don't want anyone to know. Just you and me, all right?"

"All right," I agree. She pushes herself up off the sofa. "Ruby." She turns. "Thank you for telling me. I'm glad you did."

She nods once. "Now neither of us are alone in what we are." She looks around the room. "Not quite."

Ruby goes back to where Star is sitting, ignoring the rowing shifters around her. I stand up while they're all distracted and head for the door. Jett follows, and I carry on up the stairs to the top of the building. I need some air.

It's freezing on the roof. Jett rubs his hands up and down my arms to warm me but it doesn't really work. He used to wrap his scarf around my neck. I loved that scarf. It was so warm and smelled of him. I wonder where it is now, then realize what a stupid thing it is to think about. Wondering where an item of clothing is when I don't even know where half the circus members are.

My teeth are chattering but I want to stay up here. I want to stay away from the arguing for a moment and clear my head. What are we doing here? What are we getting ourselves into? Are we really going to go marching back through the woods to the cabin with these people to save shifters we don't even know?

"What're you thinking about?" Jett asks.

I lean against his chest. "Everything," I say.

"Me, too."

I want to tell him about Ruby, but it's not my secret to share. I kind of like it just being Ruby and me who know we're the same shape. I've never met another horse.

The clang of the metal door hitting the brick makes me jump. I look over as the door swings on its hinges and frames Lucas. "I think a search party is going out for Chase and Ro—are you two coming?"

I haven't spoken to Lance or Lucas since Logan's death. It's hard to know what to say when someone so close dies. Jett leans down and whispers in my ear. "You go inside. I'm just going to speak to Lucas."

I leave the two of them together and make my way back down to the fifth floor. Glancing back, I see Jett with a hand on Lucas's shoulder, the two of them talking. About Logan?

Downstairs, I sit on the sofa between Ebony and Ursula. "What's going on?" I ask.

"Kanna told us about another building she saw near the cabin. They're wondering if Ro and Chase are in there," Ursula says. "We don't know for sure Ava gave them to the hunters, right?"

"Right," I say. "Are you going?"

"No. I went last time. Kanna's taking Tia, Dee, and Ebony."

"I'll go," I say.

Ursula shakes her head. "You're not invited."

I swallow, not sure how to respond. Why am I not invited? Because Kanna's leading the group? As if Ursula can read my mind she says, "Don't take it personally."

"I'm not," I lie.

"I know Kanna seems horrid when you first meet her, but she's actually all right. She's just . . . angry is all. I don't know her well enough yet to explain it, that's just the impression I get. Lola reins her in when she goes off on one."

"I noticed," I say with a half smile. I watch Kanna with Lola now as Lola prepares her for leaving. Ebony stands and joins them, leaving Ursula and me alone. "Does it make things easier, having Owen around?" I ask, thinking again about the shifters who still have connection to family. "A part of your family who'll always be there and always has been."

"Yes," Ursula replies without hesitation. My shoulders drop. "But even though you have no family from before, we're your family now. And you have Jett, who quite clearly adores you, by the way. He'd do anything for you, Flo. The way he looks at you . . ."

I smile just as Jett walks back into the room with Lucas by his side. Our eyes meet and Jett returns my smile, thinking it's for him. And it is. It always is.

43

WHILE WE WAIT

Lola paces in front of the windows, watching the sky.

I sit quietly, eating a bowl of soup Star made for me. Hugo and Jett are on another couch, talking about what happens next. Lucas and Lance are in the corner again. I watch the room, watch Lola pacing, and wonder how long it'll be until Kanna, Dee, Tia, and Ebony return.

Ursula sits down beside me. "Hi again," she says.

I swallow a mouthful of the warm soup. "Hi," I say.

"I hurt Pru once, you know. Shifted and bit her."

I nod, unsure what to say. I told Ursula about the tigers on our journey to the warehouse. About Lexi and Maria in the woods. About Pru and the crash. She didn't say anything when I told her, and I wonder if she's been thinking about it since.

"She made my life hell after that," Ursula continues. "I tried to apologize, but she wouldn't accept."

"Why are you telling me this?" I ask, putting my bowl down on the floor.

Ursula shrugs. "I don't know. I was just thinking about her. She was pretty awful, but I wouldn't wish her dead. I thought everyone was dead, you know. After the circus fire.

Ruby, Star, Owen, and I went straight to Iris's. We couldn't believe it when she turned us away, and when she told us no other shifters had come to her for help. Then she sent us here, to this pack. They're nice, most of the time, and it could be so much worse. Do you remember that story in the newspaper? The bears that attacked a guy outside his home?"

"Yes. It was close to Violet Bay. The hunters got the bears."

"The hunters went after the rest of the pack, too, apparently. Kanna and Lola left with Tia, Dee, Ebony, Chase, and Ro before things got ugly. Jax and Hugo weren't far behind, but had a couple near misses."

"Did I hear my name?" Hugo says, sitting in front of us.

"I was just telling Flo about your old pack," Ursula confesses.

"Ah, yes," Hugo says. "The bears were terrible. They all were, really. They had little or no control over their animal selves. We'd been struggling living among them for some time. Some members of the pack did the most awful things and never showed an ounce of remorse. When hunters finally tracked us down, taking out the two bears, we decided we had to move on. I don't know if anyone else was caught or if they got away. We only stayed with the pack so long because we thought it'd be dangerous to leave. Turns out it was just as dangerous, if not more so, to stay put. We've been doing fine on our own . . . or we had been until Chase and Ro went missing."

"They should be back by now," Lola says from by the window.

"Don't worry," Jax says, moving in to comfort her. "I'm sure they're fine."

"But the hunters—"

"They know the hunters know about us now," Jax says. "That knowledge is a good thing. They'll be more careful not to be seen. They'll be fine."

"I made you some soup, Lola," Star says, holding a bowl up to her. "Why don't you come sit with us?" she suggests. "While we wait."

Lola takes one last look at the sky and joins us on the sofas. "Okay," she says. "While we wait."

44

BROKEN GLASS

A faint glow from the fire fills the room.

Tia and Dee return without Kanna and Ebony. "Chase and Ro weren't there. They had been, though. I found Ro's string bracelet," Tia says. Tear tracks line her cheeks. "Hunters came as we left the outbuilding. Four of them. They took Kanna and Ebony. We tried to help them but there wasn't anything we could do."

"What will they do to them?" Dee asks, wiping her eyes. "To little Ebony?"

I shake my head. I can't tell her. Partly because I don't know. And partly because what I do know will bring her no comfort.

Lola covers her mouth and starts sobbing.

"There's no way we can sit back and do nothing now," Tia says. "Not while they have *four* of our group. If it was any of you, you'd want us to come. You'd count on us to come."

"It's a big risk," I say.

"They have my *sister*," Lola cries. "I'm going after her whether you're coming or not."

"I didn't say we weren't. There's just a lot to think about."

"While they torture my sister."

"We can't go until we're ready," Jax says.

"What does that even mean? When we're ready?" Lola demands. "What are we doing to get ready?"

In the yard outside, the dogs start barking.

Everyone in the room stiffens, alert. "Who's on lookout?" I ask.

"Star and Ruby are on the roof," Ursula says. She grabs Owen by the arm and the two of them head up to the rooftop. I dash to the window and squint into the darkness, searching for intruders. I can't see anyone out there, though. I can't see the dogs, either.

"Come on," Lola says, heading for the stairwell. "I'm not waiting anymore."

Tia, Dee, Hugo, and Jax follow her, so there's only Jett, Lance, Lucas, and me left in the room. We should talk about this. I think I want to go back. I know I want to do something to help. If it was Star they'd taken instead of Ebony, or Ursula instead of Kanna, I'd want everyone to step up and help, no matter what. As much as I want this whole nightmare to be over, I would never forgive myself if I walked away now. But even though we joined this new group, we're still a group of our own, and there's no reason for all four of us to get mixed up in this, to go running back there. "What are you guys thinking?" I say.

Lance and Lucas glance at each other. "That things are spiraling out of control and the hunters are winning," Lucas says.

I clench my hands into fists by my sides. "They are not winning. They are—"

A continuous popping sound cuts me off. The window beside me shatters.

I freeze for a second, then drop to the ground at the sound of gunfire, landing on shards of broken glass. Big and small pieces are stuck to my palms, caught in my hair.

I hear voices. Shouting. Inside and out. I hear a scream and the sound surfaces memories of Pru, lying facedown in glass like I am now. Will it end this way for me, too?

"Sounds like they're shooting out all the windows," Lucas yells.

"Flo, come on!" Jett shouts, snapping me back into action. I move forward, glass digging into my elbows and knees as I drag my body toward the stairwell.

The stairwell has no windows. If the hunters make it into the building and catch us in one of these rooms or on the stairs, they'll have us cornered. We need to get out fast. A fresh burst of adrenaline pushes me on and I make it to the stairs and stand with Jett, Lucas, and Lance just in front of me.

Star comes running down from the roof. "Go back!" I yell. "And don't let them see you."

She looks like she's about to cry. "But—"

I pull her into a hug. "Go on, Star. Tell the others to stay up there and hide."

She turns and runs back up to the roof without another word. The rest of us run down, forced into the darkness, scattered, unprepared.

We reach the ground floor. Only Hugo and Dee remain in the building, crouching by the door. "Where is everyone else?" I ask, swallowing my terror.

"The trees," Dee says, climbing to her feet.

Everything's gone quiet. The gunfire has stopped, the dogs are no longer barking, the gates are open. I peer out the side of the open door, searching for movement in the darkness. I see something in the trees, but I think it's Jax. I hear the chain-link fence rattle, but I think it's the wind. I hate not knowing.

"Where's Star and co.?" Hugo whispers.

"Roof. They'll be all right. I want her and Ruby in particular to stay out of this. Star's too young and Ruby can't shift. Owen and Ursula will look after them."

"I'm going," Dee says. "To my sister. Are you coming?"

Lance and Lucas go with Dee, dashing across to the fence and out through the open gate. They disappear into the tree line, easy as that. *Where are you?* I think, scanning the courtyard for the hunters. *Where are you hiding?*

"Our turn," Hugo says, slipping through the door. He ushers us out. "Go on."

Jett and I start to run, followed by Hugo. There's a shot as soon as we're out in the open. *There!* The bullet hits an old metal storage container with a deafening clang. Another bang follows just as I reach the trees, allowing the shadows to swallow me up.

I look back and find that Hugo's on the floor. He's not moving.

"*No!*" Jax cries. But it's too late. Two hunters are already swooping in and hauling him up. The other two are heading right for us, guns aimed in front of them.

"We have to go," I say. "*Now.*"

45

NO MORE SPARKLY WAISTCOATS AND HATS

Back in the woods, the night has fallen quiet.

As far as I know, the hunters have gone. But for how long? Jax is bouncing from foot to foot, eager to start moving, to go after Hugo. Lola, Tia, and Dee are just as worked up. We need to talk first, though. The last time a group went out there, Ebony and Kanna were captured.

"Why are we just standing here?" Jax says. "We have to go now!"

"We should think about this," I say. "They've caught someone every time they've attacked."

"And what will they do with them now?" Dee asks.

"There's testing, and . . ." I trail off. Have they become more desperate since our escape? They were taking Lucas and me to the labs, killing the others, so what are they willing to do since that failed? Who's going to the labs, and who's going to die? They're not likely to waste any time in moving the ones they want and disposing of the ones they don't. A decision needs to be made fast—but what is the right one? At least there are more of us this time, working together. We outnumber the four hunters.

"Flo?" Lola says, her voice high with panic. "What is it?"

"I don't know how much time we have." I turn to Jax. "You're right. We have to go. Just . . . just be careful, stay hidden. Don't let them see us until we're ready to be seen. If we attack as a team, we've got the numbers to overpower them if we move fast."

Lola nods sharply. "I'll fly ahead. Scout out the cabin and find you before we go in."

"Good idea," Jax says. "But be careful."

"You, too," Lola says. She bursts from the ground in a spiral of color, heading up into the sky. Her clothes fall off her bird form and land in a heap on the ground. She flexes her clawed feet and flies up over the trees and toward the cabin, anxious to find her sister.

The cabin is a soft glow in the distance.

We're almost there, almost back in the place where I was sure I would die. I guess there's still a chance that I will.

I've been wondering what we'll find when we get there—who we'll find. I hope those we left behind are safe. Owen and Ursula will make sure Star and Ruby are okay, that they hid in time and stayed hidden. They had plenty of warning.

Ro, Chase, Kanna, Hugo, and Ebony, I'm not so sure about. And if they are still alive, and being held in the underground cells, freeing them won't be easy. There's no turning back, though. I'm a part of this now.

"This is it," Jax says. He removes his clothes and stashes them in a bush. He shimmers out of focus as he shifts. Two legs become four. His eyes become ice-blue cat's eyes, not far off their color when he's human. His cheeks sprout whiskers. A beautiful coat of pure white and incredible dark markings take the place of his human skin. He has four large paws with razor-sharp claws and an enormous jaw with huge fangs. He is amazing—both gorgeous and terrifying.

Tia and Dee transform into sleek and slender cheetahs. Their spotted fur is beautifully glossy. They both stretch out their long, graceful bodies and hiss, watching the rest of us with their piercing yellow eyes.

They all go ahead, leaving Lucas, Lance, Jett, and me behind to change. "Everyone all right?" Jett asks.

I swallow. "I am."

"Us, too," Lucas says, bumping his shoulder against Lance's.

"And are you sure you want to do this?" Jett says.

I don't *want* to, but I'm going to. I'm not walking away until we're done here. "I am," I say again. "I have to help."

"I want to make them pay for what they did to Logan," Lucas says. "For what they did to all of us."

Lance and Lucas exchange a nod. They step apart, close their eyes, and grow wider and taller, becoming elephants. They shake, flapping their ears, then stomp away into the trees.

Jett squeezes my hand and pulls me to him. "Stay with me," he says. I'm pressed up against his body, wrapped in his arms. I wish I could just stay here like this forever, never move from this spot. "Stay close."

"I will," I whisper, meeting his eyes. "You, too."

Jett pulls his T-shirt over his head and unzips his jeans. I remove my own clothes and stash them with his. Then I close my eyes and concentrate on my shape.

For a moment I'm whipped off the earth, away from the chaos, away from the cabin. I'm surrounded by nothing, frozen then heated. When I open my eyes I'm back in the woods, standing beside a brown bear with claws like knives. No more sparkly waistcoats and hats for us. No more small bikes or flaming hurdles.

We carry on toward the cabin as animals.

46

GIRL TO HORSE

I watch the sky.

As we approach the hunters' cabin, I see Lola up there, circling. She comes into view, then disappears behind a tree. I start to wonder what it'd be like to fly—

Then I hear the first shot. I stop. Jett does the same, flinching at the loud bang.

Lola comes back into view, diving rapidly to the ground. I hurry forward to meet her. Before hitting the forest floor, she transforms back into a human and lands on her feet. She's panting, holding her hands out in front of her while she catches her breath. "I'm . . . fine." We crowd around her. "They . . . know we're . . . here."

I'd worked that much out for myself. *So what now?*

"They've only seen me," Lola continues after steadying her breathing. "They're ready for us, though, so be careful."

I have a sudden, horrible feeling that the hunters have purposefully lured us here. They tracked us to the warehouse, and even though most of us got away, they took Hugo instead of killing him there and then. Which makes me think they haven't killed the others yet, either, despite what I assumed earlier. They want us to come looking for them. They're using our friends to round up the rest of us.

I look at Jett, but I can't tell what he's thinking. I want to shift back and speak to him.

Lola jumps into the air, shifting back into her parrot form, and takes to the sky. I shift back to human, urging the others to do the same.

Once we've returned to human form, I tell them what I think—that the hunters purposefully took our friends and wanted us to come. "So the only thing we can do now is be ready for them, too," I say. "I didn't see much when I was in the cabin, but I know they have weapons. Silver bullets, silver-coated guns, nets. They'll use all of these things to slow us down and stop us."

Dee leans against a tree. Tia moves in to comfort her.

"I don't know how we could be ready for that," Jax says.

"So what do you suggest?" Tia asks him. "Give up? I'm not leaving Ro and Ebony with them. Even if we're unsuccessful, we have to try, don't we?"

"Hugo told me about your old pack," I say to Jax. "How they let go, gave in to their animal sides, and let that rule them so much they became a threat."

"They were out of control," Jax says.

"We just need a dose of that. Embrace your animal. Lola's already doing that—she's small, the scout, using her shape to her advantage."

"She was spotted . . ." Jax comments.

"Jax," Dee scolds. "Not helpful."

I hold my hands up. "This could help, if we use our individual abilities, if we give in to instinct and draw strength from our animals. Give in to your predator sides. Become the hunter instead of the hunted. With the numbers in our favor, and heightened animal skills paired with human brains, we *could* beat them. They don't have the abilities we have."

"They have weapons, though," Jax says, still unsure. I don't know how else to convince him.

"We have to believe we can do it, Jax," I say.

He shakes his head. "Right. You're right."

Tia steps forward and claps him on the back. "We can," she whispers. "We'll get Hugo back. And Chase and Ro, Ebony, and Kanna. We have to do it for them."

Tia and Dee shift back to cheetahs and take off again. Jax follows suit.

I look at Lance and Lucas, they nod. "Nice speech. Good luck, you two."

"Be safe," Jett says before they shift. He turns to me. "It really was. Do you believe we can save everyone, too?"

"We got out once," I say. "And we're at an advantage this time. I think we can."

"Good," he says. "So do I."

He leans forward, kisses me lightly, then steps back and shifts. I smile up at him and call on my own shape. But as soon as I've transformed, I hear a high-pitched yelp up ahead. Once I catch up, I find that one of the cheetahs has her paw caught in a bear trap. The hunters are obviously resorting to new means of catching us. I imagine Jett's foot in the trap and shudder.

The cheetah shifts into Dee, crying out in pain and clutching her leg. Tia shifts, too, and kneels down beside Dee. "Help me get this off her," Tia pleads.

I shift back and drop to my knees by Dee's leg. I gag and cover my mouth when I see the metal has sliced right though, puncturing gaping holes in her leg. Tia holds Dee's shoulder while Dee cries and begs me to pull it off. I put my hands around the metal, slick with Dee's blood, and try to pull it apart. Dee screams.

"Try again," Tia insists.

"I need help! Hold this side down. Jett?" He shifts and crouches down beside me. "You take this side." I put pressure on the release but it's holding out. I push, and Dee starts to scream. Tia covers her mouth. "Shh," she soothes. "We'll get it off you."

I hear a squelching sound as it starts to give, and Tia and Jett both help pry it open. Jax shifts and pulls Dee back as soon as the jaw is clear of her leg.

Gunshots fill the air again. "We have to keep moving," Jett says, shifting before Tia can argue. I do the same. The shift back to horse makes me feel nauseous. I haven't shifted from girl to horse, girl to horse, repeatedly in such a short period of time before.

Jax shifts back again, too, but Tia hesitates. "Go," Dee says, which comes out as barely a whimper. "Get Ebony, then come back."

Tia leans close to Dee. "I will be back for you," she says and kisses Dee's forehead. "When I have Ebony, I'll be back. I promise you."

Dee nods and lies back, crying silently. Tia stands and wipes her eyes, then shifts back into a cheetah. With a fierce growl, she runs for the cabin. I lose sight of her in seconds. Tia and Jax will get there first, I assume. Jett and I aren't too far behind, but I walk a little more cautiously since seeing the bear trap, looking out for any others on the way to the cabin.

When we stop, Jett and I find a spot to hide and watch, with no idea what the plan is now that we're here. Attack as one, or wait to see what the hunters do?

There's a lone hunter outside the cabin, his back to the open door. Ethan.

Where are the other three?

I have such an awful feeling in my stomach that has nothing to do with shifting so much.

Ethan watches the sky. He holds his gun pointed upward, trying to get aim on Lola and shoot her down. All around me is deadly silent. The elephants stand slightly farther back, being bigger and more noticeable than the rest of us. Tia and Jax are closest. Tia's crouched low. She looks ready to pounce.

Don't, I think. *Not yet.*

But Tia growls and stalks out into the clearing. Ethan whistles as soon as he sees her, and the other three hunters come out of the cabin and join him.

Four hunters.

Four guns.

All pointed at Tia.

She starts to run, drops low, pounces, throwing herself at the line of hunters. Quick as a flash. But they knew she was going to do that. I can see it in their confidence, their stance, their expressions. They point their guns right at Tia's chest and pull the triggers. Shots cry out into the night, rattling the silence, vibrating the earth. And the cheetah falls.

47

COATED RED

I think we are going to die.

The realization hits me. Six against four now.

The silence rings in my ears as loud as the shots. Smoke still rises from the barrels of the guns, curling in the air, twining and fluttering and disappearing like they were never there. I'm frozen in this wavering moment. It's like the earth has stopped spinning. I wish it would.

They know we're here now. They know we're hiding in the trees—they saw where Tia came from. The hunters hold their guns out for a second time and shoot blindly at the tree line.

We scatter into the woods.

I am separated from the others. Alone. Just how the hunters would want us. And just when I think it can't get worse than being lost and alone with bullets whizzing every which way, the hunters chase us into the trees, spreading out.

I run fast. I don't even know what direction I'm going in, I just *go*. I need to get away, take a moment to gather my thoughts and figure out what to do next.

When I think I'm far enough away, I shift back to human and press my back against a thick tree trunk. The bark is cold and scratches my bare back. I don't know where the others are. I don't know where the hunters are. My breathing is too loud. I put my hand over my mouth to mute the sound, but it only makes it worse.

A growl close by startles me. Then Jax skids out in front of me, the moonlight bouncing off his snow-white fur. He growls again at the hunters who approach him. Dale and another hunter hold a silver net between them, edging closer to Jax. I press my back harder against the tree trunk and move out of sight, just as they throw the net over him.

Jax writhes on the ground under the silver. It's burning, burning, burning, and I'm just watching. *I'm just watching.* But what do I do? What *can* I do?

The hunters stand over him. Dale pulls a gun from his belt. Jax shifts back to human under the silver; he withstood it for longer than I could have. He'll be dizzy now, sick, disorientated. When I was sucked out of my shape, I didn't even know what was happening around me. He'll be dead before he has a chance to realize.

I have to do *something.*

I shift back into a horse and charge at the hunters. I crash right into them and the gun goes off, but I don't know which direction the bullet travels. I haven't got time to stop to find out. I shift again, and run to Jax.

I take the net in both hands. My palms are on fire, melting, but I don't let go—not until I've peeled it off Jax's flesh. He stands up and shakes it off, his skin already healing— the scorching red lines turning a raw shade of pink.

Jax shifts again before I can blink and he's on the hunters in seconds. I don't have time to be impressed by his
resiliency and his strength. Tiger and hunter roll to the side,
bodies locked. The hunter struggles beneath the tiger's
weight. I look away as Jax raises his paw, claws out, and
slashes it down on the hunter. The hunter's screams echo
around me. One down.

Dale shoots Jax in the leg. Jax roars and shifts back, his
thigh coated red with blood. Dale aims again.

"Dale!" I yell, right as he pulls the trigger. A screech
accompanies the gunshot. Dale's head veers to the side and
he drops the gun onto the forest floor. The bullet nicks Jax's
ear. Jax howls and clasps his hand over his ear. The parrot
screeches again, swooping down and clawing at Dale's face,
forcing him to the ground. I go to help, taking the gun
from the floor where he dropped it.

I let go again as soon as my hand curls around the metal.
Silver handle. Of course. I take a deep breath and reach
for it again, prepared this time. It scalds my raw hands. I
shake, pointing the gun at Dale as he fights off Lola. I try
to hold it steady. *He's a hunter*, I tell myself. *He'd kill you
in a second.* Sympathizer or not, he was just about to kill
my friend.

I hesitate, finger on the trigger, when an elephant steps
into the clearing and crushes Dale's head beneath his feet.
I wince at the sound of crunching bones, and the way
the elephant shakes his foot to remove some part of Dale
that's splattered across the bottom of it. I drop the gun and
breathe again.

Jax is slumped against a tree trunk, blood pouring from his leg and dripping from his ear. I crouch by his side and lift his face. "Jax?"

"Thank you, Flo," he whispers, panting. "I'll be fine."

I stand while Lola's still close by. I call out to her. "Help me find Jett!"

Lola squawks in response and flies up higher into the air. I assume she's looking for him. I hope she is. I try to follow in the same direction, but it's not long before I lose sight of her.

The sound of my ragged breathing is all I can hear now. The woods are too quiet. No animals, no wind, no hunters.

I close my eyes and turn to my shape. It's there, on the edge of my being, waiting for me to come back. And I find I like it: how much stronger I feel. The stinging chill freezes my body, my bones prickle, then heat blazes. My coat travels along my bare skin. Then the world comes back, and I'm on four legs.

48

THE BEAR IN THE WOODS

In the darkness between the trees, I don't know which way to go.

Where are you, Jett?

What if he was chased like Jax? What if he's hurt somewhere and alone? What if he's . . .? I let the thought trail off. I can't think like that. I'll find him. I will.

A soft glow draws me to the cabin, forward into the light and out of the dark. I hear fighting and see Lola in the sky again. I rush on. The yellow light from the cabin windows paint the ground a buttery shade. The female hunter is on the ground, her dark hair spilling around her face like a black halo. I don't think she's breathing.

Then I see the last hunter—Ethan—on his feet. Of course *he* would be the last one. He stands over Jett, still in bear form, while Jett tries to get up. The light from the cabin throws their shadows all over the forest floor, stretched and distorted.

I start toward them, watching in horror as Ethan kicks Jett and then pulls a knife from his belt. No. *No!*

I gallop out into the open, push forward with everything I've got and more. But I can't reach him in time, and I know I can't. *No, no, no. I'm too late.*

Ethan brings the knife down and it lands in Jett's chest with a sickening thud.

Jett jerks under the pressure of the knife, arching up, then dropping back down and the hunter pulls it out again. The blade is black with blood, and I'm screaming, screaming, screaming inside. Lola screeches in the sky, an ear-splitting cry.

I charge for Ethan, but he sees me coming. He grabs for his gun, aims, pulls the trigger. It clicks, empty. Ethan drops the gun, turns and runs, and I follow him into the blackness of the trees.

49

INTO THE DARKNESS

It's so quiet.

So quiet. I stop, listen. My mind is flooded with images of Jett on the ground. He's alive. He has to be alive.

But I know he isn't.

I know he won't recover from that. I know he won't wake up.

The realization crashes into me, hard, painful, like the knife struck through me, too. It might as well have—it would hurt less than this.

I know Jett's not coming back, but at the same time I'm thinking that this can't be it. It just *can't* be. His life couldn't have left him so fast, snuffed out by the blade of a knife and the turn of a wrist. Everything Jett is can't be wiped off the planet, just like that.

And yet it was. *No*, I still can't believe it. It's so final, irreversible, and I feel so helpless. I don't know what to do.

I'm frozen in place, in time. I want to go to Jett. I want to sit by his body and cry until I have no tears left, until I'm empty, until the pain goes away.

I begin to shift to human again. I don't know if I do it by choice, or whether the human side of me overpowers the horse in my grief. There's so much about this world I don't understand anymore.

I cover my mouth and hold back a scream as my back cracks audibly. My bones feel like they're going to break, bent at wrong angles and jutting out of my skin. My shoulder's dislocated from the transformation. I try to relocate it myself, but before I can, it clicks back into place and the noise is almost as unbearable as the feeling. My shift is slow, painful.

I throw up on the ground in front of me. Strangled sobs escape my lips. A howl of grief follows, uncontrollable and insistent and full of so much pain.

I hear Ethan before I see him. My outburst must have drawn him to me. He steps out of the shadows. I'm not ready, I can't even breathe, I can hardly stand, so I turn and run, falling into shadows that might buy me some time to gather my strength.

I push through the trees and away from the cabin, away from Ethan, away from Jett. Into the darkness.

I cry as I run, stumbling and falling. My entire body is patched with mud and covered in scratches, but I can't feel their sting. All I feel is loss and the ache of every bone in my body as it completes its transformation, but even that doesn't compare to the pain in my heart. I can't live without him. How can I live without him?

I watched it happen. I watched his life be taken by a *hunter*.

The rage inside me in that moment is like a lightning storm traveling through my body, igniting my fingertips with deadly sparks. It cancels out everything else. I've never felt anything like this. Not even when the hunters caught us and put us in cells. Not even when I found out how my parents had died, and where they may be if not dead. None of that compares to what I feel now.

I stop and fling my arms out, hitting at the tree trunks with my bare hands, causing more scratches and cuts. But I don't care. I don't care. I don't *care* about the splinters or about the blood.

I just want Jett back.

I fall to the ground beside a tree trunk and nurse my injured hands. My body racks with sobs and I feel like it'll never stop. I'm lost.

Lost in these woods. Lost in this world.

I hardly notice the approaching footsteps until they get close. Steady and confident. A part of me really doesn't care anymore. *Let him come*, I think. *Let him kill me.* But I think of Jett again, and I know how much he would hate to see me giving up. So, I stand, I close my stinging eyes, and I call on my shape a final time.

50

STAY CLOSE

I land on my hands and knees, gasping and sweating.

I've attempted it three times now—shifting. I need to be a horse to do this. I need the power my shape brings to end Ethan's life. To make him pay for what he did, for *everything* he's done.

Each of Ethan's footsteps trembles through my body. I'm finally getting my chance to do *something*, to hit back, and I can't shift. The hunters have taken my parents, they've taken Jett's parents, they've captured and tortured my friends and me, they've killed most of the people I know. And now Jett. I have to do this.

Anger sparks with a crash of thunder between my bones, a scorching white fire beneath my skin. Determination pushes in when I hear the hunter's footsteps, so close now. So close that I know where he is. This is it.

My shape comes on my fourth attempt and I see the hunter before he sees me. I charge at Ethan, screaming inside.

I draw close, about to run him down, a deadly blow, when a bear lunges. Ethan slashes the knife, his attention still on me. The blade catches my shoulder. The skin sizzles at its touch and I skid and stumble, falling on my side.

My shape disappears—four legs become two, my arms cracking and shrinking, my body withering and weakening. *No! No, no, no, no.* "Ebony!" I cry. "Stop!"

Ethan turns as a growl rips from Ebony's throat. She swipes at him, but staggers back with an unseen force. *The knife.*

Ebony loses her footing and crashes to the ground. Ethan looks to me, then back at Ebony. He must see her as the more dangerous of two threats because he steps toward her, dagger in hand. My breath falters. No way is he doing this again.

I can't look.

I have to look.

I have to help. Ethan can't kill another bear.

Adrenaline courses through my body, rage churning inside. It takes over. It is everything. And I force myself to my feet.

I throw myself onto Ethan's back, reaching for the dagger. He reacts instantly, trying to throw me off, and we wrestle for it. The bear growls as Ethan tries to buck me off, his grip firm. The silver cuts into my hand. I bite down hard on my lip, determined not to let go. I release a scream as the silver cuts deeper.

Ethan swings again and I fall off him. My feet hit the ground, pain rocketing through my ankles, up my legs. I struggle to stay upright. He pushes me away, but I rush back toward him.

A smile spreads across his face, teasing. He thinks I'm an easy target and he's enjoying this. He's *enjoying* it. I reach for him and miss. With a laugh, he thrusts a hand out, silver winking in the moonlight.

I grab his wrist. Ethan's surprise is clear in his expression and he falters, hesitates for just a moment, and it's enough. It's enough time for me to shove his hand down as hard as I can and plunge the silver weapon deep into his thigh.

Ethan wails. I spin him around, grab his arms and tug, pinning them behind his back, holding him in place. Ebony comes for us. For him. Her teeth can do the rest.

I'm ready to finish him, to finish this. There's blood on Ebony's shoulder, matting in her fur. Ethan's so preoccupied by the knife in his leg, by my arms around him, that he doesn't notice her until it's too late. She rips his throat out. I let go. And he falls in a bloody heap to the ground.

I take one step back, but one is all it takes to send me crashing to my knees. They give with a crack and my head hits hard against the cold ground.

I can't move. Mud and leaves stick to my cheek. I watch Ebony make her way over to me. Blood coats her muzzle. Her teeth are bared, but her eyes are kind. Then the bear shifts to a boy.

I must be dreaming. I must be. I close my eyes. Open them again.

Jett gathers me in his arms and lifts me off the ground. "Didn't I tell you to stay close?" he whispers into my ear. His breath warms my neck and weaves through my hair.

I lean my head against his chest. Relief and confusion battle it out, tears of joy and sadness. I don't know, I don't know. All I know is he's here. He's alive.

I'm shaking so much it's almost painful.

Jett puts me down and I find my feet again. We head back to the cabin together. Lucas comes to meet us. He puts his hand to his heart when he sees us. "You two are alive," he sighs. Lucas holds our clothes out to us with his other hand.

"Just about," Jett says.

Jett and I dress quickly. Lucas holds my elbow to help keep my balance while I pull my leggings and boots on. He lets go when I'm done and I nod my thanks.

I wipe the hair from my eyes and look past Lucas, toward the casualties. Jax is sitting with his back against the cabin, his skin almost as white as his tiger fur, but he's alive. A bear and a cheetah lie side by side on the ground beside him. Tia and Ebony. Their deaths so sudden, meaning there was nothing left to pull them back. They died in their animal form—stuck in their shape forever. A slow, painful death would've caused them to shift to human and die in this form. How we die, in what shape, it matters to us. I suppose it's some comfort that it was quick. No time for suffering. But Ebony and Tia wouldn't want this. No one wants this.

I avert my gaze, Ebony's death replaying in my head. The way the knife sunk in right to the hilt, the way she arched, the sound she made.

"Th-the bear," I say, finally finding my voice. "Ebony."

Lucas turns around and takes a deep breath. "Yeah." He runs a hand through his hair. I notice he's shaking. "Hugo attacked the hunters inside the cabin and Ebony escaped. She went to find help but didn't get very far."

I cover my mouth. Jett rubs my arm and pulls me to him. "I thought she was you," I say against his chest. "I saw her die and I thought she was you."

"I'm here," Jett soothes, stroking my hair. "I'm okay. I'm here."

"But, she died. I watched it happen and I couldn't get to her in time. Where were you?"

"I was looking for you, but the woods were chaos, and everything looks the same. I couldn't find you. I got lost. I followed the sound of Lola's call and then I saw you run into the woods after the hunter. But we found each other. We're okay."

I nod. We are. We're both alive. But Ebony's not. Pru's not. Logan's not. So many of us have died. "Is everyone else okay?" I ask Lucas, suddenly worried that the body count could be higher still.

"Lance is fine. Still picking the hunter from between his toes, though," Lucas says with half a smile. I remember the elephant—Lance—crushing Dale. The sound of his skull breaking.

"Lance is in the cabin now with Lola," Lucas continues. "They went in to find Kanna and Hugo. Lola got shot in the wing, so her arm's messed up pretty bad. The bullet went right through, so it'll have started healing. Tia was shot and killed, Ebony was stabbed and killed, and I went back for Dee, but she ... well, she lost a lot of blood and it's cold out here and it took longer to find her than I thought and ... she's gone, too."

The air has been knocked out of me, squeezed from my lungs. Each word is like a punch in the stomach. *Lola got shot in the wing. Tia was shot and killed. Ebony was stabbed and killed. Dee's gone, too.* The bad news just keeps on coming with each name he mentions.

Lucas clears his throat. "They might need some help, if you feel up to it," he says. "Or you can stay out here with Jax and me and help keep watch."

I glance at the bodies. "We'll go help inside," I say, then look at Jett. He nods. Together, we approach the cabin. The yellow light pours out through the dirty windows, too bright. I cover my eyes, like I've been caught under a spotlight. "I wonder how long we were in here for," I say.

Sudden shouting comes from below and Jett hurries in. He stops in the doorway when he realizes I'm no longer beside him. "They're calling for help," he says. "They must have found Hugo and Kanna."

I take a step back rather than forward, more on instinct than decision.

"Come on, Flo," Jett says, reaching out to me. "I'm with you."

I squeeze my eyes shut. They need our help. I draw a deep breath and step inside the cabin.

51
NEVER HEAL

The smell of rotting wood is overwhelming.

I didn't get to see this part of the building before. It's just one long room, lit by two hanging lights, with a stone chimney and a log fire. There's an old wooden table in the middle of the room, scratched and worn, with four wooden chairs around it. On the table there are walkie-talkies, beer bottles, playing cards, and sheets of paper.

Jett runs ahead to a small trapdoor in the floor and down into the basement where we were held. He doesn't even pause to take any of this in. I pick a piece of paper up from the table and see myself looking back at me. I'm holding a grainy black-and-white photograph of Jett and me on the beach at Violet Bay. An arrow points to me: *Horse, female.* And one points to Jett: *Bear, male.*

"Flo!" Jett calls from below.

"Coming." I rip the paper to shreds, stuff it into my pocket, and then start down the ladder to the basement.

My eyes take a moment to adjust to the brightness of the lights that line the ceiling of the white-tiled corridor, much brighter than those in the cabin upstairs. It seemed so much bigger down here when I was being held captive.

The walls close in on me, and I put my hand against the cold tiles to steady myself. My breathing comes shallow and raspy.

The doors along the corridor are fully open. I take a moment to step inside one, into one of the cells. The lines on my wrists throb with the memory of being here, still pink from the silver. The mark on my arm where Ava cut me is still tender. I will never truly heal from this.

I step out and into the next room. This one was mine. The sheet on the bed is bundled in a bloody heap. There are red streaks on the floor. More blood—the hunter's and mine—from the struggle with the knife. The knife is still here, kicked under the bed and flecked brown with dry blood. I back out before the memories consume me.

I follow the sound of voices out of the room and back down the corridor, counting the doors as I go. The corridor snakes around to the left and I see Jett, Lola, Lance, and Hugo crowded outside the only closed door. The last one. There are only eight rooms down here. When I was in one, I'd imagined hundreds. When I ran through these corridors, I felt like there *were* hundreds. But, no. Just eight. That's it.

Lola is sitting on the floor with her back against the wall. Her hand is bloody, pressed down on her arm where she was shot. Hugo's beside her, pink lines across his face where the silver net must have made contact when they captured him. I put a hand on his arm and he takes it knowingly, giving it a little squeeze.

Lola's crying, cradling her arm to her chest. "She's in there," she weeps when she sees me. "She's lying on the bed and she isn't moving."

"She won't be able to hear you," I say. "Those doors are too thick."

"We've been knocking, too," Jett says, looking concerned. Knocking you can hear, knocking he heard when we were on opposite sides of his cell door. If she's not responding to that, that's not a good sign.

"There should be a swipe key somewhere," I say. "That's what they used to open the doors." I run my finger along the thin gap beside the handle. "I saw when I was down here. Lance, you should go get the others and search the hunters' bodies for the cards," I suggest, because I'm not sure I can do that myself right now. Dale's mush on the forest floor and Ethan's missing his throat. I shake my head and continue, "They're plastic with a sensor band."

"I'll go with him," Hugo says, pushing himself up to his feet with a grunt of pain. "Lola, you stay by the door and keep trying to stir Kanna."

Hugo and Lance are already climbing the ladders. Lola just carries on crying and I'm not sure whether she's actually listening.

"Lola? Are you going to be all right if we go look for the key?"

She nods, barely. "Yes. Go."

Jett and I carry on along the corridor as the path curves. I lead him to the small office where I first discovered Ava's betrayal. I crouched here and watched her kiss a hunter, heard her talk to him about killing shifters. The ripped-up photograph suddenly feels like lead in my pocket, weighing me down. I shudder. This is where they talked about us, our names, our shapes. This is where they plotted against us, discussing ways to kills us, to torture us with their tests and experiments, dispose of the ones who were no use to them.

Jett is holding my arm. His face swims back into focus. "Flo, what is it?"

"Hm?" I say, rubbing my head. "Let's just find the key so we can leave."

We open desk drawers, filing cabinets, look under everything that litters the desk, check all the pockets on the coat rack, with no luck. There's a small fridge on the floor, tucked under one of the desks. I pull it open and find it filled with test tubes of blood. Shifter blood, mine included. The little white labels read: HORSE, FEMALE and BEAR, MALE and ELEPHANT, MALE. I slam the fridge door closed and stand quickly. Angry and frustrated, I move back to the desk drawers.

Hugo comes rushing in, finding Jett and me in the hunters' office. "No luck with the three close by. Lance has gone with Lucas into the woods to find the one you killed," he says and I cringe. *Ethan.*

We continue to search the office until Lucas and Lance come barreling around the corner and into the room. Lance holds two swipe cards out to me. "Try these," he says.

I grab both and dash back down the corridor, skidding to a stop outside Kanna's door. I swipe the first one, which flashes red, then try the second.

Green.

Click. The door opens and Lola scrambles to her feet and bursts inside, almost knocking me over. "Is she okay?" I call after her.

Lola leans over her sister and lets out a sigh of relief. "She's breathing," she says, turning to me and smiling with tear-filled eyes.

52

WANDERERS

I took a group back to the warehouse after we got Kanna out of the cabin.

Jett, Lance, and Lucas came with me to get Star, Ruby, Owen, and Ursula. All four of them were fine. And not only that, they'd become five while we were away. Itch, one of the monkeys from the circus, had found them. He was drawn by the sound of gunfire and waited in the dark until the hunters were gone. He searched the warehouse and found the others hiding.

He told us more about the circus that we hadn't known. All the monkeys were taken or killed. My stomach twists when I think of Oscar. When I think of all of them. They got pretty far, but not many of the circus members got out completely—the hunters caught up. Itch was one of the last to leave; he saw more than any of us. He went to Iris, too, and found the pack with her information. So it's likely we are all that's left then.

I wonder what'll happen to Rain. I kind of wish we could go get her. It's too late now, though—too risky to reconnect with that life with the elders still out there. Last time I saw them, they were fighting the hunters. Then they ran. I wonder if we'll ever see them again. I hope not.

Back at the cabin, Hugo and Jax bury Tia, Dee, and Ebony. Jett goes to help them dig, while Lance and Lucas follow our earlier path in search of Logan's body. I hope they find him. I hope they get the chance to bury their brother.

Chase and Ro aren't here, and I have a feeling we'll never actually know what happened to them. They disappeared, which is something that happens far too often in our world. There are so many questions that never find their answers.

The rest of us build a campfire outside the cabin to make it a little more familiar. We clear out the cabin's rooms, burning the hunters' belongings—clothes, documents, blood samples, everything—erasing every trace of them. But we'll never be able to burn it all away—we'll never be able to erase the horror, to wipe away our memories, our connection with this place, the suffering we endured here, the people we lost.

I sit around the campfire and throw the little pieces of paper into the flames—the photograph I found of Jett and me. I watch it burn, blacken, and turn to ash, gone forever. I also found my necklace in there. The bear claw and the horseshoe rest against my skin again.

Sitting around the fire, I think back to the circus. I wonder what we'd be doing now if none of this had ever happened. Dawn is fast approaching, so I imagine we'd be waking up, preparing for a new day, some of us sitting around an unlit campfire, waiting for breakfast and a day of chores, lessons, practice. But the thought darkens as I remember what awaited us if we ever decided to leave the circus when we were deemed old enough to make that decision. It was so much worse than I thought.

I guess we're free of all that now, free of the circus, free of the people who controlled us and betrayed us, free of the pressure of performance, of the rules of the camp. But our lives aren't all that different. We're still running, still hiding, still off the grid. We've lost so many people—friends, family—but we've gained as well, and the only way to go is forward. Now that we've started to learn to embrace our animal sides, maybe what's ahead isn't so scary.

"Have you thought about where you'd like to go?" Jett asks, easing himself down beside me. His sleeves are rolled up to his elbows and his arms are covered in dirt.

I shake my head. "Not yet. But I will think. We can't all stay here, can we?"

"Not really. Do you want to?"

"Not really."

Violet Bay used to be my favorite place, but we'll all be leaving soon, together, to find a new home far away from here. Somewhere we've never been before. Somewhere the circus hasn't touched. Somewhere with no memories. Somewhere we can create new ones. Somewhere with no agents or backstreet doctors, no elders. Maybe even someplace with no hunters. Somewhere safe.

I think about my parents. I wonder if I could find them one day. Or at least find out what happened the day I was taken. Now that we know so much, maybe we should dedicate our lives to helping captured shifters instead of leaving it all behind.

Lance and Lucas dust off their jeans and join us. They put my jacket in the fire, the one we left with Logan. The one Jett used to plug Logan's wound. The one covered in Logan's blood. They must have recovered it along with his body. I'm glad they found him. They watch the jacket burn before sitting down together.

Lola stands beside me, and Kanna with her. Before sitting down, Lola drops the swipe keys into the fire, letting the plastic melt and take the memories of her sister locked in the cell, unresponsive and trapped, away with it.

Hugo and Jax next. They have nothing to burn. They both look exhausted, but I'm happy to see some color returning to Jax's cheeks.

Ruby and Itch are beside Owen and Ursula. Star comes to sit on my lap, and I hold her tight to my chest. Even though I don't know where we're going next, I know it'll be enough just that we're together. We know a number of hunters are out there, looking for us and others like us. We can never let our guards down. But now we know—we're stronger together. As humans and as animals.

This isn't exactly the life I dreamed of. We'll never have a home of our own, not really. We don't exist in this world. We're wanderers, drifters, unsettled. No roots, no family, no one but each other. But for once, I'm content with that. For once, I actually believe that we'll be okay. And I hope we find somewhere soon, a place in this world for us.

ACKNOWLEDGMENTS

As always, my first thanks go to my star agent, Isabel Atherton, who said, "I LOVED it!" after reading this for the first time early 2013, then titled *The Shapeshifter Circus*. A lot of hard work and dedication went into this project from that moment on and I'm so grateful for what it has become. Thank you for finding this story a home.

To Alice Smales, who has magical powers, for providing detailed, honest feedback, and steering me in the right direction.

To my lovely editor, Nicole Frail—I have loved every minute of this adventure together! This story means a lot to me and I can never thank you enough for saying yes.

I love being a Sky Pony author, and I'm thankful for the chance to do it all again. Thank you to the whole team for making it a real book, with special thanks to Julie Matysik for putting this in good hands, Adrienne Szpyrka for the excellent advice, Cheryl Lew for tremendous support, and Georgia Morrissey for the gorgeous cover design.

Thanks to my writing buddy, Emma Pass, who read very early chapters of this story and was excited even then.

Having people read your work is both terrifying and exciting, and a reader's support means the world. A huge thank-you to *everyone* who reads and enjoys my books, with extra thanks to: Megan Olivier, Sam and Rianna Russell, the Gemmells, the Meadows, and Scharlotte Walsh.

To Author Allsorts and Team Rogue YA.

To Anasheh and Patri, for the amazing FFBC blog tours.

To Megan Olivier (again!), for the cover reveal and so much more.

To my family, who are always excited about my books: Auntie Jan, Uncle Geoff, Claire, John, Thomas, Joseph, Neil, and Camille.

To Mum, Dad, Mike, and Dan, for encouraging me to do what I love.

To my furry assistant, Freddie, who sleeps on the job but keeps me company all the same. Love you, little guy.

And to Andy, who supports me in absolutely everything I do and takes every step with me. Love you, too!